SUZI BAMBLETT

The Travelling Philanthropist

Suzi Bamb

Broodleroo

First published by Broodleroo 2021

Copyright © 2021 by Suzi Bamblett

This novel is entirely a work of fiction. The names, characters and incidents portrayed in it are the work of the author's imagination. Any resemblance to actual persons, living or dead, events or localities is entirely coincidental.

Suzi Bamblett asserts the moral right to be identified as the author of this work.

First edition

ISBN: 978-1-8382550-0-8

This book was professionally typeset on Reedsy.
Find out more at reedsy.com

To my mum and dad
Elizabeth and Peter Bamblett

Contents

Acknowledgement

I'm grateful to my dear friend Patricia M Osborne who has tirelessly read and edited my manuscript and continues to encourage and support me through my indie publishing journey.

Thank you to my editor Claire Chamberlain for feedback, copy editing and proof-reading. A big shout out to my friends and writing buddies at Hove Friday Writing Group who have encouraged, critiqued and chivvied me along, and thanks to my beta readers - Jane Collins, Susan Morris and Maureen Utting.

I am grateful to Andy Keylock for the beautiful cover design and to Clare Coates and Sam Rumens at Marketing Pace for building me a fantastic website. Special thanks to Sam for early beta reading and continued involvement with the development of my social media platform.

Finally, I'd like to thank my partner Colin and my family and friends for their encouragement, love and support.

The Travelling Philanthropist

Prologue

The young woman stumbles along cobbled streets clutching a precious bundle to her breast. Emerging from the fog, she faces the black iron gates of the convent. Gently she lowers the child into the casket but can't let go. With a sob, she snatches him back up. Not yet. Bowing her head, she inhales his new-born scent.

Behind her, in the shadows, the man waits.

The woman looks over her shoulder. Is someone watching? Her eyes are drawn back to her child. Still she hesitates. Although the casket is lined with cloth, the wind is biting.

''Tis a cold night,' the man says.

With a cry, she spins round.

'It is after midnight.' He sighs. 'The nuns all a' bed until morning prayers.'

She stares at him. From tricorn hat to polished shoe buckles, every inch the gentleman.

'Even if the child should survive the night, he may not be given a place at the Foundling Hospital.' The man steps closer. 'The weekly lottery is tomorrow. If a black ball is drawn, they have no choice but to dispose of him. They are reluctant to take a child when they have no details of the mother, especially if he is sickly and weakened by a night out in the cold.'

1

The woman stands uncertain, her arms wrapped tightly around her child.

'I can help you,' the man continues. 'I know someone who will take good care of him. It is a boy, is it not?'

'Yes.' She finds her voice at last. 'Yes, my son.'

'He will be well looked after. Trust me.'

What choice does she have? She cannot return to her place of work with the child; they'll both end up on the streets. A sob escapes her as she thrusts her baby into the arms of the man. 'Here, take him. God bless you, sir.' She turns, her footsteps echoing as she disappears into the smog.

With the child under his black cloak, the man strides back to the waiting carriage.

2nd September 2019

The postcard lies on top of the mail. Superyachts, dazzling white against an azure sky. I turn it over to reveal familiar handwriting. 'For fuck's sake…' I drop it into the chrome pedal bin.

'Anna.' Matt tuts. 'Aren't you even going to read it?'

I ignore him, scrutinising my bank statement. 'Shit, the bank's paid my credit card balance in full. I was going to make a minimum payment this month.'

'Less interest that way.'

'But I won't have enough to last until I get paid.'

Matt picks up his keys and mobile. He kisses me on the forehead. 'Babe, I've told you, I can cover it.'

'That's not the point.' I perch on the kitchen stool. 'I hate not paying my way. It's bad enough *they* still subsidise my rent.'

Matt flips the bin lid to retrieve the postcard from my parents. 'Just read it.'

I make myself a smoothie and fill my portable bottle. I tug on my jacket and pick up my shoulder bag. All the while, the postcard taunts me from the worktop. I turn it over:

Cannes Harbour, August 2019. Spending a few days here. Haven't seen any celebrities yet. We'd love it if you could come and stay for a few days. Lots of love Mum and Dad.

I tear the postcard in half, chuck it in the bin and head for work.

* * *

The next edition of *The Tube and Eye* is due at the printers in three days' time. Gary calls a meeting. 'Where's the report I asked for on the proposed pedestrian-only areas?'

'I'm working on it, boss,' says Geoff.

'And the restaurant reviews? Jen, did we get anyone out to the launch of that new place in Northumberland Avenue?'

'Yes, boss, almost finished.'

'Christ, you lot couldn't organise a piss-up in a brewery.'

I raise my hand.

'What? Oh, thanks Anna. Two sugars in mine.' Gary loosens his collar. 'Now Rob, please tell me the feature's finished?'

My heart's thumping as I stand my ground.

Gary stares at me. 'You still here Anna?'

'I was wondering if I could write a follow-up to last month's article. The suicides?'

'Yesterday's news.'

'I thought I could link it to the teenager who jumped. Add a personal interest story…'

Gary takes off his glasses and cleans them with the end of his tie. 'Look, Anna, we do reviews, we do "What's On" pieces. This just isn't the place for in-depth features. Now, be a good girl and get me my coffee.' He replaces his glasses. 'Rob, I want that copy on my desk by noon or heads will roll.'

My cheeks burn as I walk over to the coffee machine. Gary let me proof last month's article – *Suicides from bridges*. We didn't usually cover that kind of story, but for some macabre reason he thought it might interest our readers. I'd seen Gary giving me something important to do as a turning point. Although I hadn't written the original copy, I was intrigued and could see plenty of scope for a follow-up. Now it seems things are reverting to normal. Story of my life.

I was in my teens when my relationship with Mum and Dad changed. I'd always known I was adopted, but somehow it hadn't been a big deal until then. When I was young, Mum would read me *Nutmeg the Squirrel*. I snuggled down in my bed, listening to how Nutmeg got a new home, and I felt safe. Mum and Dad didn't know who my biological father was, but they told me my birth mother wanted the best for me and that's why she gave me up. They hugged me, kissed me goodnight and whispered that I was their 'most precious gift'.

All afternoon I'm tasked with mundane chores until finally the editorial team are given permission to wind up for the night.

'Coming for a drink, Anna?' asks Jen.

'No thanks. I'm meeting a mate.'

* * *

I head for *The Black Cat*. The basement bar is heaving and the music loud. I spot Zoe chatting up the good-looking bartender and push my way through the scrum to tap her on the shoulder.

'Anna,' Zoe squeals.

We air kiss.

5

'Here, grab those crisps and I'll bring the drinks. I've bagged us somewhere to sit.' Zoe points to where she's left her jacket, sprawled across a bench seat.

We squeeze past the thirsty office workers necking their beers and make our way to the last remaining booth.

Zoe raises her glass. 'Cheers.'

I give a half-hearted smile.

'What's up?' she asks.

'My job's a dead end.' I sigh. 'Gary doesn't trust me with anything important. At my last appraisal he told me I'd get more opportunities to research and write my own stories, but all I ever do is make bloody coffee.'

'It's just a job.' Zoe raises her voice to be heard above a rowdy stag party nearby. 'If your boss can't see how valuable you are, fuck him.'

I muddle my ice with my straw.

A loud guffaw of laughter from the bar draws our attention. A group of lads sporting tee shirts emblazoned, *Nathan's Stag Do,* are pouring shots down the groom-to-be's throat. Poor guy looks half cut already.

Zoe takes another sip of her Mojito. 'So, where's gorgeous Matt tonight?'

'Work thing, leaving do I think.'

She grins. 'So, you're off the leash.'

I poke out my tongue.

Zoe throws glances at the lads until the tall, blond guy makes eye contact. She twirls a lock of her hair around her fingers.

I raise my eyebrows. 'Really?'

She laughs. 'So, you think you'll stay with the mag? Cause I might be able to get you something at mine. They're always looking.'

'I don't know. I definitely need wider experience on my CV but I don't want it to look like I can't settle. This is my third job already.'

'Well, just say the word. I do bugger all most of the month. We have a few hectic days and the rest of the time I faff about on social media.'

'I dunno. I'm not ready to give up the journalist thing just yet. Anyway, I'd be bored if I didn't have enough to do.'

Zoe plays with her paper umbrella. 'Speaking of faffing around, how are your mum and dad?'

'Still sailing around the French Riviera. I got a postcard today.'

'So, when you gonna invite me for that girlie weekend in Cannes?'

'Always up for a girlie weekend, but not with them there. Anyway, Happy Hour's nearly up. Another one?' I pull out my credit card, nodding at our empty cocktail glasses. 'Or shall we get a bottle?'

Zoe chews her paper straw suggestively. 'Perhaps it's time to have a bite to eat?'

I leave Zoe and the blond guy giving one another the eye and fight my way to the bar. An older couple are being served – probably out celebrating an anniversary with cocktails and a show. They're taking an age.

While growing up, I noticed Mum and Dad seemed older than my friends' parents. When I asked Mum about this, she explained it was because they'd had to wait such a long time. She said I was special because they'd chosen me. I couldn't have felt more loved.

7

The woman in front of me turns around and I have to lean in to hear what she's saying.

'You go first dear. We're not in any rush.'

I give a quick smile. 'No, you're all right.'

The bartender winks at me before returning his attention to the couple. 'This one's popular…'

In year nine my history teacher set us a homework to create a family tree. Mum sat with me at the dining room table as I added her and Dad's parents' names to the flowchart.

I paused, my pencil in mid-air. 'It's not accurate though is it?'

'Why?' Mum asked.

'Because you're not my biological parents.'

'We're still your parents.'

'But it's not the same. Perhaps I should add another box. Here?' I pencilled in an extra box alongside Mum's name. 'Showing my real mother?'

The bartender's waiting for my order. 'Bottle of Sauvignon and two glasses,' I say. By the time I get back to the booth, two lads from the stag-do have joined Zoe.

'Here she is. This is my best friend Anna. Anna, this is Phil.' Zoe places a hand on the blond guy's arm to indicate he's spoken for. 'And this,' she nods towards the bearded guy, 'is James.'

Zoe and Phil flirt outrageously while I try to make small talk. 'So, James, are you the Best Man?'

James grins. 'I like to think so.'

He's got a nice smile, I'll let him have that one.

'No,' James continues, 'that would be my mate curled up

in the next booth. He was sucking his thumb when I last checked.' James refills my glass.

'Aren't you drinking?' I ask.

He lifts his glass. 'Lime and soda. I decided I'd better keep a clear head if I'm to get the groom home in one piece.'

We chat amicably. James works for an investment company. Turns out he's married, the best ones always are. At eleven he rounds up the rest of the stags. They're going on to a club.

'Nice to meet you.' James gives me a peck on the cheek.

Probably for the best, I think, watching him leave.

Phil has decided to stay. I spend the next twenty minutes playing gooseberry before leaving him and Zoe cosying up together.

I check the time on my mobile – nearly midnight and Matt hasn't texted. Probably out enjoying himself. There's no rush for me to get back to the flat. My way is lit by multi-coloured fairy lights on restaurant boats along the Thames. Weaving in and out of couples sauntering arm-in-arm, I head for Westminster Bridge.

After climbing the curved steps onto the bridge, I use the torch on my mobile to read the verse on the plaque. *"Ne'er saw I, never felt, a calm so deep..."*

'It's a bit old fashioned,' Debbie had said.

'It's about sun coming up over the river, how beautiful the river is in the early morning light and how calm it makes him feel.'

'Mmm. Sounds like this Wordsworth was a bit up himself.'

We stood looking across at the London Eye.

'Have you ever been on it?' I asked her.

9

'Nope. Can't say as I ever fancied it.'

'Perhaps we could do it together sometime?'

"The river glideth at his own sweet will." I'd featured the poem in an article in the magazine, *Walking Tours around London*, one of few pieces Gary let me put together myself. I'd hoped Debbie might read it.

Shoving my mobile into my shoulder bag, I stroll across the bridge as commuters rush for their last train. A woman, standing alone by the balustrade is joined by a man. They link arms and head towards the city. I amble on. I wonder if the girl who jumped stopped to read the Wordsworth poem. Did she think the houses looked asleep? Was there nobody she could call? I note the barriers erected across sections of the bridge. They won't stop people jumping. You could hide behind them and drop unnoticed into the churning waters below…

My thoughts are broken when someone yanks my shoulder strap, pulling me backwards.

I turn my head to a man in a hoodie tugging at my bag.

'Let go, bitch,' he hisses.

My brain seems to freeze. Instinctively, I clutch my bag tightly to my chest. I stare at him. 'No.'

His eyes glint.

'Help,' I yell, but there's no-one nearby.

Without warning his fist shoots out. The blow grazes across my cheek, forcing me to lose my grasp. The mugger tears the bag from my shoulder and runs off, east of the river.

I'm gulping for air. My breath is a shudder, my limbs shaking. Big Ben strikes midnight. My body seems to fold in on itself. I reach a hand towards the carved stone balustrade.

2nd September 1752

Frederick Tweedie makes minute adjustments to the equipment while Thomas Pestlemore stands beside him huffing and puffing.

'Have patience, sir. These things cannot be hurried.' Tweedie tweaks the aperture by a miniscule amount to ensure the lens points at the darkest space between the stars.

The rotund Pestlemore leans in over his shoulder.

'Damn it, sir.' Tweedie pushes him away. 'Give me room.'

'S-sorry.' Pestlemore steps back. Gazing out across the dark waters of the Thames, he looks upwards. Using his fat thumb, he traces a line tracking the projection from the equipment to the horizon. 'Perhaps a little higher, Tweedie?'

Tweedie glares at him.

'Sorry, sorry,' repeats Pestlemore.

'Who is doing this, me or you?' Tweedie struts forward, his seniority somewhat diminished by his sticky out ears which give him a certain ape-like appearance. 'Who, sir, is the astronomer here? Oh yes. That would be me.'

Pestlemore lowers his head, looking down at his feet.

Tweedie moves to make one final adjustment. 'There, that should do it.'

'Oh well done.' Pestlemore claps his skinny friend across

the shoulder blades.

Tweedie's eyes narrow.

Pestlemore's enthusiasm cannot be dampened. He hops from one foot to the other. 'Are we ready now for the prism?'

Tweedie cups his hands. 'Yes.'

Pestlemore lifts the object reverently from its wooden case. As he holds it aloft, light from the moon catches the crystal sides. A rainbow of colour cascades far out across the rippling black Thames water.

Tweedie takes the prism and, with meticulous care, positions it at the heart of the assembled equipment. Both men step back, regarding the contraption with awe.

'It is the moment of truth.' Tweedie clasps his hands together as though in prayer. 'The culmination of months of calculations, design and planning. If the prism does not spin on its own volition, then everything has been in vain.'

The prism clunks into place and begins to rotate.

'Each component joins to make a whole,' marvels Pestlemore. 'It is nothing short of miraculous.'

The two men watch as the equipment vibrates.

'But see, the lens remains steady,' says Tweedie, 'fixed on its target.'

Pestlemore casts an eye over his shoulder ensuring the bridge men are nowhere in sight. They'd bribed the jack-a-lantern on the east side of the bridge with a jug of gin. It's vital that they are not observed.

Tweedie notes his distraction. 'It is not yet time for the west side watchman to make his hourly patrol.'

'Look.' Pestlemore points and they both peer into the depths of the blackest part in the sky where a faint light is beginning to appear.

Tweedie is mesmerised as the light grows stronger, reflecting rays back onto the bridge.

Pestlemore clutches Tweedie's arm. 'What is that?'

Tweedie squints, at first dazzled by the brightness. Slowly, at the very core, an apparition appears.

As the shape becomes clearer, Pestlemore gasps. 'Dear God. Tweedie, do you see? 'Tis a figure, slumped against the balustrade.'

3rd September

Mercy is gazing into the dark waters below. Although mist has dampened her woollen clothes, it is not yet raining. Would that it were. If she were soaked to the skin it might be easier to slip down into the water. She shivers as the last of hope deserts her body. Even God seems to have forsaken her. Nothing left but emptiness and a dull ache.

A sound invades her thoughts. Someone calling? Mercy turns. 'Tis a person, far side of the bridge. Stepping into the road, Mercy peers through the smog. Be it man or woman? A few more steps. The cry sounded female, but 'twas difficult to be certain. No, by the attire it's a fella. Can't be too careful, might be a ploy to get her close. And yet, whoever it is needs her help.

'Who's there?' When there's no response, Mercy creeps closer.

The woman opens her eyes.

Mercy crouches down. 'Take it slow, miss.'

'Debbie?' The woman's voice is a croak.

'No, miss. My name be Mercy.'

The woman reaches for Mercy's hand and pulls herself up to sitting. 'Damn, he's taken my bag. My mobile. I need to get to the tube.'

Mercy stares at the young woman. Not a pauper for she'd instinctively addressed her as 'miss'. But breeches and boots? A lady would never dress this way or cuss in such manner. Her words make no sense and yet, there's something about her. Perhaps she's a runaway? Whatever her tale, she's in distress. Can't just leave her here, gawd knows what might happen.

'Lawd, if you ain't chilled to the bone.' Mercy removes her cloak which, although damp, still retains some warmth. She wraps it around the woman.

The woman's gaze flits about before settling on Mercy's face. 'Mercy, you said?'

'Yes, miss.' Perhaps she's escaped from an asylum? Still, too late now. With her own worries temporarily forgotten, Mercy drags the woman to her feet. 'Can you walk? I'll have to take yer home wi' me and see to that head.' With an arm around to steady her, Mercy guides the young woman across the bridge.

* * *

The octagonal recesses positioned above each pier of the new bridge were originally designed for the protection of the wayfarer. Now, often used for more sinister purposes, they necessitate regular patrol by the watchmen.

Concealed in one of the domed shelters, Tweedie and Pestlemore try not to draw attention to themselves. It's a tight squeeze and Pestlemore's girth is not helping.

'Damn it, sir.' Tweedie says. 'You crush the very life from me.'

'Sorry,' Pestlemore attempts to turn sideways. 'Sorry.'

'Can you see anything?'

15

'Yes, b-but, I think we should wait a while longer.' Pestlemore's heart thumps, causing a dull ache in his chest. He wheezes. 'Did you gather everything?'

Tweedie had the forethought to snatch up what he could of their equipment. He attempts an inventory in the gloom. 'No, I am missing the alitude.'

Pestlemore sighs. 'Bother and blast.'

'Can you see it?'

'I cannot see a damn thing with this fog.'

'Move over then, sir.' They shuffle around so Tweedie can peer from their hiding place.

'Are they still there?' asks Pestlemore.

'I see two figures.'

'Both from the portal?'

'I think not.'

'Let me see.' Pestlemore tries to squeeze his head between Tweedie's arm and the stonework. 'Ow.'

'Patience, sir,' says Tweedie. 'Ah, they move away.'

The men duck back into the shelter as the figures leave the bridge. After a few moments, Tweedie creeps out and beckons Pestlemore to follow. They scoop up the remains of their abandoned equipment and, with furtive glances over their shoulders, set off in the same direction.

* * *

Anna stumbles along beside Mercy. Everything's dark, like someone turned off the streetlights. Soft drizzle refreshes her face and objects around begin to take shape, but she can't get her bearings. Where's Big Ben? As she twists her head, the thick woollen cloak scratches against her neck. The London

Eye's missing, too. Is she dreaming?

'Wait.' Anna stops and rubs her eyes.

Mercy frowns. 'Yer right shaken.'

What's that strange, metallic smell? Anna can taste it. Her head's throbbing. She raises a hand and her fingers meet a sticky mass. Her body begins to shake. 'Where am I?'

'Can't dilly dally.' Mercy glances over her shoulder. ''Tis not safe.'

Anna allows herself to be steered through streets she doesn't recognise. If this is a dream, she will wake soon. A carriage speeds past, the horses' hooves chucking up mucky water that soaks into her jeans. Uneven cobbles press into the soles of her feet. Streets, narrow and gloomy, are lit by old-fashioned streetlamps. It's dark, a thick, dense fog, like on Guy Fawkes night when the smoke from bonfires and fireworks conceals everything from view.

A horrid stench, as if drains have spewed out raw sewage, makes Anna nauseous. She stops several times and leans forward, hands on knees, but Mercy urges her on. They tramp ankle deep through mud and rotting rubbish, a sweet sickly smell wafting around them like composting vegetable peelings.

At one point, Mercy drags Anna down a side alley where they crouch in the shadows while a noisy crowd of boisterous revellers pass by. Further on, two drunks wearing historical fancy dress stagger past them. The men leer and gesture obscenely, but Mercy takes it in her stride, confidently leading Anna on.

Eventually the streets become quieter, more residential. Nothing is familiar, Anna is completely lost.

Mercy stops at the top of a flight of stone steps leading down into the basement of a tall townhouse.

'No.' Anna clutches the metal railings. Can she trust Mercy? Someone could be down there, lying in wait. But what choice does she have? She has no money and no phone. She'll never find her way back through those wretched, unknown streets.

'Don't you be fretting none. Master and Mistress are away.' Taking her arm, Mercy helps Anna down the steps where, lifting a huge metal key from a string around her waist, she unlocks the door. 'In yer come.'

* * *

The young woman steps across the stone hearth and into the kitchen. Moving towards the warmth of the range, she almost jumps out of her skin when a cat leaps up, hissing loudly.

'Shoo Jinks.' Mercy waves the cat away. 'Thinks he's Lord o' the Manor. Sit yerself down.'

The woman sinks into the chair vacated by Jinks.

Mercy lights the candles then sets to work on the range, opening first one door, then another to stoke up the fire. She puts a pan to warm. 'Might I be so bold, miss, as to ask yer name?'

'Anna,' replies the woman. 'Anna Stratton.'

'Good, that's good.' Mercy ladles broth into a bowl. 'Here, drink this, Miss Anna, while I look at yer head.'

Anna cups the bowl in her hands to warm her fingers and gingerly takes a sip.

Mercy puts a second pan on the stove. While it's heating, she brings a candlestick closer to inspect the wound under Anna's matted hair. 'Don't seem too bad.' Lifting the pan from the stove, Mercy stands it down on the bleached pine table, then, using a piece of coarse brown fabric, she bathes the wound.

'Ow.' Anna flinches as tepid liquid dribbles down her neck. 'Is that vinegar?'

'Yes.' Finishing her ministrations, Mercy seats herself down on a wooden stool. 'You'll know 'bout it the morrow, but I reckon it could ha' been worse.'

Anna glances at the door. 'I don't understand what's happening. I shouldn't be here.' Her voice is wobbly as if tears threaten.

'Nonsense,' says Mercy. 'I told yer, Master and Mistress are away so they'll be none the wiser. Anyway, couldn't have left yer there, could I?'

Anna shakes her head. She leans back in the chair and closes her eyes.

'That's it. Nothin a good night's sleep won't mend, I'll warrant. You'd best stay the night. Can't be sending yer out again, not with that head.' Mercy disappears into shadows at the back of the room. Moments later she returns, picks up the candlestick and tugs gently at Anna's arm.

With a final look towards the door, Anna allows herself to be led behind a curtain to a wooden cot where, exhausted, she lays down and falls immediately to sleep.

Mercy watches her visitor a while. Reassured her breathing is even and not laboured, she returns to the kitchen. She drops the bowls into the deep sink and settles in front of the fire. 'Hope I don't wake up to find the silver gone,' she murmurs to Jinks, who has jumped up and is kneading her lap. 'Reason enough to sleep in this chair. Make sure she don't get up to no mischief.' As she strokes the cat, he purrs noisily. 'Funny, 'aven't thought 'bout John all night. Took my mind right off 'im, finding her like that just as I was praying.'

Mercy sits forward so fast that Jinks is thrown to the floor. He stares at Mercy accusingly. Flicking his tail, he walks haughtily away to lick his wounded ego on top of the pine dresser.

'Of course, God has sent someone to help me.' Flooded with renewed hope, Mercy closes her eyes and gives silent thanks. ''Tis another sign.'

* * *

'Are you okay?'

I open my eyes and look up into the face of a middle-aged man.

'Steady now,' he says. 'Ambulance is on its way.'

The pavement's cold and hard, but something soft has been wedged under my neck. 'What... what happened?'

'You've had a bit of a fall.' The man's voice has a calming ring of authority. 'Your head's bleeding. Just stay put until we get you checked out.'

Somewhere, far away, a siren is screaming. It's getting louder. I close my eyes. What a strange dream...

'Stay with me. Don't go to sleep.' The man pats my hand.

I open my eyes again. The strange image, an old-fashioned carriage and horses, fades away. Wasn't there a woman too? Dressed in black, hair tucked up under a bonnet. Where did she go?

My head's throbbing. The traffic crossing the bridge is deafeningly loud. My eyelids are heavy. The voice of the stranger is lost as other voices approach.

* * *

A nurse loans me her phone but I can't remember Matt's number.

'It's the shock,' says the nurse. 'Can you remember anyone else's?'

I tap in Zoe's number. 'Hi, Zoe?'

'Hey party pooper. If you've decided to…'

'Zoe, I need you to call Matt.'

'What's wrong?'

'I've been mugged.'

'What? Where are you? I'll jump in an Uber.'

'No Zoe, just call Matt for me. Tell him I'm in University College Hospital.'

'Are you all right? Oh God, Anna, this is all my fault.'

'Don't be daft.'

'Should I let your mum and dad know?'

'No.'

After "family tree-gate" I wouldn't let it go. 'At least tell me my real mother's name,' I pleaded.

Mum shook her head. She must have known if she gave me the name, I'd have looked it up on Facebook. 'There's no point until you're eighteen. That's when you can find out if your birth mother wants to meet you.'

'But I have a right to know.'

'Not before you're eighteen. It's illegal to try to trace her before that.'

Dad was no easier. 'We're doing this for your protection.'

'To protect me from what? Why do I need protection from my own mother?'

21

Dad buried his face back in his *Motor Boat and Yachting* magazine.

I didn't take their word for it. I Googled. *What age do you have to be to track down your birth mother?* Google confirmed what my parents had told me. I had almost five years to wait.

'Did you manage to get through to someone?' asks the nurse.

'Yes, my boyfriend's coming.' I hand over her phone, lean back on the trolley bed and close my eyes.

Forty minutes later, Matt pushes through double doors and rushes to my side. 'What happened Anna?'

'I'm still waiting for triage. Calm down, you look worse than I feel.'

'That's probably true.' Matt rubs his hands on his jeans to dry them of sticky disinfectant gel before kissing me on my forehead. He winces as he gently examines my cheek. 'You seem remarkably upbeat for someone who just got mugged.'

'Must be the adrenaline.'

'I've been frantic wondering where the hell you were.'

'Sorry.'

'At first, I thought you'd had a few too many and gone back to Zoe's but then, when your mobile kept going to voice mail, I started imagining the worst. Where did it happen anyway?'

'Westminster Bridge.'

Matt groans. 'It's been eighteen months, Anna. Why do you keep going back there?'

There's a lump in my throat. I can't speak.

He shakes his head. 'You should have rung me.'

'I tried, there was no signal.'

'Then you should have got an Uber.'

'Do we have to do this now?' I touch my head, trying to stop the throbbing. Why does he have to go on so?

'Sorry,' he says.

I squeeze his hand. 'It's okay.'

Matt squinches his eyes. 'You know I love you?' Spotting the striped woollen scarf at the foot of my bed, he reaches for it. 'Whose is this?'

'I think it belongs to the man who found me. He called the ambulance. The paramedics said it was under my head. I ought to track him down and say thank you.'

'Don't suppose he'll want it back. Matt discards the scarf onto the plastic chair. He sniffs. 'I hate the smell of hospitals. Anyway, what's happening?' He nods towards the nurses' station where two doctors are consulting over a screen.

'They want to do a scan,' I answer, tracing the laundry numbers inked on the starched white sheet. 'If it's clear, I'm allowed home.' I grin. 'As long as someone's there to wait on me hand and foot.'

'Might make you a cuppa if you play your cards right.'

I gesture at the curtained bays and occupied trolleys lining the corridor. 'It could be a long wait.'

'Scooch over then.'

I slide across the trolley and Matt climbs up beside me. I lay my head back on the pillow and close my eyes again. Perhaps I should have let Zoe ring Mum and Dad?

I was fifteen when things came to a head. Mum knocked at my bedroom door. 'I thought you might like a sandwich as you're busy revising.' She placed the plate and a can of coke carefully down beside my science revision book. 'What's this?' She picked up the holiday brochure I'd been flicking through.

'I was going to speak to you and Dad about it tonight. Me and Zoe are planning a post GCSE trip to Magaluf.'

Mum sat down on my bed. 'I'm not sure that's a good idea.'

'Why not? Everyone's going away after exams.'

'Why don't you stay in this country. Cornwall's nice. I hear lots of young people go to Newquay.'

'We want some sun.'

'I don't think it's a good idea for two young girls to travel abroad on their own.'

'It's not just two of us. Beks and Lou are coming too. It's perfectly safe. We'll stay in a hotel, all inclusive.'

'Your dad will never agree to it.'

I thought Mum was being anxious and overprotective and I was sure I'd talk Dad round but, when he came in from work, he took her side. 'It's not a good idea Anna, you're too young to go abroad on your own.'

'I won't be on my own. I told you, there'll be four of us. You just don't trust me.'

'It's not a matter of not trusting you, it's other people we don't trust,' said Mum. 'Tom, say something.'

Dad tried to find a compromise. 'Why don't we do something together, as a family, to celebrate the end of your exams?'

Mum always said that once I had the bit between my teeth there was no stopping me. 'I'm sixteen in two months. It's time you let me do stuff on my own.'

Dad persisted, he was due to retire and they'd talked about getting a boat and sailing around the Mediterranean. 'It would be the perfect time for the three of us to go.'

'It's not fair, 'I grumbled. 'Everyone else's parents have agreed.'

'The answer's still no, Anna,' said Mum.

'Why are you being so mean? My real mother would let me go.'

Mum turned pale.

'I think you'd better go to your room, Anna,' said Dad.

As I stomped upstairs, I threw my parting shot. 'I wish I lived with my real parents.'

Two porters stand by the lift. They glance over at Matt and me, one nudges the other and whispers something. Will they tell us off because Matt's lying on my trolley? I shift my gaze to an elderly woman in a wheelchair, doubled up in pain. My cheeks colour. She should have the trolley, not me. I shake Matt's arm.

'What?' He blinks a few times, remembering where we are. 'Why don't they do the bloody scan and let me go home?'

* * *

Anna opens her eyes, then squeezes them tightly shut before opening them again. It doesn't work. When she was little, she'd sometimes fall asleep in the car on the way home. In the morning she'd wake in her own bed with no recollection of Dad carrying her upstairs or Mum undressing her. This is like that, but much worse.

The last thing she remembers is being on Westminster Bridge. Was she looking for someone? Did she have an accident? She must have banged her head because there's a dull ache, but it's no longer throbbing. This isn't a hospital, but someone helped her?

A rustle comes from behind the curtain. Anna pulls the cover up to her neck. She's not alone. The blanket scratches

25

her chin. Is this a hostel? A squat? She lifts the cover and sighs with relief to find she's fully clothed. What the hell happened last night? Must have had a right skinful. She runs her tongue around her mouth – furry, stale, metallic taste. Where the hell is she? And who is out there?

The curtains divide and someone peeps through. Black curls poke out around a frilly cotton cap. The face, strangely disconnected from its body, gives a smile.

Anna remembers. It's the girl who helped her, Mercy.

'Morning, miss.' The head does a little bob. 'There was me thinking you might sleep past noon. Come away in. There's gruel on the stove.'

Anna sits up, her brain reaching for rational explanation. She's dead, this is purgatory she must work through before getting to Heaven? Or perhaps she's lying in a coma somewhere and this is some sort of lucid dream? But it all seems so real.

She crawls off the cot and pushes through the curtain to emerge into the large kitchen. A cat eyes her suspiciously from the chair in front of the range. Anna remembers him from last night.

Mercy shoes him away. 'Come on now, Jinks, move over. Let someone else have some warmth.'

Rays of sunlight battle through the smeary basement window and Anna recognises the old-fashioned kitchen with the big black range.

The room is lit by candles. Must be a power cut, thinks Anna. Yes, that would explain the lack of streetlights last night. By the soft glow, Anna realises her rescuer is younger than she'd thought. Her skinny frame belies her strength and stamina and, although her features are sharp, she has kind eyes, shadows around them hinting at a life of hardship and disappointment.

Anna watches as Mercy tucks a dark tendril under her cap, then takes a bowl from the huge pine dresser dominating one entire wall. Where the hell is she? It's like she's walked into *Downton Abbey*.

'Come and sit, Miss Anna.' Mercy ladles a spoonful of grey mush into a bowl and places it in front of Anna with a thick chunk of brown bread beside it.

Anna lifts a spoon to poke at the stodgy porridge. It's the consistency of poly filler. She lays down the spoon and picks up the stale crust. It won't be enough to raise her blood sugar, but she nibbles politely.

Mercy watches her. 'How you faring today? How's yer head?'

Anna still feels weak and lightheaded, but she reaches up to the bump on her crown. 'A bit better. Where am I?'

'You suffered a nasty blow last night. I bringed yer home with me. Don't you remember?'

Anna shakes her head. 'Not really.'

'Don't you even remember what happened to yer?'

'I was on Westminster Bridge. I think I was looking for someone? Then... sorry, no.'

'Well, I see two men on that bridge and I wonder if they didn't 'ave something to do with it? 'Twas a good job we left when we did.'

'But where am I?' repeats Anna.

'You be in Duke Street, London residence of Lord and Lady Astley, but don't you go worrying again, cause they ain't here.'

Anna surveys the room, taking in the flagstone floor, copper pans and deep butler sink. Lord and Lady Astley? So, it's a stately home. But why has Mercy brought her here? 'What is this place? National Trust, English Heritage or something?'

Mercy frowns. 'Not from these parts are yer?'

'No, I don't think I am.'

'No, you be from some other place. I thought you was a lady when I first saw yer. Although, truth be told.' Mercy takes a deep breath. 'Now I think you might be an angel.'

'An angel?'

'Yes. Come to help me find me boy.'

'Oh no, I'm…' Anna stops. What is she doing here?

Mercy's gaze is expectant.

'The truth is, I can't remember anything.' Anna's eyes brim with tears. 'I know my name and that there was an accident, but apart from that…'

'Don't you be worrying none, cause I knows why yer here. I prayed and the Lord provided.'

'I really don't think…'

'Yes, that's it. You've been sent to help me.'

Anna shakes her head. How can she help anyone when she can't even help herself?

'Rest a bit longer,' says Mercy. 'I don't think yer quite right yet.'

Anna is suddenly claustrophobic. 'No. I need some air, to get my bearings.' She gets up and crosses to the door. Relieved to find it unlocked, she stumbles over the threshold and up the basement steps to the street.

She must be on a film set. The street is wide and cobbled with deep gutters running down both sides. Although there are no cars, there is much going on. A gentleman in old fashioned clothing walks past, giving Anna a curious look before averting his eyes. Further along, a boy rolls a hoop while other children squat in the gutter.

'Mind out the way.'

Anna, too slow, is doused by muddy water as a carriage and horses drive through. She looks up and down the street, not remembering whether they approached from left or right last night. Which way is home?

Mercy tugs at her arm. 'I don't think yer up to this. Come and have a bite more to eat.'

Anna allows herself to be led back down to the kitchen. It's like she's in a different time. She pulls away from Mercy's grasp. 'What year is this?'

'Why this be the year of our Lord, 1752.' Mercy shakes her head. 'Come, Miss Anna, yer making me fearful.'

Anna feels a wave of nausea as she slumps into the chair. 1752? It can't be. Something really weird is going on. Either that or she's gone completely and utterly insane.

* * *

My head throbs. I stretch out my arm, but Matt's side of the bed is empty. Despite our disturbed night in A & E, he's managed to get up in time for work.

There's a Post-it note stuck on top of my stack of bedtime reading. *Hi babe. Didn't want to wake you. I've left you my MacBook. Speak later x.*

Dragging myself out of bed I stagger into the kitchen, scanning around for the kettle before remembering Matt recently had a hot tap installed. The digital display on the built-in Bosch reads 09.45. No bananas left for a smoothie, so I slot two slices of bread in the toaster. With no mobile and no landline in the flat, Matt's MacBook is a life saver. I pull it from the power dock to check my iMessages.

The first one is Matt. *Hi sleepy head, I've rung your boss to tell him what happened. He says there's no need to come back to work until next week.*

There's also a short message from Gary. *Sorry to hear what happened Anna. Everyone sends their love. Just get yourself well.*

What did I expect? That I was indispensable? It's not like they won't get the October edition to print without me.

Squishing my mint tea bag against the side of the mug, I read the message from Zoe. *How are you hun? I feel sooo responsible. Get some rest. Look, if you feel up to it, we could do lunch tomorrow?*

I wash down two paracetamol with sips of tea. Munching toast, I gaze across the café style breakfast bar into the bustling city beyond. The long empty day looms ahead of me. I head to the sofa and switch on the TV.

My parents always treated me beyond my years. As an only child I thrived. Perhaps it was teenage hormones, but after the Magaluf debacle I started acting up. Everything Mum and Dad did annoyed me, and I fought them on every front. At least fifty per cent of the time I won. I knew I was hurting their feelings, but I didn't care.

I started to hang around with older girls at school, staying out late and neglecting my studies. It had always been the plan that I would go to university, but the summer of my 'A' levels things got bad. All I wanted was to leave home for good. As my birthday approached, the nerves crept in. 'Does my birth mother know anything about me?' I asked.

'Yes,' said Mum.

'You stayed in touch?'

'Not directly,' Dad said. 'It's called the letterbox process. We send a letter and a photo once a year.'

'So you have her address?'

'No, it's all done through a social worker.'

On the morning of my eighteenth birthday, Mum handed me a pink envelope. I ripped it open and inside was a card with my birth certificate. *'Deborah Brennan,'* I read out loud. So that was my mother's name. Later that day I filled in the online form on the Adoption Contact Register. I entered my birth name, date of birth and my birth mother's full name. Mum made a good show about being okay, while Dad, concerned but resigned, tapped in his credit card details for the fifteen quid fee. Now all I had to do was wait.

Three weeks passed before I received an email response. I sat staring at it, not knowing how to answer. My birth mother wanted to meet me, but what should I say? I typed, *'I'd love to meet you too'* and pressed send before I changed my mind.

'There's a letter for you,' said Mum a few days later.

The envelope was small and handwritten. Inside was a piece of paper that looked as if it'd been torn from a reporter-style pad.

'What is it?' Mum asked.

'It's from her. She wants to meet me next Saturday at three o'clock.'

'Where?'

'Bosworth House. I don't know where that is.' I Googled it on my phone. It was a women's shelter near Ashford. Was my birth mother homeless? A victim of domestic violence?

'I think we should take you,' said Mum.

'No, I'll get a train. I want to go on my own.'

Over the next few days, I scrutinised both envelope and

scrawled note. This woman had given birth to me, surely her handwriting revealed something? I grappled with questions, scribbling down things I wanted to say, then tearing up my notes. I laid outfits out on my bed, changing my mind a dozen times. All the time I could feel Mum watching me.

Bored with *Homes under the Hammer*, I turn off the TV and pull Matt's MacBook onto my lap. I draft an email, then delete it. I shouldn't, I promised Matt… I get up, make myself a coffee then return to the sofa where I redraft the message and hit 'send'.

I flick through a copy of *Elle*, giving the MacBook sideways glances. Even so, when Brenda's reply lands, I jump.

Anna, you can't keep pestering her.

It's been eighteen months, I respond.

Well, I suppose I could ask Debbie if she's prepared to meet you again.

Is she still in Bermondsey?

No.

There's a pause. Brenda must be weighing up how much to share. It's good of her to consider it after what happened last time.

The day I met my birth mother was also the day I met Brenda. She was waiting for me in the reception area of the women's shelter, wearing what Dad would call Dame Edna glasses. 'Not fat, just big boned,' Mum's voice whispered in my ear.

'Anna Stratton?' she said.

'Yes.'

'Let's sit for a moment. My name's Brenda Scott. I'm a volunteer support worker at Bosworth House. I wanted to have a little word before you meet Debbie. You've probably got lots of questions.'

I had a million questions starting with, who was my father and why did you give me up? I didn't say this to Brenda.

'Debbie's been here for almost two weeks,' she continued. 'I don't know how much you know?'

'Nothing really.'

She placed a hand on my arm, closing her eyes as if channelling her answers. 'Debbie's not had an easy life. She was very young when you were born. Back then she was mixing with the wrong crowd. Giving you up was the most loving thing she could have done.'

I pulled my arm away. I didn't want this woman telling me this stuff. I wanted to hear it direct from my birth mother.

Brenda peered at me over her glasses. 'Don't be surprised if Debbie doesn't want to revisit those early years. There are blanks in her life she either doesn't remember or can't face going back over. She's had lots of therapy.'

'What sort of therapy?'

'Debbie has mental health issues. Not unusual for someone who's lived rough, but she's doing well right now. You couldn't have picked a better time to get in touch. I'm hoping meeting you might help her turn a corner.'

'Turn a corner?'

Brenda nodded. 'Debbie's recovery journey hasn't been straightforward.'

I stood up. 'I'd like to see my birth mother now.'

'Of course, but small steps. Don't expect too much.'

After our first meeting at Bosworth House, Brenda kept in touch, periodically giving me updates. That's how I knew Debbie had a run-in with the law. If she hadn't been arrested and sentenced to three months at Her Majesty's Pleasure for some drug-related offence, she'd never have got around to contacting me again. I suppose three months is time enough to reflect on your life. Debbie wrote to me via Brenda saying she wanted to turn her life around and she'd like to get to know me. Once she was released, we met up a few times for coffee.

The MacBook pings. *Debbie's in a halfway house in Kennington. She recently went through a new programme. Let me see what I can do.*

Matt comes home early bearing flowers, chocolates and two Marks and Spencer ready meals. After we've eaten supper on our laps, he puts the plates in the dishwasher then sits down on the sofa beside me. 'Come on, snuggle up. I've never seen anyone more in need of a hug.'

I rest my head on his shoulder and he kisses the top of my head. 'Can we talk now about what you were doing on Westminster Bridge?'

'If we must.'

'You have to let it go.'

'It wasn't about Debbie. You heard about the girl who jumped?'

Matt lifts my chin to stare into my eyes. 'You weren't thinking about…'

'God no. I was hoping to do a follow-up story.'

'Because if you ever feel like that you know you can tell me. I can get you help.'

'Are you even listening to me?'

Matt holds up his hands defensively. 'Yes.'

'I'm not suicidal. I had this idea for a story speculating on the reason why the girl jumped. I thought if I could get inside her head….'

'I don't think that's a good idea under the circumstances.'

'Well, Gary didn't go for it anyway, so it's a moot point.'

Matt rubs the back of my hand with his thumb. 'Perhaps you do need to talk to someone?'

'Oh, for Christ's sake.'

'It wouldn't do any harm.'

'I have you to talk to. And Zoe.'

'So, talk to me.'

I take a deep breath. 'Sometimes I regret that I didn't get a chance to know her. How can I know who I am if I don't understand my past?'

'You're you. The girl I fell in love with.'

'But that's just it. Sometimes it feels like there are two versions of me, the girl I was growing up and the girl I am now. I'm not sure which is real.'

Matt pulls away. 'And Zoe, of course, knows both versions.'

'Let's not have that old row again. Are you pouting? Christ, anyone would think you were jealous.'

He gets up. 'You talk to her more than you talk to me.'

'You're a bloke, you don't get what it's like to have a best friend.'

He turns away from me.

'Where are you going?' I yell.

'Got stuff to do.' Matt picks up his MacBook. 'I left work early, but I've still got to finish what I had planned for today.' He heads into the bedroom.

I turn the sound back up on the TV and pretend that I'm not alone.

* * *

Anna raises a hand to wipe dribble from the side of her mouth. She rotates her neck, stiff from dozing in the chair. Day has turned to night, the kitchen is once again lit by candles and she's still here. She watches Mercy ironing clothes on a thick folded blanket on top of the pine table. It's calming, almost peaceful.

Mercy turns to reheat the cast flat iron on the range. Noticing Anna's awake, she smiles. 'I've made yer some broth.' She ladles something from the pan on the stove. 'You needs to keep yer strength up.'

Anna doesn't think sleep or food will help, but her stomach's rumbling so she holds out her hands to take the bowl. At least it's thicker than the liquid Mercy dished out before. Anna dunks the dry bread into the hot broth while Mercy resumes her ironing.

Hiding bits of unidentifiable meat under her spoon, Anna pushes the bowl aside and turns to Mercy. 'You said something about your boy. He's missing?'

'I'll tell yer, but I needs to tell the whole story.' Mercy puts the iron to one side. 'You needs to understand why I deserves to have me son back. I'm not a bad girl and yer mustn't judge me harsh. I feared God had judged me and that's why he were punishing me. I'm shamed to say I were minded to jump from that bridge last night. I'd all but given up. But now you've been sent to help me, I sees that the Lord is merciful. He's sent yer to me.' Mercy seems to be working herself into a passion. 'It's like that story the Pastor told in Church. 'Twas a test and I was yer Good Samaritan. Now, cause I helped yer, you'll help me.'

'I'm not sure how I can help but tell me anyway.'

Mercy sits on the low stool in front of Anna. 'Don't remember much about me family. I were the daughter of a water man. He shipped goods on the canals from the Midlands to London and back. Me ma worked with him. I remembers the warmth, heat from the stove and feeling safe bundled up in blankets. They couldn't keep me on the boat of course. No place for a child. By time I were five, I were in the orphanage. Not a happy time. Strict rules and I quickly learned best way to keep out a trouble was to abide by 'em.'

'You had a tough start,' says Anna.

'When I was eleven, I got lucky. I were offered a job as scullery maid working for Lord and Lady Astley. They's good and fair employers. Mrs Marsh, she's the cook, took me under her wing. It were hard work.' Mercy inspects her hands as she speaks. 'But I were grateful for food in me belly and a roof over me head.'

Anna's eyes are drawn to Mercy's callouses, the hands of a much older woman.

'When I were fourteen, a young groom were hired and me life changed. John were two years older than me. Tall, dark and handsome, I loved him the minute I saw him.' Mercy puts a hand to her heart. 'He were that shy. I'd try and strike up conversation, but he'd grab his lunch and retreat off to the yard. After a time he got brave enough to chat wi' me.' She laughs. 'How Mrs Marsh would chivy, telling me to get on. I saved all me smiles for John.' Mercy leans across to pull open the door of the stove. She pokes at the coals before throwing in another log and closing the door again. 'Came a time Mrs Marsh had to go away. Her ma had died and she were called home. Lord and Lady Astley were out of town and, cause the

37

house were run on reduced staff, me and John got to spend more time together. One day, after he'd finished his work, I asked him to stay.' Mercy blushes. 'That's when we moved things forward, if yer knows what I mean?'

Anna smiles.

'He were the love of me life. We couldn't afford no ring, but John made me a buckle bracelet out of an old bridle. I treasured that bangle like it were made o' pure gold. He had this plan that we might stay working for master and mistress as a married couple. John even worked out we could share his quarters over the stables. When we was up there I'd lay in his arms, thinking of the little ways I'd make that place our home.' Mercy wears a dreamy look before her face clouds over. 'Then comes the worst day of me life. Master had gone to visit across town and John had gone to help wi' the horses. They told me later that one of 'em horses went mad, rearing up and crashing down on a little trap belonging to mistress of the house. John had been helping fix the spoke on the wheel,' – a sob escapes her – 'he were crushed underneath.'

Anna reaches out to touch Mercy's arm. 'I'm so sorry.'

'Couldn't even cry.' Mercy waves her hands in front of her face. 'Couldn't believe I wouldn't see John no more. I remember this heavy feeling in pit of me stomach. For days I went on like I were a puppet. It were Mrs Marsh that sat me down and talked me through it all. That's when it hit me and I cried like I'd never stop.' Tears trickle down Mercy's face.

Anna, also welling up, sits forward and gives Mercy a hug.

'It were so hard. I couldn't even say goodbye. Master paid for the burial, just the basics like. We sat in the kitchen that night and Mister McCreery the butler, he poured us all a drink. He made a toast to John, I were that proud.'

'That's really nice.'

'As days went by, Mrs Marsh noticed how pale I were but she thinks it's 'cause I lost my beau. It were weeks afore she found out I had bigger problems. Remarking, she were, 'bout me putting on weight, when I sees the light dawn on her face.'

'She guessed you were pregnant?'

Mercy nods. 'Mrs Marsh were good to me though, she helped me conceal my condition. If I'd been found out I would 'ave been dismissed. When me time come, 'twas her that looked after me. For once luck were wi' me. Master and mistress was away visiting up north, so they didn't hear me screaming and carrying on.'

'Oh Mercy, how awful.' Anna couldn't begin to imagine childbirth without pain-relieving drugs.

'I were exhausted, but I got to hold my bairn for a while.' Mercy cradles her arms as if nursing the child now. 'I called him John after his pa. He had the tiniest fingers and toes and a mess of black curls. I felt such love.' She lowers her voice. 'Even more than for me beau. Ain't that wicked?'

Anna shakes her head. 'Of course not. Go on.'

'Mrs Marsh knew 'twere impossible to keep the bairn hidden. I'd lose my job and we'd both be out on the street. So, two days after he arrived, while I were sleeping, Mrs Marsh wraps him in an apron and takes him to the Foundling Hospital.'

'And you've not seen him since?' asks Anna.

Mercy's eyes shine. 'Oh yes, but I has. I been working hard over the years, I'm a lady's maid now and gets one afternoon off a fortnight. I goes to that hospital to look for my John and sometimes I sees him. I knows it's him, a mother knows these things. I stands and watches him through them black iron railings and I whispers to him, "I'm coming to get yer." One day John turns round, he looks right at me and smiles. He knows me, see? There's this bond atween us that can't be broken. John knows one day I'll come and get him.' She gazes imploringly at Anna. 'So, will yer help me get my boy back?'

Anna hugs her. 'I'll do what I can. But how? Do you just have to turn up at the Foundling Hospital and collect him?'

Mercy stands up to stoke the fire again. 'That be the problem. They tell me John's not there.'

'But how can that be? You said you've seen him?'

'They says I'm mistook. That the boy I seen ain't my John.'

There's a sinking feeling in Anna's stomach. 'Mercy, are you sure the boy you've seen is your son?'

Mercy raises her voice. 'You think I don't know me own boy? I'd know him anywhere.'

'I'm sure you're right. So, what exactly did they say? Don't they have records? Can't they check for sure?'

Mercy sits down heavily. 'I give 'em his name, but they says he's not there.'

'When did all this happen?' asks Anna.

'Yesterday morning. Lawd knows how I got to that bridge last night. I were wandering I s'pose, no purpose left. I walked until dark then I stands on the new bridge and that's when I sees the moon. 'Twere so bright, too bright for a sad night. I remember thinking I might drop down into the water and let it carry me away. Perhaps meet up with me beau? But I was afeared to jump. So, I stands there, asking God, "Why you doing this to me?" That's when I hears yer call out and I stops thinking 'bout me own problems and helps yer. Weren't till later I realised you'd been sent.' Mercy's eyes are bright. 'I think they got me boy in there. I know he's alive, I do feel it in me bones and God has sent yer to help me.'

Anna stands up. 'I don't think God has sent me Mercy. I'll try to help but please, don't get your hopes up. Perhaps they've made a mistake or perhaps they're telling the truth. Either way, there must be some sort of record.'

Even if she couldn't find Mercy's son, perhaps she could find out what happened to him and help Mercy to accept it?

'I said you was an angel.'

Anna chortles. 'I may not remember much, but I'm fairly sure I'm no angel.' She looks down at her jeans and tee shirt. 'But if we're going to the Foundling Hospital, I'm going to need something more suitable to wear.'

Mercy smiles. 'Miss Abigail has plenty o' clothes. That's what I been ironing.' She jumps up, shaking out a plum coloured gown from the top of the pile. 'We'll find something to fit yer.'

Anna paces up and down. 'We'll need a story, something to explain my presence.' Excitement bubbles in her belly. She can't do anything about her own predicament, at least not until her memory returns, but meanwhile she can repay Mercy's kindness. She just hopes Mercy doesn't get her heart broken all over again if it turns out that her child is dead.

4th September

Something stirs in Anna's mind as she lays on Mercy's cot next morning. Everything feels so out of sync but the idea of searching for someone seems strangely familiar. If only she could remember more than her name.

Emerging from behind the curtain, Anna spots a full-length mirror standing adjacent to the range. The newly pressed gown rests across the back of a chair.

'Mornin, Miss Anna.' Mercy steps down from the servants' stairs and sets the bundle of clothing in her arms on the table. She selects a camisole, corset and petticoat. 'I think these should fit yer.'

Anna pushes the corset to one side. 'I'm not wearing that.' She slips off her jeans and pulls the petticoat up over her hips.

'That's it, miss.' Mercy fastens the ties securely at Anna's waist.

Discarding her tee shirt, Anna slides the silk camisole over her head, shivering as the cold fabric floats down across her shoulders and breasts. She gazes into the mirror. Although she recognises the wide-eyed girl staring back, she doesn't feel in possession of her body. Questions run around her head. Who is Anna Stratton? How old is she? Where does she live? She glances at her hand. No engagement or wedding ring. Is she even missed?

Mercy smiles as she holds out the plum gown for Anna to step into. 'There, fits a treat.' She laces the drawstrings.

'It's beautiful.' Anna smooths down the skirt. 'You sure it's okay for me to borrow it?'

'What mistress don't know won't hurt her none.' Mercy picks up a hairbrush. 'Here, sit you down and let me do something with yer hair.'

Anna seats herself in a kitchen chair. 'Is she a good mistress?'

'Miss Abigail? Yes, a real lady.' Mercy abandons her attempt to tame Anna's hair with the brush and resorts instead to pinning it up. 'Mrs Marsh trained me up well and after Miss Abigail's lady's maid left, I got the job. I gets eight guineas a year. Course, I saves every spare penny to reclaim me boy.'

'You have to pay to reclaim him?'

Mercy sighs. 'I been told it's a pound a year I owe for 'is keep.'

'Ow.' Anna winces as a pin spears her scalp. 'But Miss Abigail treats you kindly?'

'Oh, bless you, yes. We're both the same age – twenty – got that in common. Course, Miss Abigail's promised in marriage to 'er second cousin. Keep still, miss, I's nearly done. One day Miss Abigail tells me, "Mercy, when I'm married, you'll come with me to the country estate in Yorkshire." Well I'm shamed to say I burst into tears. That's how she got to me secret. Kind she were, even remembered my beau.' Mercy steps back to view her efforts. 'There, think that'll do.'

Mercy rummages through a box of shoes on the floor. 'Miss Abigail says to me, "Mercy, you must bring your son with you. He'll be well catered for in the country and the fresh air will do him good." "But my lady," I says, "the scandal". Miss Abigail

43

shakes her head, "No, Mercy, we'll tell everyone that you're a widow." Well, 'twere the answer to my prayers.'

Mercy squats in front of Anna holding a pair of leather ankle boots. 'Now all I have to do is reclaim me boy and we can be off to start our new life. Had to wait until the household took their leave to Yorkshire for the wedding. 'Twas agreed I'd stay behind to pack up the last of Miss Abigail's clothes and travel up in a week or two's time.' Mercy eases the boot onto Anna's foot. 'Might you push, miss? I be struggling.'

'So, they've left you here alone?'

'Mrs Marsh is visiting her sister for a few days and Simkins, the lower butler, stays with his ma when his lordship's away. Simkins and me have to be in Yorkshire by the time the happy couple return from their honeymoon. We's to travel up in the coach with Miss Abigail's things. It's no good, miss. These won't fit.'

Anna shrugs her shoulders. 'Miss Abigail must have tiny feet. Don't worry. I'll wear my own.'

'You look grand, Miss Anna. You'll surely convince 'em.' Mercy lifts down a blue travelling cloak from the hook by the door. She frowns. 'Them blessed moths. Well, the day is fair,' – she passes Anna a woollen wrap – 'we'll wear shawls.'

* * *

The tube is packed. I check my Fitbit – ten past twelve. I'm late. The queue for the lift is ridiculous so I take the stairs. Halfway up and I'm regretting it. I emerge, sweaty and out of breath, to duck and dive around the tourists wandering in Covent Garden. As I reach *Bistro Bellissima*, I spy Zoe sitting at a table in the window.

'I'm so sorry.' I ease into the seat opposite.

'No probs, hun. You okay?'

I touch my cheek. 'I've covered the bruises with make-up. My head is worse.' I bend forward so Zoe can examine my matted hair and sutures.

'Ouch. I feel so bad. If I hadn't got off with Phil you'd never have headed home alone.'

'It was my own fault. I shouldn't have walked that time of night.'

'And happened to walk via Westminster Bridge?'

'I know what you're thinking, it's the last place I saw Debbie, but it wasn't just that. It was that story on the news the other day.'

'The teenager who jumped?'

'Yeah. Last month Gary published an article about suicides from bridges across the Thames.'

'Your boss is sooo weird.'

I shake my head. 'No, it was a good article actually. I was thinking to write a follow-up imagined from...'

A young girl is hovering to take our order.

'Are you allowed wine,' asks Zoe, 'or you still on painkillers?'

'I'll stick to sparkling water. Caesar salad for me, please.' I pass my menu to the waitress.

'And the same for me, but I'll have a glass of Sauvignon too.' Zoe turns back to me. 'Sorry, you were saying?'

'I was trying to put myself inside her head, imagine how she was feeling... anyway, Matt convinced himself I was planning to jump into the Thames.'

Zoe's eyes widen.

'Obviously I wasn't.'

The owner of the bistro brings our drinks over. '*Buongiorno*

45

signore. We don't usually see you mid-week?'

'*Ciao* Tony.' Zoe smiles.

Tony raises an eyebrow as he pours my water. '*Niente vino?*'

I shake my head, pointing to my sutures.

He takes a sharp intake of breath. 'I bring you *bella insalata, signorina.*'

'Thanks,' I say.

'So.' Zoe straightens her knife and fork. 'Have you and Matt had another barney?'

'Kind of.' I reach across for Zoe's glass and take a sip. 'Mmm, wish I could have some wine… sometimes he drives me nuts, wrapping me up in cotton wool.'

'Yeah, well. You know how he likes to take care of you.'

'I wish he wouldn't.'

'Then tell him.'

'I can't. I suppose he misses it. He did so much for his mum.'

'You're not his bloody mother's replacement!'

Our salads arrive and we begin to eat. After a few mouthfuls I put down my fork. 'Matt thinks I need to speak to someone.'

Zoe's eyebrows shoot up. 'What, like a counsellor or something?'

I nod.

Eighteen months ago, Zoe had suggested the same thing. When I came home from seeing Debbie, I cried for hours. 'I've destroyed my relationship with Mum and Dad, and for what?'

'Your mum and dad will come around,' Zoe said. 'You can put things right with them any time you're ready.'

'But why should I apologise? They didn't help when I needed them. Everyone lets me down. Oh God, I'm so messed up.'

Zoe thought I was having a breakdown. She persuaded me to see the doctor to get some pills. They didn't solve anything; didn't explain why my birth mother abandoned me.

Zoe's staring at me. 'You miss Debbie, don't you?'

'I think you actually have to know someone before you can miss them. But...'

'But what?'

'I miss the idea of her, the chance of getting to know her, finding out who I really am.'

'You should speak to your mum and dad.'

'I can't.'

'It must be, what, three years since they sold up?'

I sip my water. 'Yeah.'

'They still pay your rent, don't they?'

'Thanks for reminding me.'

'Sorry, it's just, well, they haven't written you out of their lives, have they? It's your choice not to stay in touch.'

'They let me down, Zoe.'

'They had your best interests at heart.'

'How is it that you see the good in everyone?' I ask.

She shrugs. 'I try. I've always got your back hun.' She picks up her wine and chinks it against my water glass. 'Cheers. BFF, right?'

* * *

The Strand is heaving. 'Ow,' says Anna as a young woman carrying a basket of eggs and butter bumps into her. Further along a bedraggled boy with a box around his neck yells into

47

her face. 'Hot baked Pippins.'

Mercy hauls Anna to one side as a man hurries past carrying an enormous trunk on his back.

'He almost knocked me into the traffic.' Anna glances nervously at the sedan chairs and carriages rushing by. To step into the road would be perilous.

'Take the wall.' Mercy steers Anna to a safer path skirting the buildings.

'Tell me more about the Foundling Hospital,' Anna asks. 'I need to know how things operate if I'm to be your advocate.'

Mercy stops in her tracks. 'What do yer need to know?'

'Well, talk me through what happened when you visited two days ago.'

'I were that nervous. Didn't know what me boy would make of me after all this time. When I rings the bell, this evil looking woman comes to the door. All dressed in black she were, hair pulled back all severe. Looks at me like I'm scum but lets me in anyway. "I'm here to reclaim me boy," I tells her. She makes me wait ages before showing me up this grand staircase. "Mister Cornelius Wilkes will see you now," she says, all hoity-toity.'

'And what did Mister Wilkes say?'

'He says he can't release my boy until I show him the bit o' cloth I was given as a receipt. Well, I don't have no cloth, but I tells him I know what date me boy was admitted. That's when Wilkes gets angry. He says the cloth is proof of who I is. "But I'm John's mother," I tells him.' Mercy takes a shuddering breath. 'Wilkes won't listen. He says if I don't leave, he'll call a constable.'

Anna puts her arm through Mercy's. 'We'll sort it out.'

Leaving The Strand, they pass through cobbled city streets bustling with life: hawkers peddling wares from huge wooden trays suspended around their necks on broad leather straps – kitchen knives, scissors, ribbons and lace, while pots and pans dangle from strings tied to their belts; street sellers wheel carts loaded with fruit and vegetables; cries of 'buy my fine cabbages' compete with 'cherries, two penny a pound.'

'I'll tell you what,' Anna says, 'when we get there, I'll pretend to be your mistress and demand they tell me where John is.'

Very soon the city gives way to open fields and they walk on along unmade roads, carefully avoiding potholes and horse dung. They seem to be circling a fort with a high wooden fence when Mercy comes to an abrupt halt. 'This is it.'

Anna stares up at three stone lodge gates providing access to a wide driveway. The large country house in front of her is not what she'd envisaged when Mercy spoke of a hospital. Still, they're here now.

They make their way up the drive and when they reach the house, Anna smiles encouragingly at Mercy. 'Are you ready?'

Mercy takes a deep breath.

Anna rings the bell.

'I think someone's coming,' whispers Mercy.

The door opens and a woman stands before them. She wears a sinister expression and stares hard at Mercy before turning to Anna and bobbing the faintest curtsey. 'Yes, miss. Can I help you?'

I can do this, thinks Anna. It's all about attitude and showing them I won't take any nonsense. 'My name is Anna Stratton and I am here to see Mister Wilkes.'

'You'd best come in. Wait here.' The woman leaves them in the entrance hall as she makes her way upstairs.

Anna glances down at the black and white checkered floor tiles. Her eyes travel up the red carpeted staircase lined with portraits. She grips Mercy's hand. 'It'll be all right.'

'I hope so.'

Anna grins. 'Not the best sort of person to work with children…'

'Shhh, she's coming back.'

'Mister Cornelius Wilkes has a few minutes before the recital. He will see you now.' The woman leads the way up the staircase and into an anteroom. 'Wait here.' She disappears again.

'This is where I were yesterday,' whispers Mercy.

'Can you hear a piano?' asks Anna. 'I think it's coming from across the landing. Sounds like they're warming up for the recital.'

The woman returns. 'Mistress Stratton, come this way.'

They're escorted into a high-ceilinged room lined with massive paintings. Anna recognises one, a Holbein. Memories stir – a school trip, an art gallery – she shakes her head.

Three men sit behind an enormous desk in the centre of the room, looking like they're about to conduct an interview. The one in the middle, wearing an elaborate grey wig, looks disgruntled. Probably because he's been dragged away from the musical event that was about to start.

Mercy hangs back by the door.

Anna marches up to the desk. 'Mister Wilkes? It is with distress and concern that I accompany my maid here today. I know you spoke with her two days ago, but I am certain you can provide us with more information.'

Cornelius Wilkes sits a little straighter and clears his throat. 'Madam, you are correct. We did indeed give your maidservant an audience two days hence. I am sorry for any distress caused to yourself, but I am afraid the circumstances have not changed. We are unable to help in this matter.'

'But how can this be?' demands Anna. 'Her child was left in your care.'

'Let us review the situation. Your maid informed us the child was admitted here on,' – Wilkes turns to the gentleman on the right – 'what was the date, Pym?'

'The 21st day of February, the Year of our Lord 1747.'

'But your maid has nothing to vouch for the fact that she is indeed the child's mother,' says Wilkes.

Mercy steps forward. 'He were wearing me love token, a buckle on 'is wrist, sir.'

'Many children are admitted wearing a bracelet of some kind,' says Pym.

'I am afraid, without sufficient proof,' – Wilkes shrugs – 'my hands are tied.'

'That's ridiculous.' Anna shakes her head. 'All this fuss over a scrap of cloth. My maid has told you she was never given any kind of receipt for her child.'

'My good lady.' Wilkes smirks. 'The scrap of cloth, as you so eloquently put it, is the receipt. One half given to the mother, whilst the other stays in the child's records.'

'But you have the date and the child's name?'

'Each child is re-named on admittance. Without the cloth and the admission number, it is impossible to trace the child. Is that not correct, Mister Pym?'

Pym nods his head in affirmation. 'Yes, therein lies the problem. We have a record of several children admitted on that day. Without the child's new name, we are unable to ascertain where this child might presently be.'

'Oh, but sir, I can tell you 'is new name,' says Mercy. 'I come to 'is baptism see, so I knows what name you gived 'im. You baptised 'im Isaac Bliss, sir. I were there.'

Wilkes and Pym exchange a glance. Pym flicks through the ledger in front of him. He pushes the book towards Wilkes.

'Ah, now let me see.' Wilkes runs his finger down a list of names. 'Yes, well, we do have a record of an Isaac Bliss. Oh, I am afraid…' He exhales deeply. Closing the book, he looks Anna in the eye. 'Mistress Stratton, all infants are despatched to the country for their first few years. Gives them the best possible start in life, you see? We do not have the facilities here. The child would have been with us a mere matter of days after your maid deposited him at our door. Sadly, although we monitor our foster homes closely, some children are inevitably lost. This may be down to a child being weak, sickly, or perhaps some hereditary disorder undetected in early months. I am afraid we cannot perform miracles. The ledger shows that your maid's son has not been returned to us, which means, in all likelihood, he did not survive.' Wilkes slams the ledger closed and turns to Mercy. 'We are, of course, deeply sorry for your loss. Now, if you ladies will excuse us, we have a recital to attend.' Wilkes stands up.

Anna scans the faces of the other two gentlemen, seated like bookends. Pym, also wigged, has been nodding throughout. Even now he is rising from his seat. The dark-haired man on the left had turned to look at Mercy when she and Anna first entered the room. He has not taken his eyes from her during the whole exchange.

Mercy is wringing her hands, repeating over and over, 'but I seen him, I seen him.'

'Mister Wilkes. My maid is convinced she has seen her son here. I fear your records' – Anna taps the ledger – 'may not be wholly accurate. I demand she be allowed to view the children in order to ascertain...'

'Preposterous,' interrupts Pym.

'I cannot allow that.' Wilkes folds his arms. 'The children here are not circus creatures. They are not animals in the marketplace to be selected at will by mothers who, realising they have made a mistake in parting with them, suddenly develop a conscience. We keep thorough records. I can assure you the child is not here, nor never has been. Not since the day he left for the foster home.'

'Well.' Anna takes a deep breath. 'Then tell us who fostered him so we might locate the family and my maid may take some small comfort from hearing of his short life.'

'I am afraid, madam, that is confidential information that cannot be released. Now, I have been patient, but we can do no more.' Wilkes strides towards the door. 'I bid you good day.'

Pym gives her a brief nod as he follows Wilkes from the room.

Anna turns to the gentleman still seated. 'Please, sir. Is there nothing you can do?'

He turns to regard Anna for the first time, his blue eyes sparkling.

Anna feels her cheeks burn. 'Right, well, thanks for nothing.' She grabs Mercy and storms from the room, Mercy leaning heavily on Anna as they make their way down the stairs.

Outside, Mercy stops on the driveway and leans against the railings, gazing at the empty lawn. 'I used to stand here and watch for me boy. I knowed, see, they returned 'em from the foster homes once they be five-years-old so all I had to do were wait. One day I seen 'im. Could tell it were 'im from his black curls. Just there he were.' She stares across as if his

53

image were still visible. 'I called to him, "John," and he looked straight at me. I like to think he knowed who I was. He ran inside when the bell rang, but it were enough and I came back whenever I could.'

Anna prises Mercy's fingers from the railing. The metal has left a red mark on her palms.

* * *

We walk along Drury lane until we reach Zoe's office. 'Well, this was a nice treat,' Zoe turns to face me. 'Shame I've got to go back to work.'

I hug her. 'It's a beautiful afternoon, I think I'll carry on walking for a bit.'

'All right for some. Message me later?'

I nod. The late summer sun is warm on my face and I'm getting used to not having a mobile. It's quite liberating not checking WhatsApp or Twitter every five minutes. My feet lead me through Bloomsbury towards Russell Square, where I veer off to skirt Great Ormond Street Hospital. The traffic here is less busy and there are fewer pedestrians, but I'm feeling something else, like I've walked this way before.

I cut through Brunswick Square Gardens then, conscious of children's laughter, follow the wall on my left to reach the entrance of a small park. Although it's like many other parks situated around London, unusually I'm confronted by a large security guard manning a turnstile. He eyes me suspiciously. 'No entry unless accompanied by a child.'

'What is this place?' I ask.

'Private playground for Coram Fields.'

'Coram?'

He gestures towards the large adjacent building.

I approach to study the plaque on the wall. *The London Foundling Hospital.* Must be a museum. The door is open, and I'm drawn to go in. As I place my foot on the first step, I feel a chill. I've not stepped into shadow and yet I'm shivering. I hesitate. Perhaps I've been here before? For the magazine? But I'd remember, wouldn't I? I sit down on a bench opposite and stare up at the building. Its history has something to do with orphans and children. But how do I even know that?

I take a few deep breaths and march up the steps. Just inside the door is a woman in a kiosk. She greets me with a smile. 'One adult is it?'

I check the time on my Fitbit. There's nowhere else I need to be. 'Yes,' I reply, pulling out a note from the cash Matt left me this morning.

Following a party of Japanese tourists, I tour the house. Moving from room to room I stop to gaze at poignant pictures of small children in uniform. All those poor unloved souls from a bygone era. I can almost hear their cries as their mothers abandon them. The sense of *déjà vu* returns as I walk up the staircase and into a large room. I recognise paintings on the walls; even the way the room is laid out seems familiar. The information board informs me I'm in the parlour. An office in the time of Coram, it was also used for entertaining. Its grandeur seems a million miles from the experience of the youngsters housed here long ago.

Back downstairs, the Japanese tourists are snapping photos of the contents in a display cabinet. I wait my turn, then stare through the glass. It's full of tiny keepsakes, love tokens left for children by desperate mothers – a button, a brooch, a scrappy note, a tiny bracelet with a padlock. I wipe a tear from my cheek.

Making my way back to the exit, I stop and purchase a copy of *Coram's Children* from the smiley lady in the kiosk. I feel connection to this place. Perhaps the book will tell me why?

* * *

'If you will excuse me, I need some fresh air,' says Janus. 'My appetite for music has somewhat waned.'

Pym rises from his seat in the chapel to allow Janus to squeeze past, while Wilkes, eager for the recital to begin, barely notices his departure.

Sometimes being a patron of the Foundling Hospital challenges one's own principles and instincts, thinks Janus, as he heads out of the building.

In the gardens he spots the two women, the child's mother visibly upset whilst her young mistress attempts to console her. Janus hesitates, unsure whether to intrude, before crossing over to where they sit.

'Well, that's that,' he overhears the child's mother remark.

'We can't give up yet,' her mistress responds.

Janus clears his throat. 'Sorry to disturb you.'

The young woman looks up and Janus is struck by her hazel eyes. 'Please. I would like to help if I can.'

The child's mother is berating herself. 'What a fool I been. What woman don't know her own son?'

Her mistress continues to stare at Janus.

Janus addresses her. 'I am a patron of the Foundling Hospital. Let me make some inquiries. I may at least be able to find out which foster home the boy was sent to. If we can find out something of his early years, perhaps that might ease his mother's sorrow?'

The child's mother continues to murmur. 'I were so sure it were me boy.'

'Let me give you my calling card.' Janus reaches into his waistcoat pocket. 'Please feel free to call on me if you would like me to see what I can find out.' He holds out a card to the woman with the beautiful eyes, then doffs his hat politely, turns on his heel and strides back towards the chapel.

* * *

I make myself a cup of Earl Grey and settle down to read. An hour later the key turns in the lock.

'You're looking brighter,' says Matt.

'I do feel a bit better.'

'What have you got there?'

'Well, you know I met Zoe for lunch? Afterwards I went for a walk and stumbled across the Foundling Hospital.'

'I think I've heard of that.'

I hold up *Coram's Children*. 'Back in the eighteenth century, poor women who couldn't look after their babies placed them in the Foundling Hospital. Most of those kids never saw their mothers again.'

Matt sits down beside me. 'Is this about them or you?'

'It's just interesting, that's all.'

He takes my book and begins to thumb through it. 'It's not the same though, is it? Debbie knew what she was doing when she gave you up and your adoptive parents gave you a fantastic life.'

I snatch my book back. 'It's about women being separated from their children through circumstances beyond their control. It's been going on for ages, centuries. There might be a story here if I add a personal angle.'

Matt snorts. 'And you think Gary will publish it?'

'I don't know.'

'I don't get why you worry so much about finding a story. It's just a job, Anna. You know I can take care of us both.' Matt kisses me on the forehead. 'I'll order a takeaway. Chinese or Thai?'

* * *

Mercy pulls off her shawl and busies herself at the range.

'Sit down, Mercy.' Anna moves the chair away from the table.

'Got to get this fire going or there won't be no hot water. No good brooding. I needs to get on with the washing and ironing.'

'Just take a minute. It's all been a bit of an ordeal.'

Mercy sits down, rubbing at her wrist.

'It's lovely that you gave John your buckle bracelet.'

'Mrs Marsh cut it down to size. It were so he'd know his ma and pa loved him.'

Anna leans against the table. 'Tell me again about seeing John at the Foundling Hospital.'

'Whenever I got a few hours off on a Sunday, I'd visit the chapel to listen to the children sing. Sounded like angels they did. Made me feel close to me boy. It were the last place I seen him as a bairn.'

'When was that?' Anna asks.

'After Mrs Marsh took him. I woke up alone and it felt like a hole were ripped right through my heart. I knew they'd

58

have to baptise me boy, so I crept out of the house and went to the chapel. I stood at the back cause I didn't want to be seen. Well, it came to John's turn and I knowed it were him cause God sent me a sign. Just as the pastor lifted him up, a ray of sunlight came through the stained-glass window and shone on his dark curls. "I baptise thee Isaac Bliss," the pastor said, "in the name of the Father and of the Son and of the Holy Ghost," and I said, "Amen" real quiet as I didn't want no-one to hear.'

'So, that's how you knew his name in the ledger?'

Mercy nods. 'I were still that faint from the delivery, I had to rest me head against a marble pillar and wait till the pastor and nuns had all gone. Then I went up to the altar and I said to God, "Dear Lord, please look after my son. Let him grow strong and healthy until I claim him again as me own." Made a promise to God that day that I'd work hard, be a good girl and one day I'd get him back. I left John in God's hands. I trusted the Lord, but he took him from me. Why do you think that is?' Mercy looks at Anna. 'Do you think it's cause I'm a sinner? I does try to be good, but perhaps I'm not good enough? Perhaps the Lord's punishing me?'

'Of course you're good, Mercy.' Anna pats Mercy's arm. 'You've been so strong.' But doubts were creeping in. Was the child Mercy saw in the gardens really her son? Could a woman recognise her child after five years?

Anna pulls out the card.

Janus Gregory, Grevil Street, London.

'Don't you want to find out about John's foster home? I have a feeling this man may be able to help.'

Mercy takes out a large kerchief and blows her nose. 'I have to get the mistress's clothes packed. Have to face it, I ain't

59

never gonna get me boy back.'

'You don't believe that. Look how sure you were earlier! Don't give up, Mercy. There's still hope. We can at least find out about John's early years.'

Mercy stands up. 'I must make ready for the move.'

'Okay,' says Anna, 'but tomorrow I'm going to see Janus Gregory.'

5th September

'Monsieur Quintar,' announces Janus's butler, William.

The Frenchman, Henri Quintar hands his hat and cloak to the butler and strides into the breakfast room. *'Bonjour, comment-allez vous?'*

Khan, who has finished eating and is drinking his tea, responds with a cursory, 'Good morning'.

'Quintar, my friend. Come in, come in.' Janus waves the publication in his hand. 'Would you credit it? Those damn fools still disrupt our plans. This sets everything back, not to mention the increased cost.'

Quintar sits himself down at the far end of the table, taking the coffee pot proffered by Janus's footman, Ned. 'I see you are in fine fettle this morning, Janus.'

'Yes, yes.' Janus lays the article in front of Quintar. 'But look, is this not typical? Lining their own pockets with no thought for the unfortunate women needing a roof over their heads.'

'Ah, *la belle* Magdalen.' Quintar tucks his napkin into his collar, as Ned places a plate of herring in front of him. *'Merci.'* While Janus rants, Quintar eats, nodding and tutting appropriately.

'I need to get over there and see Thorpe,' says Janus. 'Get things back on track. Are you coming, Quintar?'

'But of course, *mon ami.*'

'Good man, good man.' Janus gets up to leave. 'Then let us be off.'

'Might I not finish *petit déjeuner?*'

'Sorry. Yes of course.'

'I do wonder,' Quintar pours himself more coffee, 'if it might be beneficial to let Thorpe stew a while? Perhaps, if he should fear the contract in jeopardy?'

Janus mutters as he paces back and forth. 'Perhaps, perhaps.' He turns abruptly. 'Are you free tomorrow evening, Khan? I have called a Prism meeting and I would be grateful if you would join us.'

Khan inclines his head.

'Have you heard from the others, Quintar?' Janus asks.

'They have confirmed, although I fear Pym will not stay late. I hear his wife is out of sorts again.'

'Right. Listen, I will get William to fetch the landau around. Do not tarry long.'

Quintar tuts as Janus rushes out. 'Surely the man digs himself an early grave?'

Khan looks up from his paperwork. 'His irritation is understandable when others are minded to create unnecessary delay.'

'Of course, of course.'

'Janus is committed to Magdalen.' Khan dabs his mouth with his napkin. 'He is passionate about the plight of so many unmarried women, penniless and homeless, resorting to prostitution as the only way to earn a crust.'

'Magdalen is a worthwhile venture and Janus's efforts in persuading wealthy patrons to take these women off the streets and help them into gainful employment is to be commended.'

Khan gathers up his books. 'Magdalen took in thirty destitute young women last year. This new wing will double the capacity.'

'Indeed, my own endeavours to gain sponsorship are postulated upon that very premise. These architects argue endlessly about the plans, but I have no doubt that Janus will put them in their place.'

'My apologies, Quintar.' Khan glances at the clock. 'I must away to Devereaux Court. I have it on good authority that Dr Johnson speaks at noon at the Grecian.'

'Johnson is indeed a grand orator.' Quintar sets his cutlery down on his plate. 'On your way, Khan, I will see you the morrow. Janus values your sound judgment.'

After Khan has left, Quintar ambles out to the hallway where he finds Janus already donning cloak and hat.

'Ready?' Janus picks up his umbrella. The doorbell rings. Expecting the coachman, Janus opens it, almost colliding with the young woman standing on his top step.

* * *

'Oh, you're going out?' says Anna.

'Yes.' Janus stares at her. 'Regrettably I am.'

'Come, Janus.' Quintar appraises Anna. 'Might we not spare a few moments for this charming young lady? Did we not agree Thorpe may become more amenable if kept waiting?'

Janus glances at the clock in the hallway. 'Quintar my friend, as usual you are correct. We can spare a few minutes.' He strides back into the breakfast room calling over his shoulder, 'William? Change of plan. Send in more coffee.'

Quintar takes Anna's arm. 'Come, *ma chérie*.'

What a lovely room, notes Anna. Despite its dark wood panelling, French doors leading onto a terrace make it airy and bright. Paintings line the walls, while brass and silver ornaments gleam from the fireplace mantel.

The table is littered with the remains of their meal. Janus takes the carver while Quintar pulls out a chair for Anna, then seats himself opposite. A footman enters carrying a silver tray with coffee.

'Ah, thank you Ned. Quintar, would you do the honours?' Janus turns to give Anna his full attention.

'I'm delaying you.' Anna plays with the calling card in her hand.

'Not at all. Let me introduce you. This is my good friend Henri Quintar. Quintar, this is Mistress Stratton.'

He remembers my name, thinks Anna. She smiles.

Quintar reaches across and takes her hand, kissing it. '*Enchanté mademoiselle*.'

Anna studies him as he pours coffee into china cups. Good looking, goatee beard, mischievous eyes. Probably charms the pantaloons off the ladies.

'So, you are staying with the Astleys?' Janus asks.

'Who?'

'Sorry, I had assumed you were staying with Lord and Lady Astley. Although I must confess to being intrigued by your connection with their servant girl. Mercy Benson, is it not?'

He's done his homework. 'Look, it's rather a long story and I appreciate you don't have much time. Might we talk about the child? He's my priority.'

Janus raises his eyebrows and leans back in his chair. 'After you left yesterday, I re-examined the ledger. I am afraid there is no record of Isaac Bliss returning from the foster home.'

'But Mercy's convinced she's seen him. She's watched him in the playground these past few months.'

'Then I am afraid she is mistaken. The mind can play strange tricks. However, all is not lost. A further search of the records revealed the name of the foster family, a couple by the name of Shuttlebarrow. They live at Harrow-on-the-Hill. With your permission, my companion Khan and I will ride there tomorrow to see what we might discover.'

'Not today?'

There's a long pause. Anna realises her enthusiasm is usurping her manners. There's no need for this man to help them at all.

'No,' says Janus. 'I am afraid I have important business this morning.'

Anna downs the bitter coffee. Thank goodness it was only a small cup. Aware both men are now awaiting a response, she stands defiantly. 'Tomorrow then. I shall come with you, of course.'

Janus shakes his head. 'No, that would not be appropriate.'

'But I insist. I must report back to the child's mother first-hand, even if only to tell her what sort of life her little boy had. What time do we leave?'

There's a knock at the door. 'The landau is ready, sir,' says William.

Anna maintains eye contact with Janus.

'As you wish.' There's a hint of amusement in Janus's voice. 'We will call for you in the morning.'

'No.' Anna's voice is determined., 'I shall come here.'

'Ten o'clock then.' Janus stands up. 'Stay, have more coffee. Forgive me, for I must take my leave. Quintar?

65

Quintar rises slowly. He kisses Anna once more, his moist moustache tickling the back of her hand. As he lifts his head, he leans forward and whispers, '*Formidable.*' Striding out to the hallway, he collects his cloak and hat from William, pulls his walking cane from the jardiniere and follows Janus to the landau.

* * *

Three gentleman hunch over a table in a dark corner of *The Ram's Head*.

Pestlemore wrings his hands nervously, yellow sausage-like fingers contrasting against the white of starched cuffs. 'What have we done?'

Tweedie, petite and pale, struggles to lift the heavy jug of ale to refill their cups. 'Come, Pestlemore. Pull yourself together, sir.'

Pestlemore picks up his pewter cup, then places it back down on the table. He shakes his head, his fat lips quivering.

The third gentleman strokes his chin thoughtfully. 'Perhaps 'tis not all bad.'

Tweedie stares at him. 'How so?'

'At least we know the equipment works.' Their companion takes a swig of ale before continuing. 'Endorsement by the Royal Society is a step closer. Come gentlemen, we should be celebrating.'

'But the ap-p-parition.' Pestlemore shudders.

'Pestlemore is right to be concerned.' Tweedie wipes froth from his top lip. 'We know not the consequences of our actions.'

Their companion slams down his cup, spilling ale across

the table. 'Do not speak of it.' He lowers his voice. 'We must proceed with caution, that much is evident. It is imperative nothing be said. Not until I have had time to consider all eventualities.'

Pestlemore tugs at his collar. 'We have to tell Gregory. He will discover it anyway once he notices the equipment missing.'

'We have no choice.' says Tweedie. 'We must confess, and sooner rather than later.'

Their companion sighs. 'I did not say Gregory was not to be informed. Simply that there is no rush. We have a Prism meeting the morrow, do we not? It changes nothing to worry Gregory before then.' He stands, placing his hat upon his head. 'Meanwhile, see if you might trace the whereabouts of this so-called apparition.'

* * *

After Matt has left for work, I return to my research. I pore over *Coram's Children*, making notes on the admissions process. There's definitely a story here. The history of the Foundling Hospital resonates. I understand what it's like to be abandoned. How many of those poor kids ever got to meet their birth mother?

I'd followed Brenda down the corridor, where we entered a room with shabby bench seating and a coffee table loaded with magazines. A woman stood by the window gazing out, although there wasn't much of a view – just the walls of other buildings. She turned as we came in, keeping one hand behind her back.

'I'll leave you to it.' Brenda closed the door.

I stared at Debbie. She was slim, skinny even. Her shoulder-length hair hung in rats' tails, its yellowish tinge suggesting repetitive bleaching rather than natural blonde. Hazel eyes like mine.

Debbie lifted the cigarette she'd been concealing to take one final drag. Prising open the window, she chucked out the butt and fanned the air. 'We're not supposed to smoke in here, but everyone does.'

We were standing two metres apart. *Should I hug her, kiss her cheek, shake her hand?* I did nothing.

Debbie crossed the room and sat down. I took the other end of the seat.

'I meant to get you a card,' she said, 'for your eighteenth. Not easy to get a nice one around here.'

'You knew it was my birthday?' I mentally kick myself. Of course she knew my birthday.

Debbie looked into her lap. 'They sent me a photo and letter.'

It felt wrong to keep staring. I sensed I was making her uncomfortable. I turned my gaze to the painting, St Michaels Mount in Cornwall, waves crashing against rocks. All the words and questions I'd carefully prepared had gone.

'You done all right in your exams?' she asked.

'Okay, I suppose.'

'You're a smart girl.' Debbie tugged at her cardigan sleeves. 'Not like me. You off to university then?'

'No, I've signed up with a temping agency.'

She nodded.

'Just for starters. I want to be a journalist.'

'Smart girl,' she repeated. Her eyes flit round the room,

settling everywhere except on me. 'They treat you all right?'

'Mum and Dad?' I winced. Was that the right thing to call them in front of her? 'They've given me a good life.'

Debbie nodded again. 'I wondered if you'd get in touch when you got to eighteen. Knew you couldn't do anything about it before.' She stood up, moving back to the window.

Noises came from the floor below. Voices shouting and pans crashing in a kitchen.

'I'm getting a new place once I get out of here,' said Debbie. 'A job, too. My mate has an opening for me.'

'Doing what?'

'This and that. I'm getting clean.' She looked around the room again, scratching at her wrist. 'What's the time?'

I checked my mobile. 'Nearly four.'

'Teatime soon.' It wasn't an invitation.

I crossed to where she stood. 'Would you like to see photos?' I scrolled through the pictures on my phone. 'There's me with my best mate Zoe.'

'Already seen them. Looked you up on Facebook and Instagram.'

She's been watching me.

We both stared out of the window. A seagull screamed as he swooped low and landed on the window ledge covered in bird shit, cigarette butts and tell-tale ash.

'I expect you got to get off,' she said.

'Not really, I...'

Debbie moved to the door. 'Well, I'll be seeing you.' She was still talking as she walked down the corridor. 'I'll be out of here soon. Perhaps we can go up town? Once I got some money.'

'Okay,' I call to her departing back. 'See you soon?'

A bleep from the MacBook interrupts my thoughts. I click on the email to open it. Brenda has asked me to meet her at lunchtime. I put away my research, get dressed and take the tube to Charing Cross.

I walk out of the station and around the corner to Villiers Street. Brenda is already in the café, halfway through a tuna baguette. As I approach her table, she swallows an enormous mouthful. 'You having something to eat?'

'I'm eating with Matt later. I'll just have a black coffee please.' I tell the waitress.

'Well,' Brenda pauses, baguette mid-air. 'I have good news.'

Brenda's the only person I know who can eat and speak simultaneously. She should be a ventriloquist. I try hard not to look at the half-chewed dough rolling around in her mouth. 'She'll meet me?'

'Yes, it's all set up. Saturday afternoon, two o'clock.' Brenda takes a slurp of her latte. 'It's been a long time, Anna. You'll have to go slow.'

I nod.

'Debbie was upset last time,' she continues. 'The whole episode set her back.'

'I was upset too.' I sound like a spoilt brat. 'It's a relief, you know? Having you in my corner.'

'As long as it's good for Debbie, I'm on side.'

The waitress brings my coffee. 'Thanks.' I turn back to Brenda. 'Why are you so good to her?'

She puts the last of her baguette down on her plate. 'I had a daughter once. I suppose Debbie reminds me of her.'

I look away as Brenda chomps down the last couple of mouthfuls. The tables in the café are close together, the chatter of the customers loud. 'Sorry.' I get up. 'I think I need the loo.'

I keel sideways like I'm on a boat.

'Anna, are you okay?'

I reach for the back of an adjacent chair and it tilts, unsteadying the woman seated there. Her drink is upset and I watch in horror as red wine spreads across the tablecloth, while her lunch date deftly saves the bottle.

The general hubbub of the café stills. I slide back into my seat, sensing all eyes upon me. My cheeks are hot. *What the hell is wrong with me?*

Brenda observes me with narrowed eyes.

She probably thinks I'm pissed – like mother, like daughter.

'Sorry,' I mumble again.

'Just sit for a moment.' Brenda pulls wads of tissue from her handbag and hands them to the couple to mop up the spilled wine. 'Shall I get you a glass of water?'

The chatter in the room resumes and everyone carries on with their lunch. I'm aware of the waitress changing the tablecloth at the next table and a glass of water appearing in front of me. I feel distanced, like I'm being siphoned away to a hidden space within my head.

'Anna?'

I'm clawing my way back through the fog. My body accelerates fast forward and the room shifts back into focus. Brenda's concerned face is right in front of me.

'Anna?'

I blink twice.

Brenda's holding out a glass.

I lean forward and sip. The water is cool and refreshing.

Around me, the rest of the world continues as normal but I've been somewhere else. I try to recall whatever it was I just experienced but I'm chasing a dream. The harder I try to recapture it, the quicker it disperses. *Is this real? This here? This now?*

A few more sips of water and I'm a little less woozy. Pushing the glass away, I smile at Brenda. 'I'm fine, but I think I'll head off.'

I haul myself up from my seat. Brenda stands, poised to catch me.

'You'll get a cab?' she asks.

'No, I can get the Northern line from Embankment. 'I'll be okay.' I walk deliberately to the door. I don't want to appear to stagger. Leaning heavily on the handrail I take shaky steps down to street level.

Embankment Station is literally yards away. *I can do this.* I resist turning around, knowing Brenda will be watching.

On the tube I lean back in my seat and close my eyes. At least Debbie's agreed to meet me.

When I got home from that first meeting with Debbie, Mum bombarded me with questions. 'What was she like? Does she look like you? Bet she was proud to see how well you've turned out.'

'She needs money,' I told her. 'She's living in a women's shelter. She needs help getting back on her feet.'

Mum looked away. 'We can't do anything about that.'

'Why not?'

'Who's to know she wouldn't blow the money on alcohol or drugs?' asked Dad. 'Sometimes in life you have to make things happen for yourself.'

When Debbie disappeared a couple of weeks later, I demanded Mum and Dad hire a private investigator to find her.

Dad frowned. 'We're not going to do that.'

'But she's my birth mother. Suppose she's in trouble?'

'She's been in trouble for years.' Dad sighed. 'Throwing money at her isn't going to solve the problem.'

'If anything happens to Debbie…' I took a deep breath. 'It will be your fault. I'll never forgive you.'

Shortly afterwards I left home, got a job and moved in with Zoe. Despite our estranged relationship, Mum and Dad supported me, subsidising my rent with funds squirrelled away for my university degree. After a few months they concluded I wasn't coming home any time soon. The family home was sold and the proceeds split between their retirement fund, a two-up, two-down buy-to-let in Brighton, and the object of their desire, a *Beneteau Oceanis 43*. Zoe said my parents were living in a luxurious self-imposed banishment until I forgave them. I couldn't consider patching things up with them until I'd sorted out my relationship with my birth mother.

I eventually reach home. I'm shattered. Matt won't be home for a while so I turn on the bath taps, light my Ylang Ylang candles and arrange them around the tub. While the bath fills, I sit on the toilet seat. I rub my eyes. There's no way I'm going to work tomorrow. I turn off the taps and go through to the kitchen to find Matt's MacBook. Flipping the lid, I type an email:

Hi Gary. I know I said I'd come in tomorrow and ease myself back with a half day, but I don't think I'm ready. I'll leave it until Monday if that's okay.

I hit 'send', go back to the bathroom and strip off my clothes. Easing myself into the tub, I close my eyes and settle down for a soak. I won't mention my wobble to Matt, he'll only worry. It was probably low blood sugar…

I open my eyes with a start. I must have dozed off. One of the candles is spitting, the wick down to the wax. I blow it out and step from the bath to towel myself dry.

* * *

'Mister Gregory has located John's foster home,' Anna tells Mercy when she arrives back at the Astleys'. 'It's in Harrow-on-the-Hill. We're to pay them a visit tomorrow.'

Mercy looks at the piles of washing. 'But I got this lot to sort, and Simkins is coming the morrow to shift some of the trunks. I needs to be 'ere.'

'It's fine Mercy, I'll go. To be honest, I don't think Mister Gregory wanted either of us. He inferred it wouldn't be appropriate, but I told him otherwise.'

'He's met his measure in you, Miss Anna, that's for sure.'

Anna surveys the laundry. 'Well, I seem to have the afternoon free. Let me give you a hand with this lot.'

For the next three hours they wash, iron and fold Miss Abigail's clothes.

Anna stands up from packing a trunk, suddenly woozy.

'You all right, miss?' asks Mercy.

'Got up too quickly.' Anna grabs the back of a chair to steady herself.

'You best rest, Miss Anna. I'll get yer something to eat.'

Anna eats the bread and cheese and sips her ale. Why is she so shattered? She sits beside the warm fire while Mercy works on, darning and patching by candlelight.

Biting off a length of thread, Mercy holds out the moth-eaten blue travelling cloak for Anna to inspect. 'Miss Abigail replaced this long ago. 'Tis old, but 'twill do the job. Can barely see me stitches. If yer going to be travelling with the gentleman the morrow, yer needs to be dressed proper.'

6th September

Janus lays the napkin down beside his plate. 'Eat up, Khan. We must away.'

Khan frowns. 'You did not expect me to forego my morning prayers?'

'No, forgive me.' Janus pours himself another coffee. 'There is time.'

Khan helps himself to kedgeree. 'The girl is to meet us here?'

'Yes.' Janus chuckles. 'I offered to collect her from the Astleys', but she would have none of it.'

Khan stirs his tea thoughtfully. 'You came across her first at the Foundling Hospital?'

'Yes.'

'And you have not yet ascertained her connection with the servant girl?'

'What is on your mind?

Khan spreads butter onto his bread. 'Be careful, my friend. You know not her motives.'

'Khan, you worry too much. Anyway, you will be with me.'

Anna's on the top step at ten o'clock precisely when Janus opens the door. The landau pulls up and, as he offers Anna his arm, a tall black man emerges from the house to join them.

'May I introduce my good friend, Ehsan Khan,' says Janus.

Khan nods politely to Anna and climbs into the landau.

'The parish of Harrow-on-the-Hill,' Janus tells the driver.

When they set off, Anna steals a better look at Khan – brooding, cropped black hair, dark soulful eyes. If he turned on the charm, he'd be difficult to resist. But charm seems the last thing on Khan's mind as he monopolises Janus's attention, leaving Anna to content herself with staring out of the window.

They make slow progress through overcrowded streets but, once clear of the city, pick up pace as they head northwest. Soon they're passing open fields.

The driver stops at an inn to ask directions to the hamlet of Alperton. Two miles further down the road, he pulls up beside a solitary single storey dwelling. Paint flakes from faded yellow walls and the cottage windows are overgrown with ivy. 'This is the place, sir,' he says.

Anna flashes Janus a look to let him know that she won't be left waiting outside. After a slight hesitation he smiles and helps her down the steps of the landau. They walk through the small front garden to a planked timber door where a small child is playing in a puddle.

'Hello, what's your name?' asks Anna.

The little girl's hands squelch in the muddy water.

'Is mummy home?'

The child claps her hands together, then jumps up and runs off around the back of the cottage. Janus tugs at the string dangling from a bell and inside a dog begins to bark frantically. Soft feet patter towards the door, which is opened by another small child who gives them a startled look before disappearing in the same direction as the little girl.

77

Anna peers in through the door. Inside a woman sits nursing an infant while a toddler grizzles at her knee.

'Good day, madam.' Janus steps into the small dwelling. 'My name is Janus Gregory, patron of the Foundling Hospital. This is Mistress Stratton.' He brings Anna forward. 'Might I inquire as to your name?'

'I be Fanny, sir.' Glancing at the satiated infant on her lap, she pulls at her shawl to cover her breasts. 'You and the lady best come in. But be so kind as to leave your manservant outside.'

Khan raises an eyebrow.

'Oh, no,' says Janus. 'Mister Khan is a free man.'

Fanny continues to regard Khan with suspicion as he waits in the doorway.

'We are trying to trace a child,' says Janus. 'He was fostered out to this address five years hence.'

'Don't know as I can help.' Fanny shakes her head. 'Five years? That be a long while back.'

'Oh, please do try,' Anna pleads.

The toddler clinging to Fanny's skirt has stopped crying and is peering up at the visitors. Anna crouches down to his level and smiles at him. 'The child's name was John, but he was rechristened Isaac. His mother says he had a mass of black curls.'

'Can't say as it rings any bells…' Fanny stares expectantly at Janus.

He plunges his hand through the placket in his breeches to extract a few coins from his purse.

A smile creeps across Fanny's face. 'I think I does remember Isaac, as it happens. Loved him like me own.'

Anna's heart lifts. 'So, he didn't die in the first few weeks?'

'No, must have had him here all of four years. Sweet little lad. Gentle, willing, never no bother.'

'Is he still here?' Anna jumps to her feet, scanning the room as if Mercy's child might be lurking in the shadows.

'Bless you no, miss.' Fanny lays the sleeping infant in a wooden cradle on the floor. 'Poor little mite took on a fever. He passed away.'

'Oh no.' Anna puts a hand to her mouth.

'Buried him in the churchyard up the lane. The ones what are christened gets buried in consecrated ground. Those that ain't end up on a bit o' common land.' Fanny crosses herself.

Anna swallows. 'I don't suppose you remember a buckle bracelet?'

Fanny glances towards Khan, then turns her attention back to Anna. 'Not that I recall. Here, George'll show yer.' She yells out through the open window. 'George, these folks want to see the graves.'

Anna and Janus join Khan and they walk around to the back garden, where Fanny's husband is tending his vegetable patch.

George looks some years older than Fanny. His skin is weathered and what is left of his sparse hair is grey. Sticking his fork into the earth, he leaves the two small children sword-fighting with weeds and steps across his cabbages. 'This way, sir.'

Sombre as a funeral procession, they follow George up the lane towards the church. Passing through the lych gate they enter the graveyard. George shuffles towards a row of five small graves marked with stones.

'Here they be.' George tips his cap. 'We lose a few to the sickness. Poor little buggers.'

Anna gazes at the tiny mounds. 'Which one is Isaac's?'

George shrugs.

A tear trickles down Anna's cheeks. *How will Mercy bear this?*

After a few minutes, Janus clears his throat. He holds out his arm to escort Anna back to the landau. 'Take us home,' he instructs the driver.

They're quiet on the journey back to town. On the outskirts of the city, Khan breaks the silence. 'Did you find the foster parents convincing?'

'If you mean, do I think it likely that the boy died of a fever, then sadly I do,' says Janus. 'It is not uncommon.'

'But you don't believe Isaac was mistreated?' asks Anna.

'No. The Shuttlebarrows presented as caring foster parents. What has unsettled you, Khan?'

Khan shakes his head. 'Nothing, no matter.'

Janus turns to Anna. 'I have a meeting with business associates when we get back, but you are welcome to dine with us later?'

'Thank you, but no. I must break the news to Mercy.'

'Then we will drop you at the Astleys'.'

'If you don't mind, I'd like to walk and clear my head.'

* * *

Opening one eye, I squint at the digital display – 08:10. The alarm hasn't gone off. Momentary panic is followed by calm, as I remember I don't have to go back to work until Monday.

Hauling myself to a sitting position, I'm pleased to find my head is no longer throbbing. I get up and make my way to the bathroom to examine my face in the mirror. The bruise on my cheekbone has turned yellow. It will be easier to cover up.

Traces of mascara linger around my eyes and my skin is pale. I fill the basin with warm water and gently wash my face with Olay. Looking again in the mirror, I study my reflection. It's like someone else is staring back.

This other 'me' picks up a toothbrush and squeezes toothpaste along the length of the bristles. She lifts the brush to her mouth and begins to move her hand rhythmically up and down.

Ow. The bristles are sharp. I lower my hand, staring at the toothbrush, then at my electric one standing in the charger in readiness. The toothbrush in my hand is an old one of Matt's. I drop it into the chipped mug on the shelf where it jiggles before settling.

The sound of rushing water draws my attention to the sink. A torrent of water is wastefully gushing down the drain and soaking my tartan pyjamas. I turn off the tap. The other 'me' shadows my every move.

I run my tongue along my teeth and, as the minty taste kicks in, I become more present.

Wiping my mouth with the back of my hand, I walk through to the kitchen and make myself a cup of tea and a slice of toast. I sit down on the sofa to eat my breakfast, then spend the rest of the morning making notes for my story in a reporter notepad.

Around lunchtime Matt's MacBook starts ringing. I flip up the lid. It's Zoe Facetiming me. I accept the call.

'How you doing, hun?' she asks.

'Okay.' I don't tell her what happened yesterday. I haven't told Matt either. He can't find out that I've arranged to meet Brenda.

'Still in your PJs? All right for some.'

'Nothing to get up for.' I could tell her I'm seeing Debbie tomorrow, but I don't. 'Just been slobbing out all morning.'

'Want to meet up tonight?

'I can't, Matt's taking me out for a curry.'

'All right. Well, enjoy your afternoon. Catch you soon.'

I'm becoming deceitful, not just to Matt, but to my best mate. Zoe doesn't deserve that. She was so supportive when I first contacted my birth mother.

'Look,' Zoe had said, 'I know your mum and dad will be upset, but this is important. Probably the most important thing that's ever happened. You need to do this for you.'

'I know.'

'How are you going to feel if you don't take this opportunity?'

'I just…'

'What?'

'I'm scared. What if she doesn't like me?'

'What's not to like?'

'Suppose I have nothing in common with her? Suppose she's a complete and utter bitch?'

'You won't know unless you try. What's the worst that can happen?'

I make another cup of tea and sit down with my copy of *Coram's Children*. I try to research, but it's hard not to think about tomorrow.

* * *

Ned moves around the drawing room serving coffee.

'I expect Mister Khan will take some tea, Ned.' Janus helps himself to a coffee from the tray and settles himself in his armchair. 'Thank you, gentlemen, for joining me this evening. Now Pestlemore, out with it. I can tell by your face you have been up to no good.'

Pestlemore's knee shakes. 'We do have something to c-confess Gregory, but I am af-fraid you will not like it.'

'Pull yourself together, sir,' says Pym. 'Confess if you must but let us get home for our supper this night.'

Tweedie gives an exasperated sigh. 'Pestlemore, if you persist in fidgeting…'

'Tweedie,' says Janus. 'For God's sake, will you not enlighten us?'

Tweedie clears his throat. 'Four nights ago, Pestlemore and I conducted a small trial.' He glances at Janus. 'Yes, I know you warned us not to.'

'Tweedie wanted to check the adjustments to the alhidade,' interrupts Pestlemore, attempting to still his knee.

'A trial run was necessary,' Tweedie continues, 'to ensure the equipment was aligned and the measurements for the azimuthal quadrant correct.'

'But you did not have the prism,' says Janus. 'How could you conduct a trial without it?'

Tweedie averts his eyes while Pestlemore fiddles anxiously with the plush trim of the tablecloth.

Janus stands up. 'You took it?'

Pestlemore covers his face with his hands. 'We only b-borrowed it.'

Tweedie glares at Pestlemore, then turns his focus back to Janus. 'I am sorry Gregory, but it became necessary. You were away in Kent visiting your sister.'

Janus paces the room. 'The prism was in my study.'

'We came in through the g-garden,' stammers Pestlemore.

Janus spins around to face him. 'Where is it now?'

Quintar watches Pestlemore squirm. 'Is there something you wish to add, Monsieur Pestlemore?'

Pestlemore peeks through his fingers. 'We returned it. That was always our intention.'

Janus eases himself back down in his chair. 'And this opportunity to trial the equipment could not be missed?'

'It was such a p-perfect night,' says Pestlemore

'Tweedie?' says Janus.

'The gibbous was the ideal size and everything lined up beautifully.' Tweedie's eyes light up. 'You should have seen it, Gregory.'

Janus scowls. 'I would like to have had the opportunity.'

Tweedie swallows. 'The prism fitted exactly and when the light fragmented, the libration was perfect.'

Pestlemore relaxes back in his chair. His hand wanders across the side table to lift the last slice of ginger cake from the plate. 'I say, Mrs Lawson has excelled herself. Is there more?'

'Ye gods,' mutters Pym.

'Tell me everything.' Janus leans forward. 'Leave nothing out.'

'The levitron was working correctly.' Tweedie clasps his hands together. 'The dark star was in our sights and the prism rotating by centrifugal force.' He pauses. 'I checked the measurements myself. No-one could have predicted…'

'What happened?' asks Janus.

Tweedie shakes his head. 'A break in the gravitational force. The transmutation was affected by a destabilising influence.'

'And the result?'

'We called up a phantom,' says Pestlemore, cake crumbs spraying from his mouth.

Quintar gasps. *'Mon Dieu.'*

'A phantom?' Janus glances at Khan, who is listening with chin rested on steepled fingertips.

'Yes.' Tweedie nods his head.

'It was a being from another time and place.' Pestlemore's tone is hushed. 'We saw her with our own eyes.'

'Her?' asks Janus.

'Whether it be female or male, 'twas definitely some sort of spirit,' says Tweedie.

Quintar's guffaw breaks the tension. 'Perhaps Janus, these two consumed too much of the spirit themselves?'

Pym shakes his head. 'What in God's name have you done, you fools?'

'What happened to this so-called phantom?' asks Janus.

'It left, with a servant girl.' Pestlemore wipes his sticky fingers on his trousers.

'And you were not minded to follow?'

'We feared for the girl's safety, but there was the equipment.' Tweedie examines his empty cup. 'We could not leave it behind.'

'We packed everything up and went home,' says Pestlemore.

Pym stands up. 'Gentlemen, do you have any idea what mischief you create?'

'Calm yourself, Pym. Sit down and drink your coffee.' Janus tops up Pym's cup.

'Have you made efforts to trace this phantom, Tweedie?' asks Quintar.

'To my knowledge,' says Tweedie, 'there have been no

85

sightings. My God, Gregory, I wish we had not gone ahead in your absence, but we did. There is nothing we can do to change it now.'

Pym checks his watch, then sits back down. He takes a sip of his coffee. 'I agree with Quintar. The phantom must be found and returned from whence it came. We know not what repercussions might follow.'

'Do not distress yourself, Pym.' Janus pats his arm. 'We will take the necessary steps. Meanwhile, I am interested in the state of the equipment.' He turns to Tweedie. 'The destabilisation, can it be corrected?'

'The alhidade requires further adjustment,' says Tweedie. 'I believe it was simply that the force did not hold for sufficient time. It worked once and it will work again.'

'When would be the optimum time for a second attempt?' asks Janus.

'The thirteenth of the month,' Tweedie replies. 'That is when the gibbous achieves the exact same measurements.'

Janus rubs his chin thoughtfully. 'What I need you to do now is make ready for another trial.'

'You still trust these imbeciles?' asks Quintar.

'We are a team, but I shall divide the equipment.' Janus casts his eyes over his colleagues. 'Quintar, you take the levitron while I keep the prism. Tweedie and Pestlemore, adjust the alhidade and re-check all calculations. Pym will oversee this.' Janus stands up. 'Quintar and Pym, let us meet the morrow to share progress.'

'And what of the phantom?' asks Tweedie.

'Leave the phantom to me.' Janus opens the drawing room door. 'Now be gone. My soirée will be in three days' time. Do not be tardy, for Elizabeth cannot abide poor manners.'

As Pym passes through the doorway, Janus takes his arm and lowers his voice. 'I am sorry to hear Isabella is unwell.'

Pym feigns surprise. 'Unwell? No, never better. She will accompany me to the soirée.'

'It was a blue moon,' Pestlemore comments as they step through to the hallway. 'I asked young Mitchell at the Royal Society.'

Tweedie scoffs. 'Mitchell is no expert…'

'He said there might not be another for three years…'

As William shows the Prism members out, Quintar raises an eyebrow with a smirk.

Janus sits down. 'Well Khan, what do you make of that?'

'Of Jinn, there are two kinds, good and evil. If the story is true, let us pray your colleagues have not opened a door to the latter. We must trust in Allah to put things right.'

'It is good to have your faith, dear friend. At least I may depend upon you and Quintar. As for the others, for tuppence halfpenny I would bang their heads together. Speaking of gin…' Janus winks at Quintar. 'This is one of those times, Khan, when I wish you would indulge. Quintar, you will join me?'

'*Je préférerais le cognac, s'il vous plaît.*'

'Good idea. Ned, bring us brandy and I dare say Mister Khan will take more tea.'

* * *

As Anna descends the basement steps, Mercy rushes to greet her. The colour drains from Mercy's face when she sees Anna's expression. 'Well, that be that. Me boy's not coming home.'

87

'I'm so sorry.' Anna steps into the kitchen. 'Let me...' She pauses mid-sentence, interrupted by a cough from a woman seated at the kitchen table.

'This be Mrs Marsh,' says Mercy, 'back from her sister's. She knows everything. Don't have no secrets, do we Mrs Marsh?'

The large woman in a red cloak scowls at Anna, but she grunts her agreement.

Mercy pulls down the clothes pulley from above the range. 'Must get on. Such a lot to do.' She folds the items roughly, stacking them in piles. 'There's but a few days afore mistress wants me in Yorkshire. Oh.' She puts one hand to her forehead as she swoons.

With surprising agility, Mrs Marsh leaps up. She catches Mercy and helps her to a chair, then busies herself heating water.

Anna sits beside Mercy, reassuring her.

Mrs Marsh places a cup in front of Mercy. She looks Anna up and down. 'Is that the mistress's cloak?'

Anna's cheeks colour as she slips off the travelling cloak and hangs it on a peg on the wall.

Mercy takes a few sips of her drink. She turns to Anna. 'Tell me everything that happened at the foster home.'

Anna recounts the visit as positively as she can. 'Fanny and George seemed kind. At least you know John had a few happy years. We could visit his grave if you like?'

Suddenly Mrs Marsh emits a strange guttural noise, causing Jinks, his fur on end, to run for the door. 'No good,' she splutters, starting to sob. 'Can't do this no more.'

Anna fetches a glass of water, while Mercy rubs the older woman's shoulders.

Mrs Marsh's body heaves and shudders, until gradually her

sobs subside to an occasional hiccup. She wipes her eyes on the corner of her cloak. Her face is swollen and blotchy. 'I best tell you what really happened that day.'

Anna and Mercy exchange a glance.

Mrs Marsh takes a sip of water. ''Twas early morning when I took the bairn. Mercy were still asleep. Broke my heart it did, stealing away like that with him, but 'twas only way for Mercy to keep her position. When I got to the Foundling Hospital, there was a huge mob of women pushing and shoving to get to the front, all desperate to have their babies admitted. Out comes this nun holding a bag and we each had to take a coloured ball.'

'Yes,' interrupts Mercy, 'we was lucky that you picked a white one.'

Mrs Marsh shakes her head. 'No child. I drew a red ball.'

Mercy gasps.

'What difference does that make?' asks Anna.

Mrs Marsh kneads the fabric of her cloak. 'A black ball means no place. If I'd drawn a black ball I'd have had to return with the child, but a red ball means there's still hope. I waited with others who'd drawn red balls. If any of the bairns whose mothers drew white balls were found to be poorly then those with a red ball would be called forward. 'Twas a long wait and I were worried about Mercy. I knew she'd be upset when she woke to find the bairn gone. Well, we waited and waited. The bairn was fretful and I begun to think, even if I was called, they might not take him the state he were in.'

Mercy is quietly sobbing. 'My poor John.'

'Then this man comes along. Said it were unlikely there'd be space for the rest of the babies but there was transport leaving for another foundling home. He said 'twas in Kent, out in the country and even better than the London Foundling Hospital. Well, there was no sign of anyone coming back to call us in. I spoke with a couple of other women and we decided to take the man up on his offer. We swaddled the bairns and the man took them away.'

'That's why we got no cloth receipt.' Mercy grabs Mrs Marsh's arm. 'Where did the man take my baby? Where did he go?'

'I don't know, my dear. Only 'twas a place where he'd have fresh air and the chance of a healthy life.'

Mercy shakes her head. 'But Mrs Marsh, you've listened to me planning and saving all these years and you've never said nowt.'

'I never believed 'twould come to this. Thought I were giving him the best chance. I were gonna tell you that night, but when I got home you was asleep and later, when I checked, you'd gone. You went to the chapel, remember? You come back that pleased, said you'd seen him baptised. I knew it couldn't have been your John, but you were that comforted, I couldn't take that away from you. I truly believed that were the end of it.'

Tears course down Mercy's cheeks.

'When you started talking about getting him back. Well, I don't mind saying I've been torn in two. And when you told me you'd seen him at the Foundling Hospital it fair broke my heart. That's when I begun thinking perhaps you was right? Maybe they transferred him back to the Foundling Hospital when he got bigger? But hearing Mistress Anna's story about him buried up at Harrow-on-the-Hill. Well, I can't let you go thinking that.' Mrs Marsh turns to Mercy, taking her hands. 'But Mercy, it sounds like Mistress Anna's got a real gent helping her now. Perhaps he'll find your John?'

'How?' asks Anna. 'Now we know even less about where John might have been taken.'

Mrs Marsh picks up a knife from the table. 'Kept this just in case.' She hauls herself up and shuffles across to the fireplace where she begins to poke at a stone above the chimney breast. With a little persuasion it comes loose. Mrs Marsh reaches in to extract a yellowed slip of paper. 'All these years child, I been keeping this for you.'

'I can't read.' Mercy hands the note to Anna who reads it aloud.

This acknowledges receipt of one male infant. The child to be transported to the subsidiary foundling home in the town of Westerham, County of Kent. Signed this day, 21st February 1747, Jack Fripp.

'Then John might still be alive?' cries Mercy.

* * *

On arrival at *Tamarind Spice,* the proprietor's son greets us with a smile. 'Good evening Matt. Hello Anna.'

'Hi Dev,' says Matt.

Dev unrolls the crisp white serviettes and lays them on our laps. 'Beer and a glass of white?'

'Cobra for me. Anna's on water tonight. Cheers. Can you bring us some poppadum while we decide?'

Dev glances my way for confirmation.

I nod my head. 'Yes, that's fine.' As Dev leaves the table I reach for the menu.

'The specials look good,' says Matt. 'Why don't we order a few things and share?'

'Okay.' I pop my unopened menu back in the holder on the table.

Dev brings our drinks and poppadum.

'Thanks mate,' says Matt. 'Okay, we'll have a lamb Makan Palak, a Koshboo chicken, onion bhaji, sag aloo and a couple of portions of rice.'

'Pilau?' asks Dev.

'Yeah. Oh, and some samosas to start.' Matt heaps relish onto his side plate 'So, what did you get up to today?'

'Nothing really.' I pick at a piece of poppadum. 'Read a bit. Watched Netflix.'

'Well I've been busy.' Matt places a gift bag in front of me.

'What's this? It's not my birthday.' Giving him a bewildered look, I open the bag, reach in, and pull out a box containing an iPhone 11.

Matt grins. 'It's all set up. Everything's downloaded from the iCloud. Just needs a good charge overnight and you're ready to go.'

God, why does he have to fix everything? 'Thank you. Just as I was getting used to not having one.'

Matt laughs. 'Now I'll be able to keep tabs on you. Make sure you're safe.'

He's only half joking. I smile and take a sip of my water.

Dev positions the plate warmers ready for our food.

'Another one of these, mate?' Matt waves his empty Cobra bottle. 'So, you ready for work Monday?'

I shrug.

'Look Anna, if you're not well enough, take more time.'

'Perhaps I should have gone back today?'

'I told you, there's no rush.'

* * *

'I be off to me bed.' Mrs Marsh lifts her tapestry bag from the floor and hobbles towards the door. 'Mind you lock up, Mercy.'

'Like I does every night,' mutters Mercy.

'Does she know I'm staying?' whispers Anna.

Mercy's cheeks flush as she stands to stoke the fire. 'She weren't none too pleased.' She shakes her head. 'I know she done her best, but how she's kept this from me all this time.'

'I know,' says Anna.

'I thought I'd been watching me boy and it weren't my John at all.' Mercy dabs her eyes with her kerchief.

'We don't know that for sure. John might have transferred back to the Foundling Hospital at some point.'

Mercy grabs Anna's hands. 'I needs to know. Your Mister Gregory, might he be able to find the man that took me boy?'

'I don't know. I can ask him.'

Mercy eyes the travelling cloak hanging on the peg.

'It's too late now. I'll go in the morning.' Anna looks at the heap of clothes on the table. 'Shall I help you with this lot.'

Mercy yawns. 'No, miss. I can deal wi' them the morrow.'

'It's been a long day,' says Anna. "Tonight, you take the cot. No arguments.'

Mercy smiles. 'Night then, Miss Anna.'

Anna stokes the fire and settles into the chair beside the range. Jinks watches her. 'Come on Jinks.' She pats her lap, but the cat regards her with suspicion. From Mrs Marsh's room next door comes the sound of wheezy snoring. Anna closes her eyes and wonders whether a mother can really know her child when she hasn't seen him for years? A memory surfaces – a man and a woman sitting with a younger Anna at a kitchen table, their faces blurred. Are they her parents? No, there's something else… they're not her biological parents, she's adopted. But who is her birth mother? And why didn't she raise her? Anna's head throbs with the effort. She wraps herself in the scratchy blanket. Giving up on Mercy's son is not an option.

* * *

'Good evening, sir.' The butler takes his master's cloak and hat. 'I trust you had a good meeting?'

'Yes, Robert,' says Pym. 'Although it went on for longer than I expected. Is supper ready?'

'Yes, sir. Although I am afraid you will be dining alone. Madam has retired early to her rooms.'

'Thank you. I shall go up and see her. Please serve my supper in the library. The child is settled for the night?'

'Yes indeed, sir. Nanny had her supper in the kitchen this past hour.'

Pym heads up the staircase with a heavy heart. He knocks on the door of his wife's suite, calling out her name. 'Isabella?' When there's no response, he opens the door.

The room is in darkness. Isabella is sitting in front of the fireplace and does not stir as Pym enters.

'Hello, my dear.' He kisses her forehead and touches her cheek. It's cold as alabaster. Pym eases himself down on the footstool and gazes into her face looking for a hint of cognition, but there is nothing except deep, sad eyes. Only this morning she'd seemed brighter, but now… 'Isabella?' he repeats, but she remains unresponsive.

'I have been over at Gregory's.' Pym tries to maintain some semblance of normality. 'We had a meeting of the Prism group. I feel we might be close to a breakthrough.'

Isabella continues to stare into the flames.

'Isabella? My dear, this will not do. Why not come down and join me for supper? Or I could have them bring us something here? Let us sit together and while away the evening.' He reaches out to take her hand.

Isabella shrinks back. Her hand flies to her lips and her eyes flit around the room.

Pym jumps up. 'Isabella, please. The child needs you. I need you. Do not disappear again.' He moves across to the fireplace where he stands, waiting for a response. *For God's sake, Isabella.* Banging his fist against the mantle, he takes one last look at his wife before storming out of the room and making his way downstairs for another lonely supper.

Pym has no appetite. Isabella has retired early to her room every evening this week. He picks up the picture frame from the top of the piano to study it. Shaking his head, he replaces the charming still life. He paces up and down the room before making his way back upstairs, this time to Isabella's studio.

Pushing open the door he approaches the easel. He exhales sharply. Her latest creation is smothered with black paint. The brush strokes swirl round and round, creating a dark vortex. He glances at another canvas on the floor. The image is repeated. Pym puts his head in his hands. *Please God, not again.*

7th September

'Mistress Stratton.' Janus jumps up from his armchair in the parlour, his newspaper dropping to the floor.

'Am I disturbing you?' Anna asks.

'Not at all. Do sit down.'

Anna settles down on the couch by the window.

'How can I help?' Janus eases himself back in his armchair. He listens intently as she recounts Mrs Marsh's story. 'Hmm.' He scratches his chin thoughtfully. 'Fripp, you say? Perhaps I might trace him?'

'That would be wonderful. Thank you.' Anna smiles. 'I'm sorry if I dragged you on a wild goose chase yesterday.'

'I was only too happy to oblige.'

Anna passes him the scrap of paper.

Janus scrutinises it. 'It seems there are certain foundling hospital practices I am unaware of. It is in my interests as patron to find out if there is anything untoward going on.'

'Do you think the child might still be alive?'

'I could not say.' He frowns. 'I fear this Fripp may be what many call a *Coram Man*. If so, I doubt the trail will lead to a happy conclusion.' Janus gets up. 'Would you mind waiting here while I speak with Khan?'

Anna taps her fingers on the arm of her chair.

Several minutes pass before Janus returns. He's wearing his hat and cloak. 'Right, let us go.'

'Where are we going?'

'A small constitutional. Here, allow me.' Janus lays Anna's travelling cloak across her shoulders. 'There is someone I would like you to meet.'

Janus escorts her along Cross Street. After reaching the top of Saffron Hill, they cut through a narrow alley which opens out to a working yard. From an archway to the left comes repetitive hammering and the clink of metal against anvil, whilst the whinny of horses echoes from a wooden building to the right.

The ground is littered with filthy straw and muck. Anna tries not to inhale as the pungent smell of ammonia reaches her nose and mouth. She steps carefully to avoid treading in a pile of manure. 'What is this place?'

'Lewis Yard.' Janus cups his hands to his mouth and emits a shrill whistle.

A young lad of about twelve emerges from the open doorway to the horses. He glances at Anna impertinently, then executes an elaborate bow. 'Whistler at yer service, me lady.' He doffs an imaginary hat. 'Ain't lost yer touch then, Mister Greg?'

'Enough of your cheek, you whelp.' Janus reaches playfully as if to grab Whistler, but the boy ducks and dives.

Glancing over to where the smithy is at work, Whistler lowers his voice. 'Got a job for me then, Mister Greg?'

'There is someone I need to locate. A gentleman who goes by the name of Fripp.'

'I'll do me best.' Whistler spits on his hands, rubs them together and sticks out an upturned palm.

Janus raises an eyebrow. 'You know the drill.'

Whistler grins.

Janus tuts. He plunges a hand into his pouch and pulls out a coin. Flicking it, he sends it spinning through the air.

Whistler leaps to catch it.

'As soon as you can,' says Janus. 'You know where to find me.'

A loud voice bellows from under the arch. 'Whistler? There's work to be done, lad.'

'Thanking yer kindly, Mister Greg. Pleasure doing business with yer.' Whistler shakes Janus's hand. 'Nice to meet yer me lady.' With a cheeky wink, the boy scampers back into the stables.

'You certainly have a variety of friends,' Anna says as they stroll back.

'Whistler is someone I do business with from time to time. Let us just say we help each other out.'

'Wherever did you meet him?'

'It is not a pretty story. William hired someone to clean the chimneys. Whistler was what they call a climbing boy, climbing the narrowest of chimneys to sweep down the soot. His outlook was grim.' Janus sighs, shaking his head. 'Soot gets into their lungs and many are dead before they reach the age of ten. I paid off the sweep and secured Whistler a job with a local farrier. It is hard work, but the lad is always cheerful, which is why they call him Whistler. He has a way with horses too, seems to calm them.'

'He's a horse whisperer,' says Anna.

'They do seem to understand him. The farrier is tough but fair and Whistler has a chance of learning the trade. Mayhap he might survive a few more years? If he had remained where he was, he would not have whistled much longer.'

'You help a lot of people, but you don't make a big deal of it. What's in it for you?'

'The satisfaction of knowing I have done something to help? A few new friends? We do what we can, do we not?'

'We do.'

Janus picks up the pace. 'Come, I need to get back.'

* * *

From the outside, The halfway house in Kennington looks like any other block of ex-council flats. Brenda had explained that it houses recovering addicts living with supervision and support while getting their lives back on track.

The stairwell is dark and shabby. I climb the stairs, stepping carefully on the broken-down concrete treads. It's been eighteen months, will she be pleased to see me? Finally I reach the top and stand outside number twenty-three. I knock.

Debbie opens the door. 'Come in.'

To call her Debbie doesn't seem right, but neither does Mum, so I avoid calling her anything. 'How are you?'

'I'm okay.'

I notice the bags under her eyes and she's far too thin.

I proffer a small bunch of freesias. *Should I kiss her?*

'Thanks.' She doesn't take the flowers. 'I don't have a vase.'

'A mug will do.'

She signals towards the kitchenette. I walk over and open the single cupboard above the sink. I reach for a coffee mug and fill it with water from the tap. After arranging the freesias, I bring the cup up to my nose. They smell sweet and a little sickly. I look around for the best place to put them. The flat's

99

tiny, a bedsit really, much like the cramped accommodation my friends had at university. There's a sofa, which I suppose converts into a bed, and a small metal table and two chairs like those you find on a patio. The kitchenette consists of a mini sink with a microwave and kettle taking up most of the narrow worktop. I slide a pile of laundry to one side and place the flowers on the table.

'You want to sit down?' asks Debbie.

'Thanks,' I say, lowering myself down on the sofa bed. Her pillow serves as a cushion, so I move it out of the way. I wonder where she stows the rest of her bedding. There's no wardrobe, just a few hooks on the wall hung with an eclectic mix of dressing gown, outdoor coat, evening top and a couple of scarves.

'You want tea?' she asks.

'Yes please.'

Debbie pads across to the kitchenette and switches on the kettle. She drops a teabag into a mug.

'Aren't you having one?'

'No, I'll have one later.'

I look towards the flowers and realise I've used her only other mug. My face flushes with colour.

She hands me the tea. It's what Dad would call builders' tea, 'so strong a teaspoon would stand up in it'. As Debbie has no coffee table, I nurse it until my fingers burn, then set it down on the floor.

'So, you've settled in okay?' I ask.

'Yeah, it's all right.' Debbie sits down on one of the metal chairs and crosses her legs.

I wonder whether to apologise about the last time we met, but decide against it. After all, it wasn't my fault. Today we're starting over.

Loud canned laughter comes from the TV in the flat next door. We catch each other's eye and exchange a grin.

'That's Bill,' says Debbie. 'He has to have the sound up cause he's deaf and it doesn't help with these paper-thin walls. I get his shopping when I go out. His knees are bad, poor old boy.'

'Have you made any other friends?'

Her foot wiggles up and down. 'There's Tracy, number nineteen. She's a right laugh. We watched a film together the other night.'

'That's nice.' I lift my mug and take a sip of tea. 'I'm still with the magazine,' I say to avoid the awkward silence. 'And with Matt. We've moved in together. He's got a flat in Islington.'

Debbie stares at the wall, then glances towards the door. She doesn't want to know anything about me. She stands up. 'I'm seeing Tracy later. Said I'd pop round.'

Is she dismissing me? 'Well, I suppose I'd better be going.' I look at my mug, it's almost full and I don't know what to do with it.

'Here.' Debbie takes it and tips the tea down the sink.

'Is there anything you need?' I ask.

She scratches her wrist. 'No, I'm all right. Got me benefits.' Her eyes flick towards a packet of cigarettes beside the kettle.

'Okay. So, I'll see you soon?'

The door's already open. 'Thanks for coming.'

* * *

William greets them. 'Monsieur Quintar is here, sir.'

'Thank you, William. When Pym arrives, bring him into the drawing room.' Janus turns to Anna. 'I am afraid I must meet briefly with my colleagues, but I would very much like to resume our conversation and discuss what we might try next. Will you stay to luncheon?'

'Yes, thank you,' says Anna.

'Perhaps you would be so good as to wait in the study? William, ask Ned to bring Mistress Stratton tea.'

Left on her own, Anna looks around the study. A row of quill pens are lined up neatly on the desk. She leans across to see what the doodlings are on the blotter, but the numbers and geometrical shapes are indecipherable. To the right is a large hollow globe tilted on its axis within an ornate golden stand. Inside hangs a smaller sphere suspended on copper wire. Around the earth's circumference is a measuring gauge, while diagonally across it bears an engraved sash. Anna runs her fingers over the metal band – *Juillet, Aout, Septembre*. Thinner strips circumvent the globe with the letters – N, G, V, T. What do they mean?

The door swings open and Anna jumps away from the globe as Ned enters the room. He places a tea tray on the side-table. 'Will you be needing anything else, miss?'

'No, thank you.'

'Very well, miss.' Ned leaves the room. Anna pours a cup of tea and walks back over to the desk, where a decorative wooden casket catches her eye. She puts her cup down and tries the lid, but it's locked. Instead, she strolls over to examine the pictures on the wall. One looks like a telescope, whilst another pyramid-shaped drawing could be an elaborate tripod.

Anna continues to explore the study. She's running her fingers across the patina on a walnut cabinet filled with decorative tiles when the door opens.

'Oh,' – the intruder seems surprised – 'please excuse me.'

Anna recognises the gentleman from the meeting at the Foundling Hospital.

Avoiding further eye contact, Pym places an object on the desk and hurries back out.

The object is a box about twenty centimetres square. It looks like an old-fashioned camera. Dodgy photos, maybe? That might account for all the secrecy.

Anna picks up her tea from the desk and takes a sip before moving across to the French doors. Finding them unlocked, she steps out onto a terrace overlooking the immaculate garden. The large lawn is manicured and bordered on three sides by high hedges. The terrace runs the length of the house and is divided by pillars. Anna continues on to the next set of French doors. When she hears voices, she tiptoes forward and conceals herself behind an ornate metal screen to listen in on their conversation.

'You have had no luck tracing this so-called phantom?'

'None whatsoever.'

'But you believe it to be a being from another place?'

Anna's heart begins to race. A being from another place? Can they be talking about her?

'Come, Janus,' says the voice of the Frenchman Anna met yesterday. 'Surely you have not swallowed this cock and bull story that Tweedie and Pestlemore concoct to divert you from the fact that they broke in and stole the prism?'

'Borrowed. I have it back. By the way, Pym, did Tweedie give you the lens for the alhidade?'

'I have returned it to your desk.'

'And how say you of Quintar's idea? That this phantom is a mere fabrication?'

'I am inclined to agree. I have been in touch with Fielding. He assures me there have been no local reports of unexplained phenomenon.'

Anna exhales.

'Let us hope you are right. Gentlemen, you will join me for luncheon?'

'I am afraid I must be away. I have business this afternoon.'

'Of course. Quintar?'

'I would be delighted, *mon ami*, but I too have a prior engagement.'

Anna creeps silently back and watches from the study door as Janus sees his colleagues out.

'I will see you the morrow, gentlemen.' Janus catches Anna's eye as he closes the front door. He smiles. 'Sorry to have kept you. You look chilled, did you venture into the garden?'

'Yes, I needed some air.'

'Let us eat.' Janus guides her into the dining room. 'We have much to discuss.'

Anna sits down at the table. 'Is Mister Khan to join us?'

'No.' Janus seats himself opposite. 'I have sent him on a mission. He will not return until this evening.'

Ned serves the soup.

'Thank you.' Anna glances at Janus. Does he know? Is he deliberately detaining her here? Perhaps the police will arrive any moment to take her away?

'My sister Elizabeth arrives the morrow.' Janus moves his napkin to his lap. 'She is hosting a small soirée for me. She will be delighted to meet you.' He pauses. 'Is the soup not to your liking?'

'Yes, it looks delicious.'

'Good.' Janus begins to eat. 'Hopefully Whistler will turn

up trumps and we will locate this Fripp.'

Anna raises her spoon. If Janus is talking about tracing Fripp and finding Mercy's child, perhaps he doesn't suspect? She sips her soup. 'It tastes as good as it looks.'

'Mrs Lawson is an excellent cook.'

'So, what exactly is the Prism group?'

Janus puts down his spoon.

'What know you of the Prism group?'

'Yesterday in the carriage you mentioned the Prism group to Mister Khan. I assume your meeting today with Monsieur Quintar and Mister Pym has something to do with that?'

Janus smiles. 'Mistress Stratton, it is impossible to hide anything from you.' He lifts his napkin to dab his mouth. 'The Prism group is a secret society of like-minded scientists working towards a discovery to improve and benefit society. I am afraid I can divulge no more.' He hesitates before lowering his voice. 'Except to say, for some, their aim is validation by the Royal Society.'

'And how is this great discovery going?' asks Anna.

'You will tease nothing more from me.' Janus resumes his meal. 'I have already confided more to you than to any other of your fair sex.'

Fair sex, indeed. She could enlighten him with a few great discoveries.

Ned takes the soup bowls away and serves the main course.

'Pease pudding?' Janus passes Anna the dish. 'One of Mrs Lawson's specialities.' His mouth twitches. 'I might say, Mistress Stratton, you did not seem unduly disappointed when I told you Khan would not be joining us.'

Anna hands the dish back. 'I'm not sure Mister Khan likes me much.'

'It is his upbringing. Cold meats?' Janus passes her the platter. 'In Khan's defence, in his homeland women and men do not mix freely as they do here.'

'Thank you. Every time I speak, I feel like he's judging me.'

Janus loads up his plate. 'Khan and I have been through a lot together. I trust that man with my life.'

'Sorry. I didn't mean to offend. I just find Mister Khan difficult to relate to. Perhaps he doesn't like women?'

Janus chuckles. 'So, there must be something wrong with Khan rather than with yourself?'

'Well, you're obviously fond of him, so I shall make more of an effort.'

'Well said. And now, Mistress Stratton, I believe it is time for you to share. My sources tell me that the Astleys are currently away in Yorkshire celebrating the nuptials of their lovely daughter, Miss Abigail. So, what exactly are you doing in their home and what is your connection with Mercy Benson, Miss Abigail's maid?

'I'm not sure that's something I am able to confide.'

Janus smiles. *'Touché.'*

'Ahem.' William is at the door. 'Begging your pardon, sir, but the boy is here to see you. He says it's a matter of some urgency.'

'Show him in William,' says Janus.

Whistler shuffles into the room, cap in hand.

Anna notices his grubby feet are bare and she smiles. William has made him leave his boots by the door.

'That was speedy work, boy,' says Janus.

'Well, Mister Greg, yer said it were important,' says Whistler. 'This Fripp. You'll likely be finding 'im in *The Three Cups*. I hear tell he spends most of his time there between shipments, so to speak.'

'Shipments?' says Janus.

'Whatever he can make money on. Mucky fingers in lots of pies, so I's been told. Never one to pass up a deal and don't care who gets hurt.'

Janus pulls two coins from the pouch on his belt and drops them into Whistler's grimy palm. 'You are sure this is good?'

'Ain't I always? When yer ever found me unreliable?' Whistler's eyes linger on the food on the table and he licks his lips.

Janus catches Anna's eye and winks. 'William?'

'Yes, sir?'

'Take the boy down to the kitchen and have Mrs Lawson feed him. Tell her I said to send him on his way with a food parcel.'

'Thank you, Mister Greg.' Whistler is grinning as William leads him away.

'I'm guessing that's not the first time Whistler's left your house with a full belly,' says Anna. She lays down her knife and fork. 'Actually, I think I should be leaving, too. There's something I have to do.'

'You have barely touched your meal.'

'I'm sorry.' Anna stands up. 'I hadn't realised the time. If you'll excuse me.'

Janus rises from his seat. 'Of course. Take the landau.'

'No, I'd prefer to walk.'

'But you will meet me the morrow? So we might intercept Fripp?'

'Yes, I'll be here at eleven.'

Anna hurries along the bustling streets, her footsteps echoing against the cobbles. Her cheeks are flushed and her ears ringing. She'd felt the need to get out before Janus resumed his questioning. If he was to be kept in the dark, she had to come up with an explanation for her connection to Mercy. There were many plausible reasons – she was a relative of the Astleys, Mercy used to be her maid… Which would Janus believe?

* * *

Pym approaches the confessional box in the chapel. As he gets close, he realises one of the boxes is occupied. He cannot risk being overheard. Taking a seat in the third pew, he strums his fingers on the row in front. The audacity of Gregory, assuming the lead, presuming he knows best. If it hadn't been for Pym, the others would never have had the guts to attempt the trial. Where was Gregory while they were making history? The discovery is ground-breaking and the phantom proof of their success. To be recognised by the Royal Society, the first to achieve movement through space and time. As Pym imagines the ceremony, his pulse races. What an accolade.

Pym sighs. Even as his heart swells, he knows in his soul that pride is the worst sin. Did God send this phantom as a warning? Its very existence threatens to disrupt the order of the universe. As steward and loyal servant of the Lord, is it not his duty to intervene? To capture the phantom and recreate harmony?

Pym kneels and bows his head.

Finally, a woman emerges from the confessional box. Pym stands, genuflects and steps into the chancel.

The priest pulls back the curtain. He glances towards Pym, then retreats into the box to wait.

'No.' Pym shakes his head. He will not relinquish control. The best scientific discoveries are made by those brave enough to take risks. 'I am not yet ready.' He turns, tripping over the vestry mat in his haste to get down the nave.

* * *

Matt had suggested meeting at *Section 7*. It's where he and the team congregate every Saturday after the match.

When I arrive, he kisses me on my cheek. 'There you are, gorgeous. What you having?'

'A glass of white. Just a small one.'

'And a small glass of white, mate,' Matt calls to the bartender. 'Yeah, Pinot Grigio.'

As Matt pays for the round, his mate Iri turns to me. 'Hi Anna. I was sorry to hear what happened. How're you feeling now?'

I open my mouth to answer when someone pushes past. I'm shoved off balance and Iri grabs my arm to stop me falling.

'Here.' He guides me to a table. 'Sit down.'

I pull my bag onto my lap. 'It would seem I'm still a bit shaky.'

'Not surprising really.' Iri agrees.

Matt follows us over. 'What happened there? You okay? You look a bit pale.'

'I'm all right. Someone bumped into me and I was startled.'

Matt puts my drink on the table. 'Would you rather have a Diet Coke?'

'No, this is fine. I've been looking forward to it all day.' I lift my glass. 'Cheers.' I take a sip. 'So, how was the match?'

'Don't ask,' Iri laughs.

Matt punches him playfully on the arm. 'Went to penalties. It's best forgotten! How's your day been?'

'Good. Me and Zoe hit the shops.' I shock myself by how easily I lie.

'Not very productive?' Matt indicates my lack of bags.

'Zoe took everything home so I wouldn't have to lug it around.'

He lowers his voice. 'Did you ring your mum and dad?'

'I'm fine now. They don't need to know.'

Iri glances from me to Matt. 'Back in a mo,' he says, tactfully.

Matt continues to stare at me.

'Please don't start,' I say.

He sighs. 'We've been invited out tomorrow if you're up for it. A barbecue at Phil and Em's. We don't have to bring anything, just beer and...'

Matt's lips move, but I barely hear what he's saying. The bass music is so loud. Although I've only had a couple of sips of wine, I feel dizzy, as if it's gone straight to my head.

'You okay?' Matt's voice is distant. Strobe lighting from the cellar bar flickers against the tiled floor and I can't seem to look away. The chatter around me fades, replaced by rhythmic pulsing. Everything goes black.

'Hi you. You're back.' Matt's face is inches from my own.

I'm lying along a bench seat. I struggle to sit up.

'Stay put a minute.'

Iri's voice comes from afar. 'Do you want an ambulance?'

'Just give us a minute, mate,' says Matt.

I can see worry in his eyes and attempt a smile. 'That'll teach me to mix wine and meds.' I stretch out my hand and Matt pulls me to a sitting position. My ears are ringing.

A waitress comes over with a glass of water in her hand. She passes it to Matt.

'Here, just sip.' Matt holds the glass to my lips.

'I had such a strange dream.'

'Yeah, it looked like you were dreaming. Your eyes went all twitchy. That rapid eye movement shit.'

'I was in a study, there was this big desk, really old fashioned.'

'Okay, you don't need to talk. Just sit tight.'

'I'm fine, Matt. I don't need an ambulance.'

'I'm not convinced. We need to get you checked out.'

We arrive at the hospital in an Uber. Matt decided that would be quicker than waiting for an ambulance. A sign in A & E warns a two hour wait. I pick up an old *Hello* magazine and flick through it, while Matt Googles my symptoms on his phone.

'What does it say?' I ask.

'Nothing,' says Matt, but I spy the words "bleeding on the brain" before he closes the screen.

'Hello again.' The nurse who saw us on Monday night spies us from across the waiting room. 'Can't get enough of us then?'

I smile, feeling a bit of a fraud. I'm fine again now.

The nurse winks as she wheels her patient towards the lift.

Eventually I'm seen by a doctor. He reviews my scan and draws more blood from my arm. He looks into my eyes with a torch. 'Okay, go home to rest. You can take two paracetamol if you need them. No more alcohol. If you're still rough in a few days, visit your GP. The blood test results should be back early next week.' He lowers his voice as he turns to Matt. 'Of course, any sign of a seizure, don't mess around. Dial 999.'

* * *

Anna runs down the basement steps and raps at the door.

It's Mrs Marsh who opens it. She looks Anna up and down. 'Mercy?' she yells, waddling back to the sink.

'Lawdy me.' Mercy pulls Anna inside. 'Where you been all this time?'

'Let's sit down and I'll tell you.' When they're seated at the kitchen table, Anna continues. 'Mister Gregory's located Fripp.'

Mercy's eyes shine. 'So, we might still find John?'

Anna reaches out to take her hands. 'If there's a chance of tracing your John, Mister Gregory's the person to do it.'

Mercy glances over to Mrs Marsh, who's ostensibly peeling vegetables.

Anna lowers her voice. 'What?'

'Simkins comes the morrow,' Mercy whispers. 'He's to stay until we travel. Mrs Marsh says he won't take kindly to you being here.'

Anna's heart beats rapidly. 'I don't want you to get into trouble, Mercy. I'll find somewhere else to stay.'

'But where will you go, miss?'

Where would she go? 'Don't worry, I'll find somewhere.'

Mrs Marsh turns from the sink and gives Mercy a look.

Mercy stands up, clasping her hands together like a child about to recite a poem. 'I'm grateful to yer, Miss Anna, but I mustn't be fergettin' my place…'

'Go on,' hisses Mrs Marsh.

Mercy swallows. 'My place, which I is lucky to 'ave. I been tasked with packing up Mistress Abigail's things and, by rights, that's what I should be doing.' She waves a hand over the huge pile of crumpled clothes on the table. 'All this ironing and mending. Bless me, if I ain't got plenty to keep me busy.'

Anna sighs. 'When do you leave for Yorkshire?'

'Simkins has arranged the post chaise for six days' hence. If there's no news of John by then...' Mercy takes a shuddering breath. 'Then I has to accept he's gone.' She pulls a kerchief from the bib of her apron and blows her nose.

Anna pats Mercy's arm. 'If John can be found, we'll find him.'

8th September

'Morning.'

I open my eyes. Matt's standing over me. I sit up. 'Morning.' I rub my eyes.

He lowers a tray onto the bed. It's laden with fresh croissants, orange juice and proper coffee.

'Mmm. That coffee smells great.'

'Move over.' He hops into bed beside me.

Matt scans the Sunday papers while I sip my coffee and nibble a croissant. He offers me the supplement, but I decline.

'Right,' he says, chucking the papers to the side and sliding out of bed. 'How about I run you a bath? Bubbles, candles, the works.'

I'm brushing my hair when Matt says, 'I don't suppose anyone in your family ever had epilepsy?'

'In my family?' I glare at him. 'Are you for real?'

'Sorry, for a second I forgot.'

'You've been Googling symptoms again, haven't you? It's what that doctor said about a seizure. I don't have epilepsy, Matt.'

Matt opens his mouth to reply, then closes it again.

I want to hit him. 'Why are you even going there?'

He shrugs. 'I read head injuries can sometimes bring it on.'

'I haven't had a seizure.'

'Not a grand mal maybe, but you've been kind of absent these past few days.'

'Have you swallowed a medical dictionary?'

He looks up from his MacBook. 'But the doctor said…'

'Matt, I stupidly mixed alcohol with my meds. It made me dizzy. That's it. Please, drop it.'

I move to the sofa and lie down. I know I'm being unfair, but I can't help myself. I close my eyes and replay the meeting with Debbie. Brenda told me to be patient. It would take time. It's too hard.

'Anna, are you okay there?'

I open my eyes. 'Yes. Why?'

'Just checking.'

'Stop fussing, Matt, I'm fine.' I sit up and pick up a magazine, pretending to read it.

Matt goes back to his MacBook. Working I hope and not Googling symptoms. Perhaps he senses me watching him because he looks up. 'Did you want to go to this barbecue?'

'Yes, all right. I'll just freshen up.' As I apply mascara and lip gloss in the bathroom, I give myself a talking to. It's not Matt's fault. He's trying to take care of you. You're such an ungrateful bitch. Go out there and play nice.

'You've changed your shirt.' I put my arms around his neck, inhaling his lemony aftershave. 'Mmm, you smell good.' I kiss him. 'Sorry I was such a cow.'

'I'm just worried.'

'I know.'

Matt pulls me close. 'We could always skip the barbecue. Go back to bed?'

115

'No, come on. They're your mates. We've been cooped up in here long enough.'

* * *

Janus offers Anna his arm. 'Come, the weather is clement, we will walk.'

They follow the same route as yesterday, passing the alley leading to the stable yard.

'Is that where we met Whistler?' Anna asks.

'Yes, but today we venture north of Smithfield.'

By the time they reach St John's Street, the lack of conversation is awkward. Anna has to say something. 'I'm sorry I rushed off yesterday.'

'And I apologise if it was my impertinent questioning that led you to leave with such haste'.

Anna smiles. 'You were asking about my relationship with Mercy.'

'It really is none of my business.'

'But you're helping us. You have a right to know.'

'Let us not mention it again.'

Janus pushes open the door to *The Three Cups.* The tavern is abuzz. The noise hits Anna first, then the stench of sweat. Her eyes sting from a combination of pipe tobacco and smoky fumes belching from the open hearth. 'Stay close,' says Janus. The chatter of rowdy drinkers fades as he pushes through the crowd. Anna senses every eye boring into her back.

Janus approaches the landlord. 'I seek a man named Fripp.' The landlord folds his arms. Janus drops a few coins onto the counter and the landlord gestures towards the back of the tavern.

They head over to a stout man seated at a trestle table. He's laughing uproariously as the buxom barmaid perched on his lap teases him.

'Good day to you, sir,' says Janus.

The man shoves the girl to the dirt floor.

'Blunderbuss,' she retorts. She hauls herself up, narrowing her eyes at Anna, before sauntering away towards the bar.

'Fripp?' asks Janus.

'Might be.' The man drains the dregs from his cup.

Janus removes his hat. 'May I?'

Fripp shrugs. 'Please yerself.'

Janus indicates for Anna to take a seat. 'Another ale?' he asks Fripp.

'Three-penny ordinary.' Fripp scratches his nether regions and farts. A stench like rotten eggs wafts around them and Anna slides to the far end of the sticky bench. Janus catches the landlord's eye.

Anna stares at a notice pinned to the wall behind Fripp's head: *A main of cocks to be fought at James Bagley's new pit at the sign of the Bull. 10ᵗʰ day of September. Four guineas a battle and forty the main.*

The barmaid settles a jug of ale and three earthenware cups on the table. Janus pours the drinks. Moments later the barmaid returns. Grazing Fripp's cheek with her ample bosom, she places a bowl of broth down in front of him. She gives Janus a wink as she leaves.

Fripp slurps his broth like a starving man. When he's eaten his fill, he chucks the spoon into the bowl and belches. Using the back of his hand he wipes his whiskers.

Anna's stomach turns as fatty deposits dribble from his chin. She leaves her ale untouched.

117

Janus passes Mrs Marsh's receipt to Fripp.

Fripp picks it up and squints at the scrap of paper before throwing it down. He stares at Janus. 'What be yer business?'

'Did you write this?' asks Janus.

'Mayhap.' Fripp downs his ale and belches again. He seems distracted by men gathering a few tables away. Their voices rise in a cacophony of jeers and banter. One man is collecting money in a tricorn hat.

'Maybe this will help your memory.' Janus slides a handful of coins onto the table.

Fripp eyes the money. 'What is it yer wanting to know?'

'It says here you transported a child to a foundling home in Westerham.'

'Well if that's what it says, then I dare say that's what 'appened.'

Janus leans forward. 'I sent a man out there. There was no trace of the boy.'

Fripp shrugs. 'Not all of 'em survives the journey.'

Janus grabs Fripp by the collar. 'You did not take the child all the way to Westerham. You dropped him somewhere closer to home, did you not?'

Noticing the altercation, the men nearby begin to egg them on: 'go on,' 'he needs a good clout in the chops,' 'knock 'is block off.'

Janus lets Fripp go. Fripp lunges for the coins, but Janus's hand shoots out to cover the money. 'No information, no payment.'

Fripp sighs. 'Ain't no point traipsing all the ways out to Westerham when there's good folk not far from town who can take the bairns.'

Janus tops up Fripp's cup. 'I need names.'

'All right.' Fripp takes a swig of ale. 'Alfie Smythe in Barnet, Old Ma Finch over in Waltham Forest and the Shuttlebarrows, Harrow-on-the-Hill.'

Anna gasps.

Janus releases the money. 'What happens to the children after they have reached a useful size?'

Fripp grabs up the coins and shakes his head. 'I jest drops 'em off. Don't have nothing to do with where they ends up.'

Pulling a small pouch from his belt, Janus dangles it in front of Fripp's nose.

A cheer goes up as a burly giant enters the tavern. Throwing back his head, he raises his arms and roars like a lion. A smaller sprightly man steps forward. He hauls off his shirt, flexing his biceps and pecs as he fronts up to the champion. The mob descend on the man with the tricorn hat and there's a flurry of activity as they place their bets.

Janus frowns. ''Tis a fight. Let us be away.'

As Janus stands, Fripp reaches out his hand. 'Wait, mayhap it be the Grey Man you is lookin' for?'

Janus sits back down. 'Tell me about the Grey Man.'

Fripp lowers his voice. 'Grey Man travels betwixt London and Bristol. Pedlar of sorts, Jack of all trades.'

'What trades?' asks Janus

Fripp picks up the chunk of bread from beside his bowl. He chews with his open mouth revealing black, gappy teeth.

Anna shudders.

Fripp swallows, eyeing the pouch again. 'Grey Man trades in children. Collects young 'uns from poor houses, churches and foster homes. They's glad to get rid of 'em, the big 'uns eat too much and there's always more to take their place.'

'Where does he dispose of them?'

'Some's dropped at the mills, but there's a good price to be had at the ports for able workers.'

'And what of the younger children?'

'Grey Man's been known to help a gentlewoman rid herself of a problem. Out she'll come, dead o' night to hand over her precious basket.' Fripp puts on an affected voice. '"Please take care of my little treasure," she'll plead, oft with a purse of coins tucked into her basket for good measure.'

Anna inches forward. 'What happens to the babies?'

'Those that believes him a *Coram Man* says he takes 'em to the Foundling Hospital.' Fripp beckons Anna and she moves closer. He runs his tongue around his lips and cups his hand to whisper in her ear. 'Some say yer can hear the whimpers of babies drowned in all the ditches between 'ere and Bath.' Fripp sits back and guffaws.

Anna shrinks away.

'That's all yer getting.' Fripp grabs the money, weighing the pouch in his palm. He casts his eyes around for the barmaid and spots her enjoying the company of more appreciative customers. 'Come back 'ere, me darling,' – Fripp gestures to his groin, – 'and let me see what I can get up for yer.'

The barmaid laughs. Swaggering over, she mounts him as though he were a horse.

The tavern is heaving now with men jostling and yelling as they psych up the opposition. Janus picks up his hat to signal it's time to leave. Anna tries to slide out from the bench.

Fripp shoves the table forward, pinning her against the wall. 'No rush there, missy,' he leers. 'Got plenty to go round for the both of yer.' He grinds his hips and roars with laughter again.

Janus reaches across the table to take Fripp by the throat.

As Fripp is lifted into the air, the barmaid jumps from his lap and backs away. Fripp's eyes bulge.

Anna places a hand on Janus's arm. 'Leave it, he's not worth it.'

Janus releases him and Fripp slides under the table. As the crowd bray for the fighting proper to start, Janus and Anna head outside.

Anna glances at Janus. The muscle twitching in his cheek reminds her of someone. 'I thought you were going to kill him.'

'Sorry if I frightened you. I should never have taken you to that place.'

They cut through an alley bringing them out in Charterhouse.

'I can't believe Fripp mentioned the Shuttlebarrows,' says Anna.

'Khan had a feeling they knew more than they were willing to admit.'

'Was it Khan who went to Westerham?'

'He rode out there yesterday.'

Maybe Khan's not so bad. They slow to a more leisurely pace as they cross the lawns. Anna looks up at the elaborate buildings surrounding the square. 'It's nice here.'

'Yes, very pleasant to perambulate. We might take this path if you like. The trees are particularly attractive this time of year.'

'Why do they call the Grey Man a *Coram Man*? Surely Coram doesn't endorse such practice?'

'Thomas Coram has been dead this past eighteen months. Wilkes is in charge now.'

'You don't believe Fripp or the Grey Man to be in Wilkes's

employ?'

'I dare say Wilkes has heard the rumours. Such inscrutable people will be known to the authorities, but I am certain he is not involved.'

'So why isn't something done about them?'

Janus shrugs. 'What can be done? Who knows how many vagabonds use the Coram name to give them undeserved respectability?'

'Those poor babies… their mothers believe they're sending them to safety.'

'They might be the lucky ones.'

'What do you mean?'

'What sort of life do the others have? Reared in some God forsaken foster home until they are old enough to be sold on to mill owners or chimney sweeps. Or to become cabin boys and live as slaves for seven years, if they survive that long. Many do not.'

Anna wells up. 'It's terrible.'

'Yes, it is.' Janus faces her and using his thumb, wipes a tear from her cheek. 'Fripp has upset you.' He leads her to a nearby bench. 'Here, sit a while. We will watch the young men playing cricket.'

Anna sniffs. She can't stop crying.

'This is not just about Fripp,' says Janus.

'No.'

'Then whatever is the matter?'

'I… it's…'

Janus pulls a silk kerchief from his sleeve. 'Here.'

Anna blows her nose. 'Sorry.'

There's a round of applause as a young man scores a run.

If only she could tell Janus everything. Anna takes a deep

breath, then lets it out slowly. 'It's just... I don't know where I'm going to sleep tonight.'

'You cannot remain at the Astleys'?'

'It's complicated. The Astleys don't know I'm there. Mercy's only in London for a few more days and the butler returns today. There'll be dreadful trouble if he finds out she's let me stay.'

Janus pats her arm. 'Then you must stay with me'.

Her heart beats fast. 'I can't.'

'Nonsense. My sister Elizabeth arrives this afternoon, so there will be no impropriety. Now, why not return to the Astleys' and explain everything to Mercy? Do you have things there to collect?'

'Nothing but the clothes I'm wearing.'

Janus raises an eyebrow. 'No matter. Elizabeth will lend you whatever you need. Be back in plenty of time for dinner. My sister will be impatient to meet you.'

* * *

Anna takes off the travelling cloak and hangs it on the peg. 'No Mrs Marsh?'

'Gone to market.' Mercy lifts a handful of stockings from the sink and gently wrings them out.

'We got some information from Fripp. Janus will follow it up.' Anna sits down. 'He's asked me to stay with him for a few days.'

Mercy, hanging stockings on the string above the range, turns to look at her. 'Oh, miss. I ain't sure that's right.'

'It's fine. His sister arrives today from Kent, so don't worry, I'll be chaperoned.'

123

'Well, thank the Lord. I has to admit it takes a load off me mind.' She dries her hands on her apron. 'I think that calls for a drink. You thirsty?' Mercy opens the larder and retrieves a pitcher of ale. 'While the cat's away.' She winks at Anna and fills two cups. 'Cheers.' They chink cups and sip their drinks.

Mercy puts her hand to her mouth. 'But, Miss Anna, what'll yer do for clothes?'

'Janus said his sister will lend me some.'

'Even so…' Mercy gets up from the table and pulls a dark green gown from the ironing pile. 'How about this? Don't think Miss Abigail will miss it.'

'Are you sure?'

Mercy shakes it out and holds it up to Anna. 'Yes, it be a good fit, although could do with a patch here and there.'

'Thanks, Mercy. If I can borrow this gown and the one I'm wearing, and perhaps the travelling cloak, I'm sure I'll manage.'

* * *

William throws open the doors to the drawing room. 'Mrs Carmichael, sir.'

Janus stands to greet his sister. 'Elizabeth. How good it is to see you again so soon.' He kisses her affectionately on both cheeks.

'Brother, you will not believe the atrocities of my journey, and yet, here I am at last.' Elizabeth unpins her hat and holds it out to the butler. 'Tea would be lovely, thank you, William, but no cake, it will spoil my appetite for dinner. Now, let me sit and catch my breath.' She moves over to the couch. 'Come, sit beside me Janus. Have you received any replies from your

124

invitations?'

'Yes, I...'

'I suppose you have invited those staid old Prism members. Although I am happy for you to include your mysterious shadow Mister Khan, and I dare say we will not get away without the charming Monsieur Quintar.'

'Of course, I...'

'I do hope he restrains himself from emptying your entire wine cellar this time. How is jolly old London, brother? Has anything exciting happened since last we met?'

A smile plays around Janus's mouth.

Elizabeth momentarily pauses, looking at him quizzically. 'Janus?'

Janus leans forward. 'Actually, there has been a small development.'

'How intriguing. Do tell.'

'I am not at liberty to say too much, for 'tis a delicate matter, but sister dearest, I need your assistance.'

'I am listening.'

'We shall be having a house guest and you would do me a great service if you would collude with me in a little deception. At the soirée I intend to introduce her as a dear but distant relation.'

Ned the footman arrives with a tray.

'Thank you, Ned. I can manage.' Elizabeth pulls off her gloves to pour the tea. 'But perhaps you might put another log on the fire? It is most awfully chilly in here. Now tell me, Janus, exactly what have you been up to?'

'It is nothing to be concerned about but it will help me enormously if you would go along with my explanation of her presence. It is merely for a few days. I shall say she is a cousin whose visit to town fortuitously coincided with your own.'

'For shame, Janus. And here I was, thinking at last someone had caught your attention.' Elizabeth sighs. 'I fear this is another of your experiments. One of your rescued strays, I suppose.' She passes her brother a cup. 'Really, brother, we can hardly pass off one of your fallen women as a relative. I do not know if I am willing to join in such deceit.'

'Elizabeth, I cannot explain everything now so you will have to trust me. I believe you will have no trouble convincing others that she is a relation. In fact, once you meet her, I have a feeling you might rather enjoy her company.'

'Well now you have whetted my appetite. You know, I think I might manage some cake after all. Ring for Ned, would you, dear? Are you sure this mystery woman cannot be persuaded to stay for longer than a few days? Female company is just what you need, Janus. It is high time you settled down.'

'Excuse me, Mrs Carmichael.' Ned enters the drawing room with a plate of fruit cake. 'Mrs Lawson wondered if you might like a slice of her cake to go with your tea?'

'Oh Ned, you anticipate my needs so well.'

Janus chuckles. 'I do not think life with Mistress Stratton would be very settled, but you will see for yourself, for she dines with us this evening. And Elizabeth?' He lowers his voice. 'I am sure you will not mind, but you may have to lend her some clothes.'

'I must confess to being more than a little intrigued.'

'Elizabeth, drink your tea.'

* * *

Anna looks up at the clock in the hallway. Six o'clock. She stands at the drawing room doorway waiting to be announced.

The butler opens the doors. 'Mistress Anna Stratton.'

A woman with coiffured hair the same inky black as Janus's is seated on the couch. She extends her hand. 'Charmed to meet you, my dear.' Anna notes that Elizabeth is a similar build to herself. *At least her clothes should fit.*

'Come and sit here.' Elizabeth pats the place on the couch next to where she's sitting. 'Now tell me about yourself. Janus is being a perfect bore and has told me absolutely nothing.' Elizabeth throws Janus a challenging look. 'Anna Stratton, did you say? Are you related to the Strattons of Hampshire?'

'No, I don't believe...'

Janus, who had stood when Anna entered the room, sits back in his armchair and attempts to conceal a smile.

Anna sits down with some trepidation. Elizabeth leaves few gaps for response, while her eyes, intelligent and searching, flick between Anna and Janus, double checking their answers.

'Tell me, Mistress Stratton,' says Elizabeth, 'where did you receive your education? I can detect no accent. Europe, I dare say. Did you take elocution lessons?'

'No, I...'

I believe it has become fashionable there. We do our best in Tunbridge Wells, of course. An acquaintance of mine lately opened a day school for young ladies and hopes soon to receive a visit from the esteemed Doctor Johnson. He was kind enough last month to honour a similar establishment in Newstead Green with his presence. Is that not right, Janus?'

'Yes, Elizabeth.' Janus catches Anna's eye and smiles. She smiles back.

The drawing room doors open. 'Dinner is served, sir.'

'Thank you, William.' Janus rises from his chair. 'Ladies? Let us continue in the dining room.'

It's a different dining room to the one in which Janus and Quintar had taken breakfast three days before. *Who has two dining rooms?* Anna wishes she had something dressier to wear. The candles of the chandelier flicker down on the table, and the crystal and cutlery sparkle. The table is set for four.

'Oh splendid. Mister Khan is to join us,' says Elizabeth. 'You sit here, my dear. Opposite Janus.'

Khan enters the room. 'Forgive my tardiness, Mrs Carmichael.' He kisses Elizabeth's hand.

'No matter, Mister Khan. You may make amends by sitting opposite me.'

As Ned serves the soup course, Elizabeth resumes her interrogation. 'Mistress Stratton. You have not yet explained where you and Janus met.'

Unsure of the etiquette, Anna watches for the others to start eating before lifting her soup spoon. 'At the Foundling Hospital. Janus is helping a friend of mine who is trying to locate her son.'

'Ah yes. That sounds like Janus. My brother can always be relied upon when others are in need.'

Janus smiles. 'Do I detect a note of sarcasm in your tone, sister?'

'Not at all, Janus. You have been forever thus.'

As Anna watches the siblings she's surprised at the warmth and understanding they have between them. *Has she ever experienced a relationship like this?*

By the time they're finishing their main course, the conversation has turned to the soirée. 'Have all your guests responded?' Elizabeth asks.

'Khan will be able to help you there,' says Janus.

Khan inclines his head.

'Oh, dear Mister Khan. I do not know what my brother would do without the two of us looking after him.' She lifts a small, embroidered bag onto her lap and takes out a piece of paper. 'Now let me see, Mister and Mrs Skinner?'

'Yes,' replies Khan. 'Mrs Skinner says they would be delighted.'

'Thank goodness, Mrs Skinner is such a charming lady.' Elizabeth winks at Anna. 'Mister and Mrs Palmer, Mister Harbinger and his daughters, Mister and Mrs Pestlemore…'

Wasn't Pestlemore the name of one of Janus's Prism acquaintances?

Khan responds with the replies. Ned enters with the coffee tray and Elizabeth turns to Anna. 'We have a busy time ahead of us tomorrow, Mistress Stratton. There is much to organise before the soirée.'

'I am afraid, dear sister, I must disappoint you.' Janus puts his knife and fork down on his plate. 'Mistress Stratton and I have business to attend in the morning.'

'Really, Janus, this is too bad. There will be the food and the wine, not to mention the additional serving staff. You expect me to do everything myself?'

Goodness, has Janus given his sister carte blanche?

'Dearest Elizabeth, you know that you thrive on it. Anyway, Mrs Lawson, William and Ned are all at your disposal. Is that not so, Ned?'

'Yes, sir.' Ned pours the coffee.

'Hmm,' says Elizabeth. 'Well, Ned, I am afraid I have a long list.'

Janus winks at Anna. 'I promise there will be plenty of time for the two of you to discuss outfits.'

'Do you imagine all women talk about is clothes?' Anna retorts.

Elizabeth turns to her. 'Janus tells me your clothing trunk was lost in transit?'

'I… well… yes,' says Anna.

'Do not fret, my dear. I keep a wardrobe here. I am sure I can find you something suitable.'

'Khan,' says Janus, 'that may be our cue to retire.'

* * *

When we arrive at Em and Phil's, there's a Post-it note stuck to the door: *We're in the garden. Come in through the side gate.*

Em holds her arms out wide, pulling me in for a hug. 'OMG Anna! What a terrible thing to happen. Are you all right?'

'Getting there.'

'What can I get you to drink?' asks Phil.

'Just a soft drink please,' I pull on my cardigan. 'Diet Coke or something?'

'Beer for me.' Matt follows Phil down the garden.

Em leads me towards the patio. 'The girls can't wait to see you.'

All eyes are on me as I sink into one of the comfy seats.

'Well?' says Em. 'Tell us everything.'

I shrug. 'He came out of nowhere. He was yelling, telling me to give him my bag…' They listen as I continue to recount my mugging story.

'I can't believe you fought back,' says Marcie, Iri's girlfriend. 'You go, girl.'

'I didn't exactly fight. I just didn't let go.'

'Phil told me Matt's been beside himself with worry,' says Em.

'Poor Matt, he's been doing a great job looking after me.'

'Lucky you.' Marcie throws Matt an appraising glance.

'Quite frankly, I'm amazed to see you up and about,' says Em.

'I'm fine,' I say, but I know I'm not. My head's throbbing again. I look across to Matt larking about with his mates. It wouldn't be fair to suggest going home yet.

I listen to the girls nattering on about *Love Island*, bitching about the contestants and arguing which of the boys will turn out to be a player. *When did their conversation become so superficial?* I wish Zoe were here.

'Burgers are ready,' yells Phil.

The girls haul themselves up and head over to the buffet table. I walk across to Matt.

He nuzzles into my hair. 'You okay?'

'Bit of a headache.' I smile.

'Okay. We'll grab a bite, then get away early.'

'Have some of this pasta.' Em passes me a bowl. 'Marcie made it.'

'I'm sorry. I should have brought a dish of something.'

'Oh, my goodness, you've had more than enough to contend with.' Em gives me a quick squeeze, before heading off to check everyone else is eating.

I'm not hungry, but I spoon pasta into my bowl and add salad. Picking at my food, I watch the guys larking about by the barbecue.

'How burnt do you like your sausages, Iri?' Matt yells. 'I don't think Phil's quite finished cremating these yet.'

'Keep complaining and you could find yourself going vegan

131

tonight, mate,' Phil retorts.

The guys don't bother with plates. Or salad, it seems. Matt's tucking into his third burger and pulling the ring from yet another can of beer when I sidle over and whisper in his ear. 'Can we make a move soon?'

'Sure babe. Soon as I've finished this beer.'

Another half hour passes and Matt's still laughing with his mates. Absentmindedly he reaches down to grab another beer from the bucket of ice.

'Matt,' I say.

He turns, giving me the look, the one that says, *don't show me up*.

I wander over to the patio, lay back in a recliner seat and let the girls' chatter wash over me as I close my eyes.

We'd only been together a couple of months when Matt told me he wanted to take care of me.

'What if I've ruined things with my parents?' I'd wailed, opening up to him about the situation with Debbie, Mum and Dad.

'You're in a new relationship now. I'm all the family you'll need. Everything will be all right, babe.'

He reached for me, but I pushed him away. 'How can you say that? You can't know things will be all right.'

'We'll work this out.'

'I have to sort it out. It's my life.'

'I'm trying to help.'

'I know, but you can't fix everything.'

Matt didn't give up and it wasn't long before he wore me down. I moved in. He's been looking after me ever since.

Someone lays a hand on my shoulder. I jump. Opening my eyes, I see Em standing over me.

'Matt's going to take you home, love.' Em says in a soft voice. 'I told him you look done in.' She holds out her hands to pull me up.

Matt mimes raising a glass to his mouth and points in my direction. The guys guffaw and Phil claps Matt on the back.

'What was that about?' I say, as Matt unhooks the side gate.

Matt laughs. 'Oh, I told them I had to take you home 'cause you'd had one too many.'

I turn on him. 'I've been drinking Diet Coke all evening.'

He holds up his hands defensively. 'Okay. Chill out.'

'If you don't want to leave yet, I can get myself home.'

Matt takes my arm. 'It's fine. I might watch the match for a bit when we get in.'

* * *

Elizabeth leads the way upstairs. The staircase is wide and carpeted, and the candles on the wall flicker from a draught sneaking in around the front door. Anna wonders who lights them all. Must be a fire hazard.

'My dear brother maintains these rooms for when I am in town,' says Elizabeth. Her bedroom is cosy and warm. Someone has lit a fire and the bedding has been turned down in readiness. Elizabeth crosses over to a beautiful walnut armoire taking up one entire wall. She pulls open both doors.

Anna is stunned by the array of fabrics and colours. 'Wow!'

Elizabeth begins to rummage through the multitude of dresses. 'I am sure I have something that will fit you.' She pulls out a gown of magenta satin and holds it up. 'Oh no,

133

that will not do at all.'

Anna reaches out to feel the fabric and it crackles at her touch. The gown is entirely the wrong colour for her. It looks like a bridesmaid's dress. 'It sounds as if there will be many guests attending this soirée.'

'Janus has invited his Prism colleagues and there will be a number of ladies, of course. You are not the first damsel in distress that Janus has saved.' Elizabeth pats Anna's arm affectionately. 'Bless you, no. I am afraid his ventures do little to help his reputation. Not that it bothers him. Janus has a knack for rescuing young ladies from the most terrible calamities.' Elizabeth's voice is muffled as she all but disappears behind her gowns. 'Many is the time I have arrived here to find a strange woman supping with Janus, wearing my clothes, even sleeping in my bed.'

'What happens to them?' Anna asks.

'Well, that is never the end of it. Janus does all he can to ensure they get a fresh start – a change of clothes, a roof over their head and the reassurance that someone cares.' Elizabeth backs out and explores further along the rail. 'I am sure I had something in blue.'

'Blue might be good,' Anna's voice is hopeful.

'Janus helps children, too. Not just foundlings. He set up a scheme for young boys to become recruits with the navy and he has rescued others from master sweeps around the city and found them work. It is not unusual to find him engrossed with one or other of his good works. Ah, what about this?' Elizabeth hauls out a layered gown in pale lilac. 'I have to admit, I rather thought you were one of his projects yourself.'

Anna holds the dress up. The skirts billow. It reeks of lavender. 'Perhaps I am.'

'Nonsense, my dear. I do believe I shall have to call Clemmie.' Elizabeth crosses to the fireplace and pulls a cord. 'Now that I have come to know you, I can tell you are nobody's project. You are a strong young woman. I fear you will terrify his male guests.'

'Why?' Anna lays the lilac gown down on the bed.

'Gentlemen like a woman they can keep in check. Sadly, independence of thought is not a quality admired in society.'

'Will your husband be attending the soirée?'

'Ernest? No, I am afraid it is not his sort of thing, but he tolerates me coming up to town to play hostess. I usually manage to visit friends and enjoy a little shopping while I am here. Ernest, bless him, never complains. I dare say he is glad of the peace.' Elizabeth peals with laughter. 'Perhaps we might shop together? You do have such an eye for fashion. Is that the Parisian way to fix one's hair?'

Anna pats her unruly mop and looks away.

'I shall enjoy spending time with you, my dear. Getting to know you better. Where is that girl?' Elizabeth tugs the cord again. 'Tell me, should I be excited? Are you and Janus...'

'Oh, no,' says Anna.

'But you are blushing! How charming. Take no heed, my dear, I see I have made you uncomfortable.' Elizabeth's eyes twinkle. 'How delicious it will be to see the reaction of the Harbinger sisters.'

'The Harbinger sisters?'

'Yes. They have rather lain claim to Janus, you know? Their father donated a fortune to the Foundling Hospital with hopes of marrying one of them off. Sorry, my dear, do I upset you?'

'No, of course not. So, has there been anyone special in Janus's life?'

135

'Well, Ramia of course. The love of his life.' Elizabeth crosses to her dressing table and sits down. 'His Persian princess, very beautiful, quite captured my brother's heart. Unfortunately, she was promised in marriage to the Sultan.'

'The Sultan?'

'Yes, it was a few years ago now.' Elizabeth gazes at her reflection. 'Janus was working for the East India Company. While on his travels across Persia, he met Ramia and fell in love.'

Anna moves closer. 'Did she feel the same way?'

'Apparently yes.' Elizabeth has a faraway look in her eyes. 'They sought to find ways to be together, but it is extremely dangerous for a man and a woman to meet alone in the East.' She sighs. 'It was all very sad.'

'Why? What happened?'

Elizabeth turns to look at her. 'Janus made plans to smuggle Ramia away, but the plot was discovered. He could not bear the thought that she might be punished, so he took the blame himself, concocting a story that he had tried to kidnap her against her will. The Sultan's love for the princess was so great he was willing to believe the lie and Ramia was cleared of any indiscretion. Janus, however, was lucky to escape with his life.'

There's a knock and Elizabeth's maid enters the room. 'Sorry ma'am, I was down in the kitchens.'

'Clemmie,' says Elizabeth. 'I am sure I had a gown that would be right for Mistress Stratton. The teal, I just can't seem to...'

Clemmie runs her fingers through the garments, quickly locating the gown in question.

'Yes, that one,' says Elizabeth. 'Now tell me, my dear, what do you think?'

'It's lovely.' Anna holds up the gown, stroking the luxurious velvet.

'Brings out the colour of your eyes. It will be perfect for the soirée,' says Elizabeth. 'And I do believe there was a day dress.'

Clemmie, still standing by the wardrobe, pulls out a toffee-coloured garment.

'Oh, I knew you would find them, Clemmie,' says Elizabeth. 'Now, please show Mistress Stratton to the guest room.'

Clemmie lays the gowns over her arm. 'If you'd like to come this way, miss.' She leads the way by candlelight along the corridor and up a small flight of stairs. Stopping outside a door, she opens it up to reveal a pretty room decorated in sunshine yellow. Draping the dresses carefully across an armchair in front of the window, Clemmie turns to Anna. 'Will you be needing anything else, miss?'

'No, that's fine thank you.'

Clemmie bobs a curtsey.

Left alone, Anna gazes out of the window. In the dark streets below, a carriage goes by and someone shouts as they leap aside to avoid being mown down. Anna turns back and looks around the room – a tall four-poster bed, a washstand with china jug and matching basin depicting a pastoral scene and an ornate mirror. She crosses to the mirror and stares back at her twin. She's stuck in a parallel world. *When will she feel herself again?*

Reaching up behind her back, Anna wriggles and contorts as she struggles to unlace her bodice. She should have asked Clemmie for help. Finally, ribbons loose, she steps out of the gown and tiptoes across the creaky floorboards to the washstand. She pours a little water into the bowl and splashes her face. After patting her face dry, she turns to stare at the

137

four-poster bed. How is she going to get up there? She walks around the other side and discovers a small set of steps.

Clambering up, Anna finds the bed delightfully soft and feels like the princess in a story she loved as a child. She thinks back over what Elizabeth told her about Janus and his Persian princess. It sounds like a fairy story. Does that sort of thing happen in real life? She rolls over but can't settle. Why is the bed so high? Is it to keep its occupant higher than the rats? Anna shudders. Now she hears the patter of tiny claws scuttling along inside the walls. She leaves the candle alight, just in case.

* * *

In his study, Janus swirls his brandy in the glass. 'Come on, Khan. Out with it, man. What is it you wish to say?'

Khan stirs his tea. 'Is it wise you have the girl to stay?'

'There is no impropriety. She will be chaperoned while Elizabeth is here.' Janus frowns. 'Mistress Stratton believes you do not care for her.'

Khan shrugs. 'It is not my place to have an opinion. I wonder though, at your fascination?'

Janus snorts. 'I am not fascinated.'

'You seem rather obsessed.'

'Khan, my friend, you are mistaken.' Janus sips his brandy.

'My concern is that you might neglect your other projects. For instance, you have not mentioned Magdalen in two days.'

'There will be time enough for Magdalen when Mistress Stratton has gone.'

'So, she does have plans to leave?'

'I assume so.' Janus sighs. 'Once she has completed her quest for the missing child, there will be nothing more to keep her here.' He throws back his brandy and stands up. 'I think it is time I retired. Do not stay up too late my friend.'

* * *

Tweedie is enjoying a cup of coffee in front of the fire. It is peaceful in the house now that Mrs Blaine, his housekeeper, has retired for the night. His boy, who is kneeling beside Tweedie's armchair, starts when the bell on the front door clangs. Tweedie pats the boy's head and goes to answer it.

'Oh, it is you,' says Tweedie. 'I am not used to receiving callers so late. You had better come in.'

His visitor steps into the entrance hall and puts an arm around Tweedie's shoulders. 'Let us go into your parlour.'

Tweedie perches on the edge of the chaise, while his visitor takes the comfortable armchair by the fire. He rubs his hands to warm them, then looks around the room, taking in the prissy ornaments and trinkets. His eyes alight on the young boy quivering by the window. 'Ah, there he is. Quite popular with the ladies, I gather? I wonder, Tweedie, if I might have done better to have kept him myself? Still, now you have had your grubby mitts on him he is somewhat less appealing. Does you like yer master, boy?'

The boy stands wide eyed, trembling.

'I am not sure, Tweedie.' The visitor laughs. 'Looks like he could do with a bit more meat on his bones. Perhaps you should fatten him up for Christmas? A nice little nibble, eh?'

Tweedie examines his fingers.

'Or mayhap you prefer 'em a little delicate? Makes 'em a little more compliant, eh?'

The boy steps sideways to hide behind the drapes, leaving only the tips of his velvet slippers peeping out.

The visitor laughs again. 'Tweedie, the boy disappears before my eyes. Does he fear I mean to eat him?'

'Leave the boy alone.' Tweedie's voice is barely more than a whisper.

'Do not look so worried. I can maintain a confidence. Discretion between friends is a good thing. I am a man of the world. I have seen it all before.' The visitor runs his tongue around his lips. 'Believe me, there is nothing you thirst for which cannot be found on the streets of the best cities in the world. And yet, there are some…' – he sits forward, lowering his voice – 'some members of society who might not understand. Might even be a trifle shocked, sir.'

Tweedie stands up. 'What is it you want?'

The visitor lifts a silver jug from the coffee tray. He raises it to his nose and pulls a face. 'A little sour, Tweedie, that is what your life has become. I fear this milk is about to turn.' He pinches his nose, replacing the jug on the silver tray. 'Suppose your esteemed acquaintances at the Royal Society were to find out about your dalliances? They are men of the world to be sure, but they do not like to have their noses rubbed in it. In polite society some might frown on the misuse of a child for evil and perverted lustful desires.'

Tweedie turns pale. His hands clench and unclench by his sides.

'No, it would not do, would it, Tweedie?' says his visitor. 'All your dreams, hopes of becoming a fellow of such esteemed society dashed, so to speak. But fret not, for there is no need for anyone to learn of your dirty little secret. Are we not friends? I look out for you and you look out for me. Who knows? I might even be persuaded to find you another young companion when this one is no longer fresh. For your part I ask but the smallest of favours in return.'

Tweedie glances across to the curtain where the boy is hiding. He nods.

'You see?' The visitor smiles. 'That was not so difficult. Now, there's a warehouse down at the wharf…'

After outlining his plan, the visitor stands to fasten his cloak. 'I must take my leave. You will tell no-one of this conversation for, if you do, well, let us just say you would not like the consequences.'

Tweedie sits back in his armchair and mops his brow with a silk kerchief. A tiny movement from the drapes causes him to look up. 'Come, boy.' Tweedie's tone is not unkind. He pats his knee for the boy to join him and absentmindedly fondles the boy's dreadlocks.

9th September

Anna stretches her arms then sinks back into the feather mattress. It's far more comfortable than Mercy's straw cot. On opening her eyes, she pulls the bedcovers up to her neck. Fresh clothes are lain out on the armchair. How did she not hear Clemmie creep back in?

After checking she's alone, Anna climbs down from the bed and looks around the room. She's dying for a wee. Under the bed she finds a chamber pot. She pulls it out, admiring the Chinese design with its gilded flowers and birds. Far too good to pee in but, needs must. Anna keeps glancing at the door as she squats to relieve herself, then slides the pot back ensuring nothing spills.

She crosses to the washstand. Clemmie must have emptied the bowl and refreshed the water during the night. Anna picks up the jug and fills the bowl. She undresses, hanging her slip on the back of the chair, and washes her face. The water's freezing. The lady engraved on the jug is clearly hardier, smiling as she dips her toes into a woodland stream. Anna splashes water under her arms. *Oh, for a hot shower.* She pulls a glass stopper from the bottle beside the bowl and brings it to her nose. *Roses.* Anna applies a few drops liberally around her neck and underarms.

The low temperature in the room causes her to shiver. She dashes to the chair and retrieves the clothes. After slipping into the silk undergarments, she steps into the freshly ironed day dress. The satin fabric, dull brown in last night's candlelight, now reflects a pleasing sheen of purple and blue hues. Anna smiles as she runs to the mirror, lifting and flouncing the skirt. She groans when she sees her hair. *What a mess.* After dipping her fingers in the wash bowl, she prods and pulls at the stray tendrils before shoving the whole lot up in her hairband.

Anna enters the breakfast room to find Janus and Monsieur Quintar seated at the table. She squints from the sunlight pouring in through the French window where Mister Khan is sitting, sorting through some papers.

Janus rises to greet her. 'Good morning. Please, join us.'

'Might I say, my dear.' Quintar fingers his moustache. 'That gown is most becoming.'

'Thank you.' Anna sits opposite him and smooths down her skirt.

Janus pours out a bowl of hot chocolate and passes it to Anna. 'I trust Elizabeth's maid did not disturb you when preparing your clothes?'

'Not at all.' Anna takes a slice of spice bread from the plate. 'I slept well.'

Janus smiles. 'Good, good.'

Quintar's eyes meet Anna's. 'Might I ask, Mistress Stratton, if you would do me the honour of saving me a dance this evening?'

Anna feels her cheeks flush. 'Oh, I'm not sure I shall be dancing.'

Janus frowns. 'A wise decision Mistress Stratton. You do well to avoid Monsieur Quintar's advances. He is somewhat of a rogue when it comes to the fairer sex.'

'*Mais oui*, but I am afraid this is true.' Quintar sighs. '*J'adore* women and the English women are particularly beautiful, *n'est-ce pas?*' He spreads marmalade thickly onto his bread. 'Of course, the Parisian woman has a certain *je ne sais quoi,* for she is the height of all things fashionable, but London women are more sensual. I prefer my women soft to the touch. Parisian ladies can be very angular.'

Janus raises an eyebrow. 'Quintar, enough. You will make Mistress Stratton blush.'

'*Je suis désolé*, Mistress Stratton. What can I say? I am but a man.'

Male chauvinist more like. Anna turns to Janus. 'Where is your sister this morning?'

'Elizabeth will join us later. You will find she is more night owl than lark. Unless rising early for the coach to Tunbridge Wells.'

'It's kind of her to lend me some clothes.'

'You will find Elizabeth most benevolent.'

'Her husband is a doctor?' Anna asks.

'Yes. Ernest Carmichael is renowned in Kent. My sister is very content there as long as she is able to come to town once a month and meet with her friends in Mayfair.'

Quintar nods. '*Les Bas Bleus.*'

Anna raises an eyebrow.

'Elizabeth is a member of the *Blue Stocking Society,*' explains Janus. 'Their doctrine is to engage in rational conversation.'

'Good for them.' Anna sips her chocolate.

'Have a care, *ma chérie.*' Quintar wags his finger. 'Madame

Carmichael will be inviting you to take tea and cake with her pretty *petticoteries*.'

Anna smiles. 'And I should be delighted.'

Janus laughs. 'Perhaps it is you who should take care, Quintar? Elizabeth would not take kindly to you describing her friends in such manner.'

Quintar bows his head. 'Janus, *mon ami*, you are, of course, correct.'

Janus pushes back his chair. 'Right Quintar. Did you not say you have business to attend? Mistress Stratton and I have a visit to make.'

'My sedan is ordered for ten o'clock.' Quintar helps himself to more coffee. 'Madame Carmichael will be most upset to find you have whisked the charming Mistress Stratton away.'

Janus grins. 'That is exactly why we are setting off early.'

Leaving Quintar to finish his breakfast, Janus and Anna make ready to leave. William helps Anna with her travelling cloak. Khan joins them in the hallway.

In the landau, Khan sits opposite Anna. She attempts to engage him in conversation. 'Where are you off to then, Mister Khan?'

'Slaughters.' He doesn't elaborate and avoids eye contact.

After a short ride they arrive at St Martins.

'What did he mean by slaughters?' Anna asks once Khan has alighted. 'Is Mister Khan visiting an abattoir?'

'Abattoir?' Janus frowns. 'Slaughters is a Coffee House. A place for gentlemen to while away a few hours in conversational politics.'

Anna giggles. 'Mister Khan will much prefer spending time with gentlemen rather than sitting in the carriage with me.'

Janus grins. 'Come now, admit it. You will miss his company.'

He's handsome when he smiles. 'So, where are we going?'

'After meeting with Fripp, I have decided we should pay the Shuttlebarrows another visit. Do not fear, I shall have you back in plenty of time to ready yourself for the soirée.'

* * *

Pestlemore lifts the metal plate from the furnace and sets it aside. Returning his attention to the already cooled specimen, he carefully transfers the white powdery residue to the measuring vessel, chewing his lip thoughtfully. The mass of phlogiston generated is significantly higher. Turning to the journal where he meticulously records the volume of calx derived from each combustion, he adds new figures to the final column.

'There's someone here to see you, Thomas.' Pestlemore's wife pushes open the door and ushers the visitor into the basement laboratory.

Pestlemore wipes his palms on his trousers and extends a hand. 'My good fellow, this is indeed a p-pleasure. Come in, come in.'

His visitor declines to shake hands.

'It is an honour, sir, that you visit me here in Addles Street.' Pestlemore lifts a tray of receptacles from a wooden stool and wipes it with a cloth. 'Please, take a seat?'

'I prefer to stand.' The visitor eyes the phials and bottles on the workbench with disdain.

Pestlemore smiles. 'Of course.'

'You will be aware,' the visitor says, 'that Gregory has

become somewhat distracted of late.'

'He does seem to have his mind on other things.'

'It is since the arrival of a certain Mistress Stratton. Gregory has become obsessed with assisting her search for a missing child.'

Pestlemore takes off his glasses and wipes them on his coat. 'I am not sure what that has to do with…'

The visitor smashes his fist down on the work bench. 'Pestlemore, you cod head. Don't you realise her presence puts the whole project in jeopardy?'

'How s-so?'

'If Gregory does not approve the second trial of the equipment by the end of the month, the application for fellowship with the Royal Society cannot be lodged until next year.'

'Gregory was most d-displeased when we p-previously took matters into our own hands. I don't think we should act again without his approval.'

The visitor scoffs. 'Gregory does not know what is good for him. He is infatuated with the woman. As his friends it is up to us to act in his best interests. It is imperative the project gets back on track.'

'What do you p-propose that we do?'

The visitor waves at Pestlemore's potions. 'I want you to create a concoction to help rid us of this problem.'

'B-but I understand that Mistress Stratton is little more than a girl.'

The visitor snarls. 'You will help me with this or be damned.'

Pestlemore shakes his head.

'If you do not assist, things may take an unfortunate turn. Rather a sad life your bachelor friend Tweedie has, do you not agree? You have a good set up here, Pestlemore. Nice

147

home, comfortable wife. 'Twould be a shame if things were to change…'

Pestlemore drops his shoulders. At that moment Sarah returns with a tray of coffee.

'Not for me, thank you. I will let myself out.' The visitor strides upstairs, his black cloak swirling behind him.

'Well?' Sarah turns to look at her husband.

Pestlemore covers his face with his hands.

* * *

I paste on a smile as I enter the offices of the *Tube and Eye.* It's a normal Monday morning with the others engrossed on their computer screens.

Dan spins around in his chair. 'There she is. We've missed that smiley face.'

I hang my jacket on the back of my chair and place my shoulder bag in the bottom drawer of my desk.

Jen comes across to hug me. 'Hi, how're you doing?'

'I'm okay.' I nod at my clear workspace. 'Thought I'd have a stack of jobs?'

'It's your first day back,' says Jen. 'Gary said go easy on you.'

I sit down, pull some files from my drawer and pretend to be busy.

Gary walks past. 'She's back. Fetch me a coffee?' He winks. 'No one else makes it the way I like it.'

I deliver the drink to his desk.

'Thanks.' Gary takes a sip but doesn't look up.

I hesitate for a moment, then return to my workstation. I'm shuffling papers when my mobile rings.

Brenda's on the other end of the line. 'Any chance you can

meet me in Costa this morning?'

In a low voice I answer, 'I don't know. I've only been back at work five minutes.'

Brenda's enjoying her latte and a Danish pastry when I arrive at *Costa*.

'I'll go and grab a drink.' I join the queue and watch Brenda breaking her pastry into small pieces. She shoves them in her mouth one by one, alternating with slurps from her coffee glass.

After being served by the barista, I carry the tray with my black coffee back to the table to join Brenda.

She looks at my drink. 'You're not eating?'

'I've a sandwich back at work. I assume you want a debrief from my meeting with Debbie?'

Brenda holds up one finger.

I wait while she finishes her mouthful.

'Sorry, I didn't want to alarm you on the phone.' She brushes pastry flakes from her skirt. 'There's been a bit of an incident at the halfway house.'

'An incident? What do you mean?'

Brenda leans forward giving me a sickly blast from her milky drink. 'You do understand, Anna, there are rules that recovering users must adhere to.'

'What's happened?'

'It seems there was some kind of altercation.' She looks at me pointedly. 'On Saturday night. The police were called.'

Is she blaming me? 'Debbie's been arrested?'

'No, Debbie hasn't been arrested.'

I exhale with relief.

'Debbie recently befriended another woman who lives

149

there.'

'Yes, she told me she's made a friend. Tracy isn't it?'

'Yes, well I'm afraid Tracy is not a good influence. They arrived home late on Saturday night and very much the worse for wear. One of the residents complained about the noise so Tracy gave him a black eye. Another resident called the police and Tracy was arrested.'

'Then it's not Debbie's fault.'

'We don't know how involved Debbie was. She ran off before the police could apprehend her.' Brenda sits back. 'I suspect she knew they'd carry out drug and alcohol tests.'

I sip my coffee. 'Do you know where she is?'

'No.' Brenda sighs. 'But I've a fair idea who she's with.'

'Who?'

'Some guy she turns to in times of trouble. He's bad news.'

My heart thumps. 'Where can I find him?'

Brenda shrugs.

'So, what happens now?'

Brenda drains the froth from her latte glass. 'I can't do anything for her if she won't help herself.'

'Perhaps she'll speak to me? I might be able to get her to talk to you?'

'I'm afraid we're running out of options. There are only so many times they'll take someone on a rehab programme. Debbie's rather used up her lifelines.'

'You can't give up on her.'

'It's not a question of giving up on her. She knows the score. In effect she's opted out of the programme. Sometimes, my dear, there's nothing that can be done.'

'Debbie hasn't just left the rehab programme, she's...' I sniff and wipe my eyes with my sleeve. *She's abandoned me all over again.* I blow my nose on my paper napkin. 'You told me once that Debbie reminded you of your daughter?'

There's a pause before Brenda answers. 'Yes.'

'What happened to your daughter?'

'Things didn't end well for my Laura.' Brenda closes her eyes. 'She got mixed up with a bad crowd. She was only fourteen when they groomed her, got her dependent on drugs and doing all sorts of things to feed her habit.' Brenda shudders. Opening her eyes, she looks down at her skirt and rubs at a grease spot. 'Look, I'd rather not talk about it. I'm going to have another coffee. Do you want one?'

'No, I've got to get back.'

Brenda gets up. 'Last I heard,' – she lowers her voice – 'this guy was living in a squat.' She hesitates before adding, 'not far from the *Pie 'n' Mash* in Deptford.'

Back in the office after my early lunch, I scroll half-heartedly through my emails. I glance around to check no-one's watching, before pulling my reporters' notebook with research notes on *Coram's Children* from my bag. I'd planned to talk to Gary about my ideas for the foundling story. If I gave it a contemporary twist, perhaps even a happy ending? I sigh. Who was I kidding? Matt's right, Gary won't be interested. Nobody's ever interested.

My mind wanders back to that day out with Debbie. It started well – window-shopping along Oxford Street, followed by lunch and a walk along the Thames. The Embankment was my idea. How was I to know the significance?

'That's where you were,' Debbie said as we stood on Westminster Bridge.

I turned to look in the direction she was pointing. 'St Thomas' Hospital? When?'

'When you was a baby. They had to do tests. Something wrong with your heart. I never did find out what. Poor little mite, you were only six weeks old. Too young for all that paraphernalia, wires and tubes everywhere. That's when I knew I couldn't do it.'

'Do what?'

'Look after you. I decided there and then there was no way I could bring up a kid. Especially one so sick.'

'You left me there?'

'I knew there'd be better people out there who could love you. Give you the sort of life you deserved.'

'But I was poorly. I might not have survived.'

Debbie said nothing.

'How could you abandon me?' I yelled. 'I could have died in there all alone.'

Debbie shook her head. 'They let me know you was all right. We was apart anyway while you were in hospital and that made it easier to let you go. I'd got used to it, see? You not being with me.'

'I don't understand how you could just give me up.'

I sigh. Stop replaying everything, Anna. Shoving my notebook back in my bag, I do a Google search for *Pie 'n' Mash, Deptford* and come across an article: *Café threatened with closure by council. "They must stop encouraging squatters and homeless people to our area," said one local resident...* I switch to Google maps, satellite view. It looks like the area around the café is mostly residential. Perhaps the squat's still there? A ping on my PC. I check the new email. It's from Gary: *9th September.*

5.00 pm – Editorial Meeting. All staff to attend. Great, that's all I need. I let my head drop forward onto my desk.

'Are you all right, Anna?'

Shit, I didn't hear him approaching. 'Sorry.' I give Gary a small smile. 'Bit of a headache.'

'Get yourself off home then, and don't come back until you're properly fit for work.'

* * *

'I've told yer all I know.' Fanny Shuttlebarrow's cheeks redden. 'Why do yer keep asking these questions? We done nothing wrong.'

Janus takes a deep breath. 'How do the babies arrive?'

'The Foundling Hospital brings 'em and, when they's big enough, they takes 'em back. They's well cared for. We gets regular visits to check we're treating 'em right. The little lad you asked after? He'd have gone back just afore he were five years old if he hadn't passed away. My George sorts all that out. He's round the back. You'd best speak to 'im.'

A noise coming from outside causes Anna to peer through the grimy window. 'There!' She points to where George is legging it across the fields. He must have been crouching against the wall to listen.

Janus flies through the door to make chase. George stumbles on uneven ground. Janus is on top of him. Hauling George to his feet, Janus marches him back to the cottage.

'Why did you run?' asks Janus, brushing the soil from his clothes.

'Don't rightly know. Guess I thought you was complaining about summat.'

'We got nowt to be shamed of. Always treats the kids right.' Fanny nudges her husband. 'Tell 'em, George. Them that survives goes back to the Foundling Hospital.' She folds her arms, waiting for George to confirm her words.

George shuffles from one foot to the other. 'In all likelihood.'

'What does that mean?' Anna frowns. 'Either they do or they don't.'

'Well, some might go t' other places,' George mumbles.

Fanny glares at him. 'Silly old fool.'

'What other places?' Janus's tone is fierce.

George scratches his head. 'Sometimes it all gets a bit confusing like, remembering where they've come from. There's other transportation, some goes back on that.'

'But the Foundling Hospital pay you.' Janus grabs George by the scruff of his neck. 'Just what game are you playing?'

Fanny shrieks. 'Keep quiet, you old bugger.'

The children tremble and huddle together.

'We should continue this outside.' Janus drags George towards the door.

'No,' Fanny shouts.

George stares at her, shaking his head.

'Wait.' Fanny steps around her grizzling small charges. 'Don't yer go hurtin' him.' Muttering to herself, she lifts an earthenware vase down from the shelf above the fire. 'Truth be told, I don't recall no Isaac, but there's this.' She tips the vase upside down and an assortment of trinkets lands on the table. 'There, just be takin' it.'

Anna rummages through the haul – two brooches, an assortment of coins, a silver cross and chain. She pulls out a tiny buckle bracelet. Spotting what she's found, Janus releases George.

Fanny throws herself to the floor, dissolving into theatrical sobs. 'Have pity, sir, George didn't mean no 'arm. The silly old devil's all I got.'

The children creep forward to form a whimpering, wailing circle around Fanny.

'The Foundling Hospital pays us for every child Fanny wet nurses.' George is quivering. 'They's supposed to go back when they's five.'

'But I am guessing not all children make it,' says Janus.

George shakes his head.

'What does that mean?' asks Anna.

'It means George has been doing rather well,' says Janus. 'It must be lucrative. Firstly, he is paid by the Foundling Hospital, then by some unscrupulous go-between.'

'Someone like the Grey Man?'

Janus nods. 'As much as fifty per cent of the workforce in factories, mills and mines are children, and they will all pay on point of supply. People like George earn twice.'

'So, John was taken as child labour?' Anna's eyes are wide.

'That is what we need to ascertain.'

Anna picks up the buckle bracelet. 'Well, we know he was here.' She crouches down beside Fanny. 'Fanny, where did John go?'

Fanny reaches out to finger the bracelet. 'He were a good bairn, no trouble…'

Janus pulls George to his feet. 'You know, Shuttlebarrow, that I shall be reporting your racket to the governors of the Foundling Hospital. It would go better for you if you were to tell us all you know about the whereabouts of the lad.'

George pales as Janus towers above him. 'Is it the Grey Man who collects the children?'

155

George's voice is quavering. 'I don't know where 'e takes 'em.'

'Where might I find him?'

'I'd tell yer, sir, if I could. It's not like I've anything else to lose. Our livelihood's gone now for sure.'

'What's to become of us?' sobs Fanny.

Back in the landau, Anna sighs. 'What will happen to them now?'

'I shall inform the Foundling Hospital. They will receive no more foundlings from there.'

'Where do you think the Grey Man took John?'

Janus shrugs. 'Most likely to a mill owner or chimney sweep. We need to locate the Grey Man, but this is not a job for today. Elizabeth wants you back in good time for the soirée and I have other business to attend.'

'Business more urgent than John?'

Janus shakes his head. 'No, but I do have other projects and Khan has reminded me that I have been neglecting my responsibilities.'

* * *

As I leave the office, I check the time on my Fitbit – twelve thirty. I call Zoe. 'Have you had lunch? I wondered if you wanted to grab a drink?'

'Monday lunchtime?' She laughs. 'Hell yes.'

We meet in *All Bar One*. I order two glasses of Sauvignon.

Zoe lifts her wine glass. 'So, you're officially back on the booze?'

'Yeah, sod it.' We chink glasses. 'Cheers.'

'Good to be back at work?' she asks.

I pull a face. 'I got sent home. Headache.'

Zoe points at the wine. 'Then is this wise?'

'I didn't actually have a headache.' I sigh. 'It's no good. You know I can't keep secrets from you. You can't tell Matt, but I've been in touch with Debbie.'

Zoe looks at me wide eyed. 'Spill.'

I sip my wine. 'I went to see her Saturday.'

'And Matt doesn't know?'

'No, and you're covering for me. I told him we were shopping.'

'That's fine.' Zoe glances at the half empty glasses, 'but we're going to need more wine.' She disappears off to the bar.

I wait for her to return and sit back down. 'Debbie was in a halfway house.'

'Well that's good, right?'

'Yeah, but something's happened. She's got mixed up with another woman there and this other woman, well, it sounds like she assaulted someone.'

Zoe exhales. 'Shit.'

'Debbie's done a runner. I spoke to Brenda this morning and she told me Debbie turns to some bloke when she's in trouble. Apparently he's bad news. I have to find her.'

'Do you know where she is?'

'Deptford, I think. And, seeing as I've now got the afternoon off…'

'You're going there?'

I nod.

Zoe checks her mobile. 'It's nearly two o'clock. I have to go back to the office but I can probably get away early. Give me a couple of hours.'

I reach across and touch her hand. 'It's okay Zoe. I have to do this on my own.'

'Please be careful. If this bloke is dodgy, you don't know what you might walk into.'

'If Debbie doesn't come back, she'll be thrown off the programme.'

'She's a grown woman, Anna. You can't make her do anything she doesn't want to do.'

'Yeah, that's pretty much what Brenda said.'

It's twenty minutes on the DLR to Deptford Bridge. I step out of the station and head for the High Street. There are several residential roads leading off and I walk each one in turn. Most of the houses are well maintained but here and there I come across one boarded up. The neighbours must have been pissed when squatters moved in.

After a couple of hours my feet are killing me. I've counted seven houses that could potentially be the squat, but despite the lunchtime wine, I'm not feeling brave enough to start knocking on doors. I retrace my steps to the small parade of shops near the station where I'd noticed a café. I go inside.

'Black coffee, please.'

I pay and take my drink to a small table in the window. *What was I thinking?* I gaze out as I sip my coffee and spot a homeless man sitting in the doorway of a betting shop opposite. He has a grubby sleeping bag beside him and he's swigging from a bottle. *Will Debbie end up like that?* It's mid-afternoon and the few people ambling along the pavement ignore him. A woman strolls along pushing a buggy; she's probably killing time before the school run. Stooping, she drops something into the man's lap. *That'll go towards his next drink, no doubt.*

The woman continues along to the SPAR off licence. She struggles to lift the buggy through the door. Another woman coming out of the shop stops to help her. *Wait.* I sit forward. *That's Debbie.*

My heart begins to thump. I grab my jacket and drop fifty pence on the table. I sense the guy behind the counter watching me as I lurk inside the door. *Just take your tip, mate, and mind your own business.*

Even from fifty metres away, Debbie looks rough. Greasy hair and clothes crumpled like she's slept in them. I watch her turn right down East Street and, when she's rounded the corner, I leave the café and cross the road to follow her. It's one of the roads I walked along earlier. Supposing we'd passed each other? What would I have said?

I keep my distance like I'm a private detective. When Debbie stops, I duck behind an Ocado van and wait while she rummages in her white plastic bag. She pulls out a packet of cigarettes, lights one up and moves on.

The driver of the van comes out of the house he's delivered to. He slides three empty crates into the back and secures the rear doors. Giving me a funny look, he walks around to the driver's seat. He's going to pull away. If Debbie looks back now, my cover's blown. But she's taking her time, enjoying her fag. She stops again, glancing up and down the road. Taking one last drag, she chucks the cigarette butt and disappears around the side of a large, detached property.

The van driver turns the ignition. It's now or never. I break cover and head along the road to the house. The front door and windows are boarded up and the timber is covered in graffiti. *Blah, Blah, Blah* is scrawled across one downstairs window board, while another is emblazoned with *FUCK YOU* in two-foot high lettering. Not exactly welcoming. My legs shake as I step onto the driveway. Weeds push up through the tarmac and the rubbish bins overflow with plastic bags and beer cans. I feel sick. I wonder who she's living with. It could be a bunch of alcoholic drug addicts. Supposing Debbie doesn't want to see me? She made it clear on Saturday that it was time for me to leave.

I check the time on my phone – ten past five. Matt will be home in an hour. It's late now to be visiting. Turning around, I head back to the station.

* * *

Elizabeth is a master party planner. Anna understands why Janus leaves the soirée arrangements to his sister.

Anna trails around in awe as Elizabeth oversees the cleaning, catering and dressing of the buffet table.

Elizabeth turns to Anna. 'How are you with flowers?'

Anna stares in trepidation at the beautiful blooms and foliage. Although her flower arranging skills are limited, she does her best, filling three huge vases. Elizabeth is gracious with her compliments.

'Let us have the silver cutlery, Ned,' Elizabeth says, 'and Anna, my dear, come and help me select the glassware. I was considering the Venetian, but perhaps the French balustre might be safer…'

Back in the drawing room, Elizabeth instructs the footmen to roll up the carpets and move the chairs to the sides of the room. 'We need maximum space for dancing.'

'Dancing?' Anna had hoped Quintar was joking. She's pretty sure she has no idea how to dance.

'Of course.' Elizabeth smiles. 'But do not fret. It is not compulsory. Although, my dear, I fear you might break a few hearts if you decline.' Elizabeth looks around the room. 'There. I think we can leave the staff to complete the finishing touches. Come with me to my rooms. We must ready ourselves.'

This takes 'glamming up' to a whole new level, thinks Anna, as Clemmie arrives armed with a basketful of concoctions.

Clemmie scrutinises Anna's face. 'Perhaps a freckle wash, miss? It improves the complexion.'

'No thanks.' Anna's rather fond of her freckles.

Despite Clemmie's pleas, Anna declines a corset but accepts a camisole as compromise. Clemmie helps Anna to roll on the silk stockings and shows her how to fix them in place with a garter. So many layers. Petticoat and underskirt before they even get to the gown. With the combined weight, Anna will not be able to walk, let alone dance.

Elizabeth, sitting in front of her table mirror applying rouge, glances across at Anna. 'You look beautiful. Didn't I say that colour would suit you?'

'Thank you. You look lovely too.' *Although the painted-on beauty spot might be going a tad too far.* Anna gazes at her own reflection in the mirror, barely recognising the glamorous woman staring back. She shivers.

'Are you cold?'

'No, I'm fine. This gown is perfect.'

'You know, my dear?' Elizabeth rises from her dressing table stool. 'I believe you should accompany me to *The Salon.*'

'*The Salon?*'

Yes. Just a few of my friends, fellow philosophers really. I shall be taking tea with them this week and I fancy you would make quite the impression.'

Elizabeth and Anna stand side by side at the top of the stairs. Elizabeth magnificent in her red gown, a jet-black wig piled high and dressed in sparkling firmaments. Although Anna declined a wig, Clemmie doused her hair with orange water before backcombing it and pinning it in a style appropriate for the occasion.

Elizabeth reaches out to touch the tendrils at the nape of Anna's neck. 'My dear, this continental style is quite charming.' Lifting a painted fan to her face, Elizabeth gives a coy smile. 'Come, it is time for us to make an entrance.'

Janus is chatting to William in the hallway when Anna and Elizabeth glide down the staircase. He looks up at the ladies. 'You both look exquisite. Come, not a moment too soon, people are already arriving.'

Elizabeth steps forward to greet the first of the guests while William opens the front door to more. Janus takes Anna's arm and guides her to a recess behind the staircase. 'How are you?'

'I'm fine.'

'Yes, I believe you are.' His eyes appraise her.

Anna shivers with excitement.

'Just smile, enjoy yourself and let Elizabeth do the talking. I will be watching over you and will come to your rescue should you need me.'

Anna's cheeks flush with pleasure as Janus leads her into the drawing room. She gasps. While she and Elizabeth have been beautifying themselves, the staff have transformed the room. The buffet table is resplendent – silver platters of thinly sliced cold meats, glass dishes of jellies and syllabubs, china bowls heaped with raspberries and strawberries. At the centre sits an enormous pyramid of sweetmeats – candied fruits, marzipan, crystallised ginger and Turkish delight. Overhead, the glass chandeliers twinkle brightly with flickering light from a hundred candles. The whole effect is magical.

Elizabeth's gown rustles as she approaches. She takes Anna's arm. 'You must forgive me, Janus, but I need to introduce "our cousin" to your guests. Come, my dear. She looks charming, does she not?' Elizabeth winks mischievously at her brother as she leads Anna away.

'Cousin, let me introduce you to Janus's colleagues. This is Nathaniel Pym and his dear wife Isabella.' Elizabeth smiles at the couple. 'How wonderful it is to see you both tonight.'

Pym takes their hands in turn, air kissing them with a slight dip of his head. 'Ladies.'

Ned appears at their side with a tray of drinks. They all take a glass, apart from Pym's wife who stands demurely at her husband's side. Isabella has the fine cheekbones of a beautiful woman, but she is painfully thin and her soft yellow gown does nothing to detract from the paleness of her skin.

'It was Mister Pym,' enthuses Elizabeth, 'who was instrumental in securing Hogarth's paintings for the Foundling Hospital. He also championed the first performance of Handel's *Messiah* in the chapel.'

Anna is open mouthed. 'How very impressive.'

Pym accepts her praise with nonchalance while Isabella gazes ahead, a blank expression on her face.

Elizabeth skillfully intervenes. 'My dear Isabella. How is your painting? Really Anna, you must see Isabella's work. She creates charming pictures, delicate designs with such fidelity to accuracy. Isabella captures the very essence of fragrant little flowers and her butterflies seem to fly from the canvas.

163

Have you completed any more masterpieces of late?'

Isabella shakes her head. She stays silent for a moment before answering in a low murmur. 'You would not like my recent work.'

Anna is waiting for Isabella to elaborate when her attention is drawn by the newest arrival.

Henri Quintar greets Elizabeth and Anna enthusiastically, dispensing with formal greetings to kiss them on both cheeks. 'Mistress Anna. *Enchanté.* I am so pleased you are to spend a few more days with us.'

Anna smiles wryly.

Quintar looks the ladies up and down. *'Mesdemoiselles, mais oui*, you are visions of loveliness.' He spots Isabella moving into the shadow of her husband. 'But dear lady, how wonderful to see you. I was beginning to think Pym had locked you away.' Quintar's voice is filled with bonhomie, but as he reaches for Isabella's hand, she shrinks back, looking up at her husband expectantly.

Pym pastes a smile upon his face, his brusque tone betraying his irritation. 'Quintar.'

Quintar is not to be discouraged. 'My dear Isabella, you look a little pale. Would you like to sit down? Pym, why don't you fetch your wife a drink?'

'Isabella is fine,' assures Pym.

'Really? I am sure a little spirit would be just the tonic. Bring the colour back to those pretty cheeks. Please, allow me to fetch you a glass of something.' Quintar snaps his fingers and Ned steps forward with a tray of drinks.

Isabella glances at Pym. He gives a barely perceptible nod and she reaches out to take the proffered glass. Lowering herself onto a chaise, she holds her drink at arm's length.

'I have always loved this room,' says Quintar. 'It is made for entertaining, *n'est-ce pas*? If I were Janus, I would hold a soirée every week.' He downs his drink before moistening his fingers to reshape his moustache. 'Now my dear Elizabeth, I am recently returned from visiting *ma mere* in Paris. I have brought you *un petit cadeau*. I know how you ladies adore such trinkets. I have left it with William to await your pleasure at *petit déjeuner.*'

'Monsieur Quintar, you spoil me.' Elizabeth winks at Anna from behind her fan.

The conspiratorial expression reminds Anna of someone. A name springs to mind: Zoe. But who is Zoe?

'*Mais oui*, I know how to please the ladies, this much is true. Pym? You spoil your lady too, I am sure.'

Isabella's face is composed. Pym's is unreadable.

Quintar waves another footman forward. This time he takes a brandy, downing it in one before clearing his throat. 'Pym, forgive me, but I must steal these delightful ladies away. We must circulate.' Quintar takes Elizabeth on one arm and Anna on the other, whisking them towards a livelier group.

The room fills fast. Small clusters of guests chat and laugh, while footmen move unobtrusively between them offering wine and spirits. Two women arrive and Elizabeth moves to greet them. She introduces Anna as her cousin and the women chat politely. It quickly becomes apparent these are the friends Elizabeth meets whenever she's in town.

Anna looks around. Her eyes alight on two people who've just entered the room. She has never seen a couple more similar in build. The gentleman's head bursts out from a tight neckline, his jowls hanging loose like a turkey. Wire-rimmed glasses disappear into fat cheeks and his velvet jacket fails miserably to meet across his vast chest. His wife's lavender gown is corseted so tightly that her ample bosom is in danger of an avalanche.

Elizabeth follows Anna's gaze. 'That is Thomas Pestlemore and his wife Sarah,' she whispers. 'Poor man, I fear he is most dreadfully hen pecked. Come, let me introduce you. Thomas, Sarah,' she says as they approach. 'Allow me to introduce our dear cousin, Anna Stratton.'

Pestlemore turns to look at Anna. He becomes flustered, his focus everywhere but at her. In contrast, Sarah screws up her piggy eyes to scrutinise Anna from head to toe. Her continuous gaze exerts authority and Anna finds herself giving an involuntary bob.

Triumphant, Sarah turns to her husband. 'Thomas, would you have me starve? Fetch me food before I waste away.'

Pestlemore scuttles off in the direction of the buffet.

'Cousin, you say?' enquires Sarah. 'Why have I not heard of you before?'

'I'm just visiting…' begins Anna.

'Anna is a distant cousin,' says Elizabeth. 'Much loved and always welcome in our home. Ah, I see the Harbinger sisters have arrived. Let me call them over directly. Jane, Ursula, come and join the ladies.'

As predicted, Jane and Ursula regard Anna with immediate suspicion, their conversation polite but strained. After a few awkward minutes, Ursula casts her eyes towards the door and exclaims, 'Oh, do look. Mister Tweedie has brought his little lad.'

Anna turns and notices a strange looking man lurking in the doorway. As the ladies make a beeline for him, Anna spots the object of their attention, a young black boy, hiding behind his master. Both man and boy are dressed in identical dapper outfits.

'Mister Tweedie,' says Ursula. 'Might we play with your little lad?'

Tweedie inclines his head.

'Come Anna, look,' says Jane, 'is he not pretty? See his curly hair.'

Anna watches helplessly as Ursula and Jane pat the little boy's dreadlocks, petting him as though he were a poodle.

'Look at his dear little waistcoat.' Ursula fingers his buttons.

'Oh, and his darling cravat,' coos Jane.

'Excuse me for a moment.' Anna makes her way across to the conservatory where she stands to survey the room. Tweedie, having abandoned the boy, is deep in conversation with Pym, while Isabella sits mute by his side. Perhaps she's not allowed to speak in public? Over by the fireplace, Quintar has gathered a circle of admirers and is noisily regaling them with stories of Paris.

Janus appears at Anna's side with two glasses of punch. 'Are you all right?'

She gestures to where Ursula and Jane have been joined by other ladies, all laughing and teasing Tweedie's boy. 'That's making me uncomfortable.'

Janus sighs. 'Such lads have become quite the fashion accessory. Many in high society see nothing wrong in keeping a child for their amusement and status.'

'And what happens to the child when he's no longer cute?'

'A good question. They must find another way in the world. Some are kept in the employ of the household, but many are cast out onto the streets when their owners tire of them.'

'Can you do nothing to stop this?' Anna glares at the ladies.

167

'Tweedie will intervene when he deems the lad has had enough.'

As Janus speaks, Tweedie seems suddenly to remember the boy. He clicks his fingers and the lad scuttles across to join him. Tweedie places his hand on the child's head, marking his ownership. The ladies move away, chattering and giggling together.

Quintar has also been abandoned, his listeners having grown tired of his tales. He calls over to Janus. ''Bout time you treated your sister to one of 'em, eh Janus? Nice little black fella to sit on her knee? Mad for 'em in Paris, of course.' His voice is slurred and yet, as a footman passes, he grabs another glass of brandy and throws it down his throat. 'Bring 'em in from Persia I believe.'

'Good old Henri,' mutters Janus. 'I can always count on him to entertain the guests.'

'Full of dogs and shit, Paris,' says Quintar. 'These little black fellas don't cause near as much damage. Daresay you might locate one for her in the Foundling Hospital? One or two of 'em might be just the ticket.'

Janus hands Anna his glass before stepping towards Quintar. Elizabeth, Anna notices, is approaching from the other direction. Once Janus and Elizabeth have Quintar in a pincer movement, Elizabeth announces loudly. 'Come, Monsieur Quintar. It is up to you and I to get this party enlivened. Let us have some music. Will you not accompany me?' She takes Quintar's arm while Janus supports the other side. Together they manhandle him to a couch behind the piano where he slumps in a drunken stupor as the music and dancing begin.

After establishing Quintar will cause no further problem, Janus moves back to join Anna by the conservatory doors.

Anna hands Janus his drink. 'That looked like a well-practised manoeuvre.'

Janus chinks his glass against hers.

'Have you known Monsieur Quintar for long?' asks Anna.

'About three years. We met at a talk at the Royal Society. I asked the speaker a question and afterwards Quintar came over to introduce himself. We share interests in common and we have worked on mutual projects over the years. Quintar has many contacts and we are currently raising money for the new wing at the Foundling Hospital. It is just when he is a little cut that he believes himself to be everybody's friend and becomes something of a liability.'

'And Mister Tweedie?'

'The man is a brilliant astronomer. None to compare. What he does not know about the stars and their orbits.'

'He's not married?'

'No. His home is run by a very efficient housekeeper. He has the lad of course, for company.'

Anna shudders. 'I find him a bit creepy. I can't quite put my finger on it, but he makes the hairs on the back of my neck stand up.'

'I agree he is a funny sort, but nothing for you to be worried about. We would struggle in the Prism group without his expertise.'

Anna sips her punch. 'And what of Mister Pestlemore?'

'Pestlemore and Tweedie are the best of friends. Almost joined at the hip. I sometimes wonder why Sarah does not put her foot down.'

'Mrs Pestlemore looks as if she's holding court.' Anna nods to where Sarah Pestlemore is amusing a small group of female guests, whilst her husband stands attentively at her side.

169

Janus follows Anna's gaze. 'Yes, Sarah certainly draws a crowd.'

There's a burst of laughter from Sarah's circle as she admonishes Pestlemore publicly, probably not for the first time.

Janus grimaces. 'Her stories are rather trivial, hence the largely female audience.'

Anna prods him. 'Not all ladies feed on trivia.'

Janus grins.

'Poor Mister Pestlemore.' Anna shakes her head. 'He seems very much at his wife's beck and call.'

'Yes, it is clear who rules the roost.' Janus drains his glass. 'But Pestlemore, too, is a valued member of the Prism group.'

'What exactly does he do?'

Janus lifts two more glasses of punch from a passing footman's tray. He hands one to Anna. 'Pestlemore is an apothecary by trade, but his real passion is alchemy. He spends hours in his workshop trying to perfect the process.'

'Alchemy? Isn't that making gold?'

'Yes, though much good it would do him. If the poor fellow did manage to make gold, Sarah would fritter it away in no time.'

'Perhaps it's an excuse for him to spend time alone in his lab?'

'Oh, I believe Sarah fully supports his ambition. What wife would not?'

'Not all women think everything in life is about money. There is such a thing as enjoying spending time with one another.'

'You think Pestlemore has an enjoyable life? He was bullied for years at school and then ended up taking a wife to keep up the tradition. The strange thing is, I do believe he adores Sarah and would not have her any other way. But let us not argue.' Janus gestures to where the footmen are moving chairs to create more space. 'Would you like to dance?'

'No, thank you,' Anna smiles. 'I prefer to people watch.'

'Well, at least we have that in common.' Janus chinks his glass against hers once more. 'I must say, Mistress Stratton, you do remain something of a conundrum.'

I'm something of a conundrum to myself, thinks Anna.

'I suppose I should circulate or Elizabeth will never forgive me.' Janus bows, leaving Anna to observe the guests from a distance.

When she spots Cornelius Wilkes approaching with Pym, Anna moves along to the other end of the conservatory. She feels no inclination to engage with them. Neither were helpful at the Foundling Hospital. She's standing closer now to Tweedie and a couple of times catches him glance in her direction, but when she returns his stare he looks away. Anna notes that Tweedie declines alcohol, taking tea instead. His hands, unusually thin and delicate for a man, hold the cup daintily with a crooked little finger and he nibbles his food like a mouse, touching a silk kerchief delicately to his lips to catch the crumbs.

The guests become louder as their level of intoxication increases. Anna's attention is drawn by an incident involving Nathaniel Pym and his wife. Isabella's drink has spilled and Pym's castigating a servant. 'You blithering fool,' Pym is shouting, 'look what you have done.'

Janus strides across to intervene. 'Come, Pym. No harm done, old fellow.' He guides him into the conservatory.

Left alone, Isabella stares at the stain spreading across her gown while the footman, on his knees, mops at the wine soaking into the rug.

'What a bully that man is,' Elizabeth whispers to Anna as she passes by. 'Why Isabella puts up with him I really do not know.'

Anna glances at the clock. It is past midnight. How long do these things go on for? She yawns and rotates her ankles. She's been standing for hours and the evening slippers she borrowed from Elizabeth are killing her. Slipping through the open French doors, she crosses the terrace and steps out onto the lawn. She pulls off the shoes and wriggles her toes in the wet grass to soothe her throbbing feet. Anna stares up at the stars in the dark sky. Where is she? Where did she come from? As she gazes at the heavens, she has the strangest sensation of looking down a telescope. She blinks. It's almost as if her own self might be looking back from the other end. She shivers.

Two men deep in conversation walk up from the far end of the garden. Wisps of cigar smoke waft towards Anna. Instinctively, she ducks behind a camelia bush.

'The matter is resolved?'

'My sources confirm palms have been greased.'

'Undoubtedly Gregory is unaware. Do we know the extent?'

'Not yet.'

'Would that there were another way. Gregory is a man of the highest moral integrity.'

'But I fear he does not always recognise his best interests.'

'You will send word as soon as it is done?'

'With every possible haste.'

'I hope I can count on your absolute discretion.'

The men head back inside.

Anna creeps towards the terrace. There's no-one in the conservatory, the men must have re-joined the other guests. Anna slides her feet back into the slippers, steps inside and moves back into the drawing room.

'Are you all right, Mistress Stratton?' Ned asks.

'Yes, thank you, Ned.' Anna helps herself to another glass of punch from the tray.

What were the men discussing? And should she tell Janus?

10th September

Anna wanders into the breakfast room. 'Good morning,' she says to Janus and Khan.

Janus rises from his seat. 'Good morning, Mistress Stratton.'

'Please, don't get up.' Anna pours herself hot chocolate from the jug on the side table. 'I slept heavily. Am I dreadfully late?'

'On the contrary. We did not expect to see you for some time.' Janus sips his coffee. 'Elizabeth rarely appears before noon after a soirée.'

Anna takes a slice of fruited bread and carries her plate over to join them.

Khan drums his knuckles against the table.

'Sorry,' Anna asks, 'am I interrupting?'

'Not at all.' Janus passes her the butter dish. 'In fact, I was explaining to Khan how I gained new information last night from a conversation with Wilkes. There is a man, goes by the name of Denton, who has a wool business south of Colchester. I gleaned that Denton has set up his own apprentice house. Twice a year he comes down to London to visit the Foundling Hospital and takes young boys back to be trained as weavers.'

'You think this Denton has John?'

'Well, we know he has not acquired him from the Foundling Hospital, but Denton may have more than one source. Perhaps he has dealings with the Grey Man?'

Anna places her knife on her plate. 'Can we find out?'

'It is a long shot but,' – Janus glances at Khan – 'Khan and I had just agreed to ride to Colchester today. And no, before you ask, you may not accompany us. A carriage and horses would take days but, with fresh horses at *Gallows Corner* and *The Ship* in Chelmsford, Khan and I could be back by tomorrow afternoon. In return you can do me a favour. Stay here with Elizabeth. She hates it when I go out of town. With you to amuse her she will be a kitten.' Janus pushes back his chair and stands up. 'Khan, we must away.'

Anna half rises from her seat. 'Janus, before you go, I need to talk to you.'

He sits back down. 'You can speak in front of Khan. What is it?'

Khan is listening.

Anna hesitates. 'It can wait.' She follows them out to the hallway where they don travelling cloaks. When Khan goes ahead to ready the horses, Anna grabs her opportunity. 'Janus, last night I overheard a conversation. A plan to resolve something on your behalf.'

Janus chuckles. 'Well, that is good of whoever it was.'

'Greasing people's palms was mentioned.'

'That does not surprise me. It is the way of politics and business.' He pats Anna's arm. 'Man talk.'

Man talk? 'It sounded as if they were doing something behind your back.' Anna lowers her voice. 'One of the men was Khan.'

Janus laughs out loud. 'We have no secrets. If it was Khan, I am not the least bit worried. He always looks out for me. Come now, we must be off. You have your own duties to attend.' Janus slams the front door behind him.

Anna returns to the breakfast room to finish her meal. It makes sense for the men to ride to Colchester alone, but it's unfair she must stay behind and entertain Elizabeth. Anna sighs. It must be like this all the time, women having no say.

'Ahem.' William clears his throat.

'Yes, William?'

'Mrs Carmichael sends her apologies. She is rather tired after last night's soirée and suggests you might rearrange your shopping expedition? After resting she hopes to be well enough to join you for a light supper.'

Anna stands up, brushing crumbs from her skirt. 'In that case I am going out for a while. If Mrs Carmichael should ask, I'll be back this afternoon.'

* * *

Pym is working through the mountain of paperwork on his desk when his butler knocks on the study door. 'You have a visitor, sir.'

Pym sighs. 'I suppose, Robert, you had better show him in.'

The visitor strides into the study. 'Might I have a few words?'

'I am rather busy. Will it not keep for the morrow?'

'I am afraid it will not.'

'Then you had better make it quick.'

The visitor sits down. 'How is Isabella?'

Pym stares at him from across his desk. 'My wife is well.'

'And the boy?'

'He is fine too, but I am sure you do not come to Salisbury Square to ask after the welfare of my family.'

176

'Indeed. The fortuitous arrival of your son was unexpected, was it not?'

'How so?'

'Come, sir. I know that you and your lovely wife have suffered many disappointments. It was imminently sensible to keep her recent confinement quiet until the happy event.' The visitor makes himself comfortable in the chair. 'Pym, we both have secrets. It would be a pity, would it not, if certain facts were to become public?'

Pym glares at him. 'Do you threaten me, sir?'

'I believe it to be in both our interests if a few things were resolved. Take the girl Gregory spends so much time with. Together they obsess over a child missing from the Foundling Hospital. 'Twould be no bad thing if Gregory's interest was to wane. We do not want him uncovering things that do not concern him.' The visitor sits forward. 'I have set certain wheels in motion, but I fear, without your experience and oversight, my plan will not be carried through to a successful conclusion.'

'And if I help you, that will be the end of it? You will leave me and my family alone?'

* * *

'Can you get away for a while?' Anna holds up the wicker basket. 'I've brought a picnic.'

'Give me a minute.' Mercy tugs off her apron. 'I'm just popping out for a while, Mrs Marsh.' Mercy pulls a woollen shawl over her shoulders and follows Anna up the basement steps. 'Didn't hear from yer yesterday, Miss Anna. Is there any news?'

'I'm sorry, Mercy,' Anna says as they make their way through Halburn yards. 'I wanted to get a message to you, but Janus was hosting a soirée last night and I was expected to attend.'

They arrive in St James's Square. 'Let's sit over there.' Anna points to a nearby bench. She pulls a folded kerchief from the basket and unwraps the buckle bracelet.

'But this be John's!' Mercy grabs the bracelet, hugging it to her heart. 'Where did yer get it?'

'We went back to the Shuttlebarrows.'

Mercy's eyes are wide. 'Do this mean me boy is dead?'

Anna takes Mercy's hand. 'John was with Fanny and George for perhaps four years. They may not be the most upright of foster parents, but I believe Fanny has a kind heart. She certainly seems to care for the children she looks after.'

'So did John go back to the Foundling Hospital?'

'We don't think so. We're trying to find out where he was taken. But don't you see Mercy? We're getting close. Now,' – Anna unpacks the food – 'I've apples and cheese...'

Mercy shakes her head. 'I'm not hungry.'

'You've got to keep your strength up. You'll need it for when we bring John home. Maybe I can tempt you with some of Mrs Lawson's excellent lemon cake?'

'I has a bad feeling. If me boy's lost his love token, how do he know I love him?'

'He knows.' Anna holds out a slice of cake. 'Janus is doing all he can. He and Mister Khan have ridden to Essex on John's trail. I can't stay long as I'm supposed to be keeping Janus's sister company while they're away.'

Mercy takes the cake; it lays uneaten on her lap. 'There's not many days left before I has to leave for Yorkshire. If your Mister Gregory don't find me boy by then...'

* * *

'Bye babe.' Matt kisses me on the forehead.

I rub my eyes. 'Oh, you're off?'

He looks back from the door. 'Yeah, I've got to go. Now you stay put, remember. It's too soon for you to go back to work.'

Matt slams the front door.

I jump out of bed and head for the bathroom. I stare at myself in the mirror. 'You're such a fucking chicken.' I slope back into the bedroom and check my phone. There's a text from Zoe. *Please tell me you got home safe.*

I tap into my mobile. *I got home safe. I'll call you later.*

Throwing on some clothes, I go into the kitchen and make myself a smoothie. I stare out of the window as I sip my drink. *I have to do this.* Discarding the glass in the sink, I pull on my jacket and head for the train.

I take the Northern line to Bank, arriving at Deptford Bridge too early. Debbie won't be up yet. I go back to the same café and nurse another coffee. The guy behind the counter glances over a couple of times and I stare back. *Yes mate, it's that weird girl from yesterday.* He's not getting a tip today. I keep checking the time on my mobile.

I leave at ten, retracing my steps to the squat. At the edge of the drive I pause, take a deep breath and walk bravely past overflowing bins. Nitrous oxide cartridges are strewn on the ground and, *oh God,* a discarded syringe. It doesn't mean anything. *I can do this.* Damn it, my way is blocked but I can't give up now. I squeeze between an old mattress and broken fencing panels. When I reach the side door, I lean my ear against it to listen. The pulse of heavy metal music pounds...

Suddenly the door's yanked open. I fall inside and hit the

floor. 'Ow.'

A giant man, like a bouncer, glares down at me. His face and arms are covered in tattoos and he's wearing a biker bandana on his head. I curl into a ball.

'Who is it?' asks Debbie.

The man hauls me up from the floor like I'm a rag doll, digging his fingers into the flesh of my upper arms. *I'll have bruises tomorrow.*

Debbie's facing me. 'Anna?'

The bouncer guy is holding me by the shoulders. He smells like he hasn't washed in an age. 'You know her? Jeez Debs, I told you, no visitors.'

'She's all right. Fuck's sake Bri, let her go.'

He releases me with a shove, and I reach out for Debbie's arms to stop myself falling. Her welcome is far from warm. 'What the hell are you doing here?'

Debbie boils water on a primus stove as I sit in a tatty garden chair. My eyes adjust to the dark room. It must have once been a grand reception area with its large stone fireplace. Bay windows and double French doors look out over a long-abandoned garden and the musky smell of damp accompanies a wainscot of mold creeping up the walls. Underfoot are patches where the parquet flooring has been stripped bare.

'Turn that fucking music down, Bri.' Debbie passes me a drink of tea.

I cradle the warm mug in my hands.

Debbie lowers herself down on the filthy mattress, sitting cross-legged. 'Bri's all right. He misses playing his guitar. We've no electric, the radio runs on batteries.'

Bouncer Brian turns the radio off. He pours water into

a bong and perches on the window seat grinding cannabis between his fingers.

'Chuck us some weed, Bri,' says Debbie.

Brian throws a tobacco tin and she catches it. Prising open the lid, she rolls a joint.

'What are you doing here?' I whisper.

Debbie lights the spliff, takes a deep drag, then exhales. 'I think that was my question?'

'Looking for you. Brenda said you'd left the halfway house.'

'Didn't have much choice once that silly cow Tracy decided to lay into that bloke.' Debbie offers me the joint.

I shake my head.

She shrugs. 'Mind you, he was being a prick.'

Brian packs the bong bowl with cannabis. Suddenly he yells 'Boo,' and when I flinch, he laughs. Putting his lips to the mouthpiece, he uses a lighter to burn the weed. The place reeks of marijuana, but at least it goes some way to mask the smell of body odour. Brian sits back and inhales deeply.

'So, you're okay?' I ask.

'Right as rain. Aren't we?' Debbie glances at Brian who has his eyes closed.

'Brenda says you're not in trouble. She says she'll help get your bedsit back and find you a job.' I'm not sure this is entirely accurate, but I'm desperate to get her out of this place.

Debbie shakes her head. 'I'm not coming back. Too many rules. Can't live like that no more. Anyway, me and Bri are planning a trip. Once we've got the dosh together.'

I glance around the hovel they're living in: the floor a polluted sea of pizza boxes and empty beer and wine bottles. 'What about me?'

Debbie takes another drag. 'What about you?'

'I thought we could get to know each other.'

Brian snorts as he relights the bong.

Debbie's gaze wanders the room before returning to me. 'Why? If you passed me in the street and didn't know who I was, would you even give a second glance? Look, you found me, we met. It's not like we've things in common, is it?'

* * *

Anna steps into the hallway and unfastens her cloak.

'Mistress Stratton, you have returned.' William closes the front door. 'Monsieur Quintar is here. I told him Mister Gregory was out of town, but he asked if he might speak with one of the ladies of the house.'

Anna frowns. 'I'm not one of the ladies of the house.'

William clears his throat. 'I explained that Mrs Carmichael was indisposed and that you would not be back for some while, but Monsieur Quintar insisted on waiting. Perhaps you would rather I send him away?'

'No, William.' Anna hands him her cloak. 'Give me a minute, then show him into the parlour.'

Two minutes later Quintar breezes in. 'Ah, Mademoiselle Anna. *Merci, merci. Je suis désolé.* My behaviour last night...'

'It's quite all right, Monsieur Quintar. All is forgotten.'

'Now I know that you are indeed an angel.'

'Please join me by the fire. Would you like coffee?' Anna catches William's eye.

'I will send Ned in directly.' William closes the door as he leaves.

'Actually,' says Anna. 'I'm pleased to have some company. Janus left for Colchester this morning. I was to entertain Mrs

Carmichael but she's out of sorts so I'm rather at a loose end.'

'*Enchanté, mademoiselle.*' Quintar makes himself comfortable in an armchair. 'But Madame Carmichael you say, is out of sorts?'

'I'm sure she will soon recover.'

'Please give Madame Carmichael my best wishes. I hope that she took some small pleasure from *mon petit bouquet?*'

'Oh, your gift? I'm not sure she's seen it. I'll make sure she receives it on waking.'

'*Très bien.*'

'Please, Monsieur Quintar. Tell me more about yourself.'

'*Mais oui.* What would you like to know?'

'Well, you're a member of the Prism group…'

'*Oui* and I have the upmost respect for my fellow members.'

'What is your particular area of specialism?'

'Mathematics. *J'ai adore.* You see, mathematics is not an abstract thing, it permeates everything. In this life we are surrounded by it, *n'est-ce pas?* Every leaf, every creature, every measurement of our bodies. There is beauty and completeness in each formula and proof. At the Academie in Paris I studied the works of Descartes and Pascal.' Quintar puffs out his chest. 'Like many scientists and mathematicians, my faith was challenged by emerging new ideas. If you could only understand the delight it gives me to see mathematics in motion. It is when we come to realise and accept, that we truly grasp the power and energy at its source. But enough of this, mademoiselle, for I fear I bore you.'

'Not at all. Your passion for your subject is commendable. Monsieur Quintar, you've known Janus for some time. I'd like to know more about him.'

'Janus is my great friend; we share many interests.' Quintar

183

strokes his moustache. 'Forgive me, mademoiselle, but I suspect that you have an ulterior motive.' His eyes twinkle. 'What you really wish to ask me about concerns matters of love, *n'est-ce pas?*'

Anna blushes. 'Well perhaps, but first I'm curious. What is the nature of the relationship between Janus and Mister Khan?'

Quintar settles back in the chair. *'Mais oui.* If it gives me an excuse to while away a pleasant hour in your company, I am *un petit chiot.* However, I fear you will cast me aside once you realise that I cannot tell you everything your heart desires to know.'

Anna smiles. 'You might reveal a little?'

'*Oui, ma chérie*, for I see your appetite will not be quenched by my charms alone. I fear, if I should delay longer, you will have me turned out of this house a broken-hearted man.'

Ned arrives with a tray of coffee.

'Thank you, Ned. I will pour,' says Anna.

'Very good, Mistress Stratton.' Ned leaves them alone.

'So, to business.' Quintar sits forward. 'I will share what I can. A few years ago, Janus was employed by the East India Company. This necessitated much travel and he spent several years in the east. Indeed, that is where he made his fortune, although he has done well since returning to England by way of fortuitous investments and tremendously successful projects… but I digress.'

Anna hands him a cup of coffee.

'*Merci.* Whilst on his travels, Janus met a princess.'

'Ramia?'

'I see, mademoiselle, you are already familiar with this story.'

'Elizabeth told me a little.' Anna sips her coffee nonchalantly.

'He fell in love with her and they were going to run away together but the Sultan found out.'

'So you know, *ma chérie*, that Janus was imprisoned to await his fate.' Quintar sips his coffee. 'It was during this time that he shared a cell with a young blackamoor.'

'Mister Khan?' asks Anna.

'That is when God intervened.' Quintar places his coffee cup on the side table. 'A huge earthquake' – he claps his hands – 'a mere day before the execution. The prison was destroyed and the guards ran away. Janus and Khan escaped and, after a terrible journey, finally returned to England. Khan could not return to his homeland so Janus took him in. He has supported him ever since.'

'What crime did Khan commit?'

'No-one knows this for sure.' Quintar shrugs. 'Some small matter deemed unlawful – *haram* I believe the Moslems say?' He smooths his moustache with his fingers. 'I must warn you, *ma chérie*, there is something strange about Khan. These Arabs are not to be trusted. Ever since meeting Janus I have taken it upon myself to look out for him. I fear Khan may turn out to be – how do you say – a snake in the grass?'

'Mister Khan doesn't think much of me, that's for sure,' says Anna.

'*Exactement*, and what man could not fail to be charmed? As I say, there is something about him…' Quintar sighs. 'But there you are, *ma chérie.* Khan is never far from Janus. The two suffered heaven knows what atrocities together and remain committed to each other. It is rather like a marriage, *n'est-ce pas?*'

'What became of Janus's princess?'

'I assume the Sultan married her and she lives with his many wives, raising his many children.'

'Do you think Janus still has feelings for her?'

'*Je ne sais pas*, he does not speak of it. Janus is a very disciplined man. Perhaps he feels he did not act rationally? Or he does not like to be reminded of that period in his life? A man in love takes mad risks. He will do anything to protect his lady.'

'And there has been no-one since?'

'*Non*. There have been plenty of ladies who have tried, but to my knowledge no-one has touched his heart. Why are you so interested, *ma chérie*? *Mon Dieu*, you have eyes for him yourself. What of my heart, which I offer up upon a platter? How cruelly you taunt me.' Quintar clutches a hand to his chest and slumps forwards. '*Je suis desole*.'

* * *

Anna knocks on Elizabeth's bedroom door.

'Enter,' says a weary voice.

Anna approaches the bed. 'I wondered if you'd like me to send something up? Ned said you didn't eat any lunch?'

Elizabeth's eyes are closed, her cheeks flushed. 'Bless you, my dear.' She raises a hand before dropping it limply back down on the counterpane. 'I could not manage a thing.'

Anna holds out the small posy. 'Monsieur Quintar sends his best wishes. He was most anxious you should receive his gift.'

Elizabeth opens her eyes and gazes at the flowers. 'A Parisian nosegay. Monsieur Quintar is such a charming man.' She closes her eyes again, lifting a hand to her brow. 'I am sorry. What must you think of me?'

'It's fine,' says Anna. 'We've all been there.'

'Really?' Elizabeth frowns. 'I fear I ate something which did not agree with me. Perhaps the fish?'

'More than likely.' Anna hides her smile. She places a hand on Elizabeth's forehead. 'You do feel hot. Shall I open the window?'

'Oh no, sweat it out, that is what my Ernest would say.'

'Perhaps Ned should send for a doctor?'

'No, my dear. I will be right as rain the morrow. Perhaps you might keep me company for a while?'

Anna pours water into a glass from the jug on the bedside table. 'Here, drink this.'

Elizabeth waves it away.

'You should drink,' says Anna.

Elizabeth shakes her head.

Anna pulls up a chair and sits down. She picks up the book laying on the bed. 'Would you like me to read to you for a while?'

Elizabeth nods.

Anna opens the novel, *Pamela – Virtue Rewarded,* and begins to read. She's barely finished a paragraph when Elizabeth waves her hand. 'You know, my dear, I fear I am not up to this after all. I think perhaps I will rest.'

Anna places the book on the bedside table. 'I'll come and see you again later,' she whispers.

* * *

'Excuse me, Mistress Stratton.' William stands in the parlour doorway holding a silver platter. 'You have another visitor.' He walks across to her armchair.

Anna puts down the book she's reading and takes the calling card from the tray. *Nathaniel Pym,* she reads. 'Did you tell him Mister Gregory is away?'

'I have relayed that information to Mister Pym, but he asks if he might take a few moments of your time?'

Anna hesitates. Although Pym's a respected member of the Prism group, he's so dull and sombre. But perhaps he has something important to say? 'Okay, William. Please show Mister Pym in.'

'Would you like tea?'

'Yes,' says Anna. 'Thank you.'

Anna checks her reflection in the mirror above the fireplace and smooths down her hair. In the absence of make-up, she pinches her cheeks.

'Mistress Stratton?'

She turns from the mirror as Pym enters the room. *Damn, did he witness her vanity?* 'Mister Pym. What a pleasure. Won't you join me for tea?'

'Mistress Stratton, I am sorry to disturb you. I came here to see Gregory, but William informs me he is gone to Colchester?'

'Yes. He has unexpected business.'

'It is somewhat inconvenient that he did not let me know. No matter. I wonder if I might take this opportunity to impose upon your time?'

Anna inclines her head. 'Please sit down.'

Pym crosses to the fireplace but remains standing. Realising he's waiting for her to sit, Anna settles on the couch. Pym seats himself in Janus's armchair.

Ned arrives with a tea tray.

'Thank you, Ned,' says Anna, 'I can manage.'

'As you wish, miss.' Ned closes the parlour door.

Anna lifts the heavy silver tea pot. Pym's stare is unnerving. The pot wobbles as she pours. 'Do you…'

'I wonder…'

'Sorry,' says Anna.

'No, after you.'

'I was going to ask if you take sugar? I don't seem to have any on the tray.'

'No, thank you.' Pym takes the proffered cup. 'Gregory has left you on your own?'

'Yes. As I said, he has business to attend.'

'I was unaware of any venture in Colchester?'

'Perhaps I've got it wrong.' Anna lifts her cup, trying to appear nonchalant. 'How is your wife?'

Pym splutters. 'My wife is well. Mistress Stratton, might I get to the point?'

'Please do.'

'As you know I have been tasked by Gregory to make inquiries about a missing child. I regret I have nothing new to report.'

'Oh,' says Anna. 'I'm sorry to hear that.'

'Yes.' Pym sits back in the chair. 'A complete dead-end I am afraid.'

'That's disappointing.'

'Quite so.' He clears his throat: 'Mistress Stratton. Might I ask if the business taking Gregory out of town today is connected to the matter I have been asked to investigate?'

'I'm afraid I really couldn't say,' replies Anna.

'I am concerned that Gregory may get into a situation where he finds himself out of his depth.'

'I'm sorry, I'm not sure I understand?'

'Well, let us just say the people involved are rarely the sort of people that Gregory would want to be dealing with.'

'And how would you know that?' she asks.

'I am simply making the point that if these people, whoever they may be, are mixed up in some illegal scheme, they will not want to risk discovery. I fear Gregory may be digging up a hornet's nest and I wondered if you might intervene? Ask him to let the matter drop?'

Anna notes how Pym grips his teacup. Her heart races. 'I hardly think I have the power to tell Janus to drop something once he's got his teeth into it. He'll not rest until he uncovers the truth.'

Pym sighs. 'I am sorry to hear you say that. I was hoping you might have a little more influence.'

'No. I'm afraid Janus is definitely his own boss.'

'Well, Mistress Stratton, I have taken up enough of your time.'

Anna stands to see Pym out.

'I wonder if I might prevail upon you to keep my visit to yourself?'

'I don't think I'd feel comfortable doing that.'

'As you wish.' Pym hurries from the room. Moments later the front door slams.

What was that all about? Anna replenishes her cup and takes her tea across to Janus's study where she spends the next hour perusing his books.

Late-afternoon, Ned knocks at the door. 'Will you be needing anything, Mistress Stratton?'

Anna smiles. 'No, thank you. How is Mrs Carmichael?'

'Mrs Carmichael says she's not feeling brave enough to venture downstairs this evening. Mrs Lawson wondered if you might prefer your supper served in the parlour?'

'That's a good idea. I don't want to eat in the dining room alone.'

'Then I'll build up the fire for you, miss.'

* * *

A post chaise, skirting the north of the city, traverses eastward. After a clandestine journey of some two miles or more, it pulls up in front of a large house.

The gentleman lifts the hood of his lady's cloak, covering her hair and face. 'Keep it like this, my dear.'

The lady allows him to lead her along a passageway to the side of the building. She waits patiently as he rings a bell.

The door is opened by a matronly woman who escorts them wordlessly along a corridor and down four steps into an anti-chamber.

The gentleman guides his lady to the seat. 'Wait here, my dear. I will be but a few moments.' He exchanges a glance with the matronly woman who assumes a wide footed stance at the bottom of the steps.

The lady adjusts her hood and takes off her gloves. Her gentleman told her someone was in need of their help but he'd not been drawn further. Whatever can be keeping him? She tuts. This waiting area is scarcely a room, it does not even have a window…

The gentleman returns with another man. 'My dear, this is Doctor Hasler. He is here to help you.'

The lady stares up at her gentleman. 'To help me?'

The doctor speaks, 'Mrs Browning? It is a pleasure to have you stay with us.'

The lady stands, shaking her head. 'Oh, but I am not Mrs Browning...'

The doctor takes one of her arms while the matronly woman grasps the other. The lady is flanked either side.

'No.' She looks back, waiting for her gentleman to explain their mistake.

Her gentleman gazes at her and shakes his head.

Together the doctor and the woman bundle her up the steps, manhandling her along the corridor in the opposite direction to the door through which they entered. Although they hold her arms, the lady struggles and kicks. A door opens and two men join them. One places a cloth over her mouth and nose. The lady tries not to breathe but the man holds it firm whilst the other lifts her legs.

They half carry, half drag her up a staircase and along another corridor. Despite her dazed state, the lady tries to stay alert. 'Where you taking me?' she cries. Her voice is not her own and her words befuddled, as if she's drunk too much gin. They pause to adjust their hold. She notices doors line both sides. From within comes banging and the distant caterwauling of women.

They come to a halt. A key is turned in a lock. The lady is shoved forward, thrown to the floor. With practiced movements, her captors step swiftly from the room. The door slams and the key turns once more.

Sitting up, the lady peels her palms from the sticky floor. She raises one hand, and her nostrils flare as she recognizes the stench of urine. Clambering up from the filth, she wipes her hands on her skirt. As her eyes grow accustomed to the gloom, she realises the room is more of a cell, its walls the same dirty yellow as the corridors they passed through. There's a cot with a straw mattress and a wooden bucket in the corner. Meagre light comes from a narrow opening near the ceiling which, despite being too high to reach, is barred.

Her heart beats fast. Her head spins.

From somewhere close comes a blood curdling scream, like an animal caught in a trap.

The lady rattles the latch. 'What is this place?'

Her cry echoes along the corridor and manic laughter bounces back.

She thumps and kicks at the door. 'Let me out.' Soon her voice becomes a whispered prayer. 'Dear God, let me out.'

* * *

Doctor Hasler returns to the gentleman waiting in the anti-chamber. 'She seems very confused.'

'Yes, I am afraid she is. As I explained, this is not the first time I've had to have my wife incarcerated. Although this time she is much worse. You will need to keep her isolated. I fear she is a danger to herself as well as others.'

The doctor scratches his beard. 'She is clearly distressed.'

'You have not met my wife before, Doctor Hasler?'

'No. Doctor Jamieson dealt with her when she was previously admitted. Sadly, I never had the pleasure of meeting the good doctor either, his new post in Edinburgh scarcely being local. However, I have read his notes. Doctor Jamieson's detailed analysis has been most enlightening.'

'There has been much deterioration since Bella last received treatment.' The gentleman puts a hand to his brow. 'It is only recently she started to make these strange claims.' He breaks into a sob. 'She no longer knows she is my wife.'

193

'Please do not distress yourself, Mister Browning. You have my word we shall do all we can.'

'And I can count on your absolute discretion?'

'That goes without saying.'

'I am, of course, extremely grateful and will ensure you are well recompensed for your trouble. Please, do not be surprised by what she says. It may sound completely strange.'

'Mister Browning, there is nothing your wife can say that will shock me. I have heard it all before.' Doctor Hasler walks him to the door.

The gentleman turns. 'I will come to visit.'

'As you wish.' The doctor places a hand on his arm. 'Meanwhile we will take good care of her.'

'Thank you, Doctor Hasler. It means the world to know my Bella is safe and secure.'

* * *

Anna hears voices in the hallway. She lifts the supper tray from her lap and stands up as the parlour door opens. 'Janus, you're back already…'

'My apologies, Mistress Stratton,' says William. 'It is not Mister Gregory. I am afraid you have yet another visitor.'

'Really?' Anna sits back down. 'It's like Piccadilly Circus today.'

'Sorry, Mistress Stratton?'

'Never mind. Who is it?'

'Mister Tweedie.'

Not her favourite person. Yet Janus had been adamant that Tweedie was indispensable to the Prism group. Anna sighs. 'You'd better show him in.'

'Shall I take your tray, Mistress Stratton?'

'Yes please.'

Anna smooths down her skirt before turning to smile at her visitor. 'Hello, Mister Tweedie. You do know that Mister Gregory is out of town?'

'Yes indeed, dear lady,' Tweedie says, 'but I am afraid this is something of an emergency. We felt you might want to know straight away. I understand Mister Pym called on you this afternoon? I am here to inform you that his investigations have suddenly become fruitful. He has this past hour received some new information.'

'Really? Do tell me, Mister Tweedie. Is it reliable?'

'Well, dear lady, I cannot say for sure.' Tweedie licks his lips. 'But there is a gentleman who comes to the city on a mere number of occasions each year. Mister Pym's source says he will be in the locality tonight, but only for a few hours. This gentleman is involved in the relocation of young children and he might shed light on the whereabouts of the little lad you seek. But, with Gregory away, what can we do? I fear the chance will be missed as the gentleman may not return for several months.'

'Then we must seize the opportunity, Mister Tweedie.' Anna leaps up. 'Are you able to take me to this gentleman?'

'Oh no, dear lady. I do not think this the sort of matter you should involve yourself with. Whatever would Gregory say?'

'I assure you he'd expect nothing less of me. If you know where this man is, you must take me to him immediately. Come, let us go.' Anna's already at the door.

William has been hovering anxiously.

'William, I have to go out urgently. Don't worry, for Mister Tweedie will accompany me. Can you fetch my cloak please?

And my boots?'

'But Mistress Stratton,' William says, 'the hour is late. I am not sure Mister Gregory would…'

'And if Mrs Carmichael should awake, please tell her I will explain everything on my return.'

Anna hurries down the steps with Tweedie and within minutes they are racing through the dark streets in Tweedie's phaeton. On the way, Anna plies Tweedie for more details, but he becomes increasingly vague. After his confidence in the house, he seems nervous and evasive. Anna concludes it must be due to them having no chaperone and forces herself to stop questioning him. As the carriage rocks, to and fro, she holds on to the window strap to stop herself toppling into him. Tweedie too hangs on for dear life.

'We're going south of the river?' asks Anna as they cross the Thames.

'Yes, not far now,' Tweedie answers.

What do I say when we arrive? Will this man even engage with a woman? 'Perhaps, when we get there, I should let you do the talking, Mister Tweedie?'

Tweedie stares out of the window into the darkness. 'As you wish, Mistress Stratton.'

Anna was expecting a tavern, but the phaeton pulls up behind an abandoned warehouse. She peers out into the gloom. 'Is this it?'

Tweedie avoids eye contact.

Useless man. Anna swings the carriage door open and is surprised to see Pestlemore standing at the bottom of the steps. 'Mister Pestlemore.'

Pestlemore holds his arms wide as if to greet her.

Anna clambers down. 'I didn't realise you were…'

Pestlemore brings one hand up to cover her mouth whilst the other grabs the back of her head. She struggles in vain as a rag is held firmly against her mouth and nose. It smells sickly and sweet. Then nothing.

* * *

I lift the spaghetti Bolognese, Matt's favourite, off the hob and lay two places at the breakfast bar. This should put him in a good mood. I turn off the main lights, leaving a romantic glow from a strip of LED fairy lights draped above the window.

'This is great,' Matt says when I sit down. He clinks his beer glass against my sparkling water.

I wait until he's several mouthfuls into his meal. 'Don't go mad, but I've been to see Debbie.'

Matt puts down his cutlery. 'When?'

'Well, I've seen her twice actually. Once at a halfway house and…'

The muscle under his cheekbone twitches. 'When?' he repeats.

I squirm in my seat. 'Saturday.'

'The day you had that funny turn at the pub. Christ's sake Anna. I told you, seeing that woman does you no good.'

I stare down at my bowl. *This isn't going well.*

'Twice, you said. You've seen her again?'

I chew my fingernail.

'When?'

'Today. I didn't have a choice. Brenda rang. There'd been an incident involving the police. It seems Debbie ran away.'

'Good riddance.'

'I found her.'

197

'Where?'

'Deptford. Staying in a squat with an old friend.'

'Squat? Crack den more like. Bet she's using again. Please tell me you didn't go there?'

My cheeks flush.

'Fuck's sake.' Matt pushes his bowl away, switches on the main lights and paces the kitchen floor. 'Anything could have happened to you.'

'Well it didn't, I'm fine. But Matt, you should have seen this place. They've no electricity, no heating.' I burst into tears.

Matt hauls me from the stool and wraps me in his arms. 'I'm sorry babe. I don't mean to get angry. I worry about you, that's all.'

I gaze into his eyes. 'Matt, could Debbie stay here?'

He pulls away. 'Absolutely not.'

'It would only be for a little while. She might not even want to, but if she did, perhaps I could get her back on track? Into another rehab programme?'

'There's no way you're bringing that drug addict to live in my flat.'

'She's my mother, Matt. If it was your mother…'

His eyes narrow. 'Are you seriously suggesting there's any comparison between…'

'Sorry. I know it's different.'

Matt takes a deep breath. 'Debbie is not your mother, she's just the woman who gave birth to you. You don't even know her. Your real mother and father are killing time on a yacht in the south of France. They keep reaching out to you, begging you to forgive them. Honestly? You don't know how lucky you are. When are you going to give them a break?'

'I know Mum and Dad love me, but they should have helped.

198

I might have got to know Debbie. I might have been able to...'

'Been able to what? I'm sorry Anna, but your birth mother's a drug addict. Your mum and dad were trying to protect you. They didn't want you having any involvement with her. They did what they thought was right.'

'I'll never forgive them for not giving me a chance to...'

'For Christ's sake.' Matt grabs his keys from the hook by the door.

'Where are you going?'

'To get more beer.' He slams the door.

I'm in a tent. Women dressed in veils swirl round and round. Men sitting on cushions are watching them. I'm amongst the dancers, chiffon veils brushing against my face. Suddenly I'm a child playing in the sheets on Mum's washing line. I'm caught up and the more I fight, the more entangled I become. I'm suffocating...

I wake in a panic and walk my fingers across the bed. Matt's not back. The digital alarm blinks 23.45. He's punishing me.

* * *

Whistler leans against the wall in an alley off Grevil Street. When Mr Greg told him to keep an eye on things, he'd expected a quiet night. How wrong he'd been. It had been two hours since the dandy and Mistress Anna came running down the steps. If Whistler hangs about much longer someone will mistake him for a fagger looking to break in.

He sighs. He had been about to head home when the dandy arrived, casting furtive glances up and down the street afore knocking on the door. It was only when the dandy emerged ten minutes later with Mistress Anna in tow that Whistler realised something was off. He watched them climb into the waiting phaeton and head east.

Whistler cusses. If he'd had Ole Peggy with him, he could have followed. He pulls his collar up around his neck. All he can do is wait. It's gonna be a long night.

11th September

Anna tries to move but her hands are tied behind her back. What the fuck happened? Opening her eyes to darkness, she cries out. 'Help.' Wriggling about she finds her ankles are also bound. She calls again. 'Help me.' Her voice echoes. Where is she?

She can't just lie here. Rocking herself backwards and forwards, Anna inches across the cold, damp floor. Her body jars. A thick leather strap around her waist digs into her ribs and hips. It must be attached to something, for she's reached the limit.

Her head throbs and her mouth's dry. She desperately needs a drink of water. What the hell is that stench? She can't even cover her mouth.

Heavy footsteps make their way towards her. Who's coming? A glimpse of light shines through as the door swings open. Anna lies back down and squeezes her eyes closed.

Someone breathes close to her ear. Alcohol and sweat assail her nostrils. 'Still away wi' the fairies,' he mutters. He moves away, slams the door and slides a bolt. As he climbs the stairs, she hears him wheezing. Muffled voices drift down confirming her jailer is not alone.

Anna opens her eyes again. Now accustomed to the dark,

she scans the area. A basement, the only light from a small dirty window above her. Twisting and wriggling, she inches backwards creating slack in the rope securing her. Rocking side to side, she brings her knees forward. After a few attempts she swings herself to kneeling. She tugs against her waist restraint, sobbing with frustration. It's securely fastened and wriggling her hands makes her wrist bindings tighter. If she had a wall, she could try pushing herself up to a standing position, but the brickwork is too far away to reach.

It must have been Tweedie and Pestlemore. They waited until Janus was out of town. But why would they plot against her? Anna curses her stupidity. It was such an obvious ploy to get her out of the house. She fell right into their trap.

Water laps against the outside walls. Of course, they'd crossed the Thames. That explained the fishy smell. Hopefully the basement doesn't flood. Her dress is damp. Anna shivers. What will happen when her jailer returns and finds her awake?

* * *

The church bell chimes midnight, then one o'clock. Whistler walks up and down. Mistress Anna hasn't returned. He whistles softly. Should he knock on the door and ask Mister Greg's butler if the outing was legit? But it's fearful late. The old boy's probably gone to bed. Whistler recognised the phaeton. He'd seen it many a time when shoeing horses. The dandy's house is not far away...

Using alleys and cut throughs, it takes Whistler less than ten minutes. He doesn't have long to wait. The phaeton pulls up outside and the dandy jumps down, but there's no sign of Mistress Anna.

202

'Refresh the animals,' the dandy shouts to his driver. 'We are not yet done for the night.'

Whistler races back to the farrier's yard to collect Ole Peggy. Who knows how far the next journey might take him? He returns just as the dandy emerges from his house with a blanket draped over his arm and carrying a wicker basket.

What's afoot? Whistler squeezes his legs against Ole Peggy's sides and shortens his reins. As the horse breaks into a trot, he whispers reassurances. 'You don't mind the late hour, do yer gal? Tis a treat to be out in the fresh night air.' The phaeton picks up speed and Whistler eases Ole Peggy into a comfortable canter while keeping distance to avoid detection.

The phaeton pulls up at Coxes Wharf. The dandy alights with his load.

Whistler steers Ole Peggy around the side of the building and dismounts. 'Easy gal,' he murmurs, scratching her forelock. 'We got to wait a bit. Find out what's going on.'

Ten minutes later, the dandy's back, accompanied by a stout gentleman who Whistler recognises as another regular at Mister Greg's. The two men climb into the phaeton.

'Home,' yells the dandy to the driver.

Still no sign of Mistress Anna. Whistler tethers Ole Peggy to a wooden post and works his way around the building. Finding an unlocked door, he creeps inside, passing through two derelict warehouses before hearing voices ahead. Ducking behind a stack of barrels, Whistler inches forward.

Two vagabonds perch on upturned boxes. One is wrapped in a blanket while the other, by the light of a candle, rummages through the wicker basket the dandy delivered. 'Ere, want some bread and cheese?'

'Supposed to be for our guest, ain't it?'

'So's that blanket, but what she ain't seen won't be missed. Anyway, she's still out cold. I'll have me a bite of supper then I'm minded t' get down there and keep 'er company. Warm 'er up like.' The man guffaws, shoving his friend so hard he almost topples him from his box.

Righting himself, his friend returns a toothless grin. 'Give us some ale then and mayhap I'll join yer.'

Whistler leaves them passing a brown flagon of ale one to the other. He backs up and heads outside to resume his search. From their conversation it sounds like they're holding Mistress Anna below ground. On the riverside of the building Whistler spots a row of hatches used for deliveries from the water. He tries the first flap, but it's securely bolted. Moving along to the next, he notices the wood around the hinges is rotten. He pulls a hoof-pick from his pouch and jabs, prising away small pieces of wood until he makes a hole. Whistler squints down into the darkness and gives a low whistle. 'Mistress Anna, are yer in there?'

Was that a distant reply?

'Wait,' Whistler calls. 'I'm gonna get yer out.' Returning to Ole Peggy, he removes a length of rope strapped to her blanket. Fixing one end to her harness and the other to the handle of the hatch lid, Whistler takes hold of Ole Peggy's bridle. 'Easy gal.' He grimaces as the horse's hooves clink loudly against the cobbles. 'That's the way.' The rotten wood groans. Ole Peggy loses her footing, then braces herself to step forward again. There's a crack as the rusty hinges give. The lid comes away.

Whistler removes the rope from Ole Peggy's harness and approaches the hatch. 'You there, miss? I'll lower down a rope. Grab it and I can pull yer up.'

Her reply is muffled.

'What?' yells Whistler

The sounds from the Thames, useful in covering the noise of the breaking hatch, is masking Mistress Anna's words. Whistler looks at Ole Peggy. 'Nothin else for it, old gal. I'm gonna have to go in.'

Ole Peggy snorts.

Whistler tugs on the metal frame surrounding the hatch. Seems solid enough. He secures the rope and lowers himself into the musty cellar.

* * *

Anna gulps down a sob. She can't stop shaking and her right ankle throbs from the tight bindings. From above she hears scratching. *Oh god, not rats.* No, it's someone trying to break in. Tiny flakes of wood rain down on her. Anna looks up. There's a pin prick of light from a small hole way above. She hears a low whistle. Whistler.

'Help,' Anna calls in a croaky voice.

Everything goes quiet. A few minutes later she hears movement – hooves on cobbles, a creaking sound, then a sharp crack as wood gives way.

Anna shakes splinters from her hair. Blinking, she watches Whistler lower himself down to land with a soft thud.

'Hello, Miss Anna,' he whispers. 'Soon 'ave yer out of 'ere.'

Whistler's fingers explore her bindings. 'They're too tight,' says Anna. 'You won't be able to loosen them.'

Grinning, Whistler pulls a small knife from his pouch and sets to work sawing through the rope.

'Thank you.' Anna rubs her wrists and ankles.

Whistler moves forward again to slide his hand under the leather strap around her waist. The blade slices through the leather as if it were butter. Whistler grins from ear to ear. Anna flings her arms around him. He backs away, suddenly shy.

'Thank goodness, Whistler. How did you know I was here?'

'Followed that dandy gent. Had to wait 'til they was gone afore I could rescue yer though, and I don't fink we should 'ang around too long.' Whistler looks up at the hatch. 'We've gotta climb out through that 'ole.'

'Oh, I don't think...' says Anna.

Whistler casts his eyes around the basement and spots some wooden crates. 'I'll stack these.' He slides the crates across the floor to create a pyramid. 'I'll go first, just t' check they's sound.'

Anna nods her head. 'Be careful.'

Whistler clambers on top of the crates and grabs the rope. 'Once I'm out, I'll throw the rope back down and pull yer up.'

'I'm quite heavy. I'm not sure you'll manage on your own.'

'That's all right. I got me some help.'

A few minutes later, Anna is standing on the cobbled street admiring Whistler's accomplice.

'This be Ole Peggy,' Whistler says. 'Couldn't ha' rescued yer without her.'

'She's a beauty.' Anna holds out her hand towards the horse's mouth. The horse nuzzles it, hoping for a treat.

Whistler blows into Ole Peggy's nostrils and the horse whinnies back. 'Good gal, but you've a little more work this night.'

Ole Peggy stamps a hoof on the cobbles.

'She'll carry the both of us.' Whistler moves to the horse's side and links his hands to give Anna a leg up.

'I've ridden before, but never without a saddle.' Anna puts her left foot into Whistler's hands and hauls herself onto the horse's broad back.

Whistler clambers up in front of her. In moments they've left the river and are riding along almost deserted streets.

Whistler turns his head. 'Where to, miss?'

'Grevil Street. I'll be safe there now. Janus will be home tomorrow.'

'Today yer mean, don't yer?'

Anna rests her head on Whistler's shoulder. 'Why do you call your horse Ole Peggy?'

'See how she flies? It were Mister Greg told me about Pegasus the flying horse. Said yer can see her high up in the skies.'

Whistler brings Ole Peggy to a halt outside Janus's house. He holds Anna's hand as she dismounts to the pavement.

'Goodnight, Whistler, and thank you. I'll make sure Janus knows how much you've done for me.'

Whistler blushes. 'Mister Greg asked me t' keep an eye out.'

William opens the door as Anna limps up the steps. 'Mistress Stratton. Thank goodness you are safely home.'

'I'm fine, William.' She turns to smile at Whistler. 'Thanks to my hero.'

Whistler doffs his invisible cap and canters away into the early morning dawn.

* * *

Two gentlemen lurk in an alleyway off Beauchamp Street.

Tweedie hurries to join them. 'I have spoken with Gregory's kitchen maid. It seems the girl has returned to the house.'

'You imbeciles,' growls the gentleman in charge. 'Can you do nothing right?'

'Sorry, b-but it was not our fault,' stammers Pestlemore.

Tweedie shrugs his shoulders. 'The men employed to keep watch say they have no idea how she managed to escape.'

'You should have kept watch yourselves. When the girl tells Gregory who was responsible you will both be implicated.' The gentleman rubs his forehead. 'This bodes well for no-one.' He glares at them. 'You had better ensure my name is kept out of this or I will make it my mission to deal with you most severely.' He storms off, his black cloak swirling behind him.

'What are we g-going to do?' stutters Pestlemore.

Tweedie rubs his chin. 'I am not sure we have been party to the whole story, my friend.'

'What do you mean?'

'I believe there may be more at stake. Has it occurred to you that Mistress Stratton may not be simply a distraction? Have you not wondered about the timing of her appearance?'

Pestlemore nods. 'It was just after our trial of the equipment, was it not?'

'That is so. I am beginning to suspect that Mistress Stratton may be our phantom.'

'If you are right...' Pestlemore shivers with excitement.

'If I am right,' says Tweedie, 'then it would be better if she were to stay. The Royal Society would be most interested.'

'But Gregory wants a second trial in two days' time. He may intend to send her back.'

Tweedie pats Pestlemore's shoulder. 'Then we must endeavour to prevent that from happening.'

* * *

After breakfast, Elizabeth comes to join Anna in the parlour. 'My dear. William tells me you have had a fall. What a pair we are.'

'I'm all right,' says Anna, 'although my ankle's a little swollen.'

'You have eaten some breakfast?'

'I'm fine, I've had some tea.'

Elizabeth sits on the couch and examines Anna's ankle more closely. 'You need to rest it. Are you sure you would not fare better upstairs?'

Anna shakes her head.

'Ned, move that footstool closer so Mistress Stratton might keep her ankle elevated.'

'Yes, madam.' Ned slides the footstool into position.

'Now, my dear, lift your foot onto there.'

Anna does as she is bid.

'Good. You see? I have learned a few tricks from my dear Ernest.' Elizabeth takes a seat in an armchair.

'And how are you feeling?' asks Anna.

'Oh, much restored, my dear. A day in bed is the solution to most of life's ills. Now, I think I should cancel my visits this afternoon for I cannot possibly leave you alone.'

'No, you go. I'll be fine.'

'Well, Ned, I think we both need a quiet morning. What is on the menu for luncheon? Perhaps a little chicken broth followed by one of Mrs Lawson's splendid rice puddings?'

* * *

All night I toss and turn. In the morning Matt's pillow is still plumped. Did he come home? Perhaps he slept on the sofa? A fuggy smell in the living room confirms he did. I lift the cushion, soured with the faint smell of sleep dribble. There's no breakfast bowl in the sink and his gym kit's gone. He must be avoiding me.

I sit at the breakfast bar and call Brenda on my mobile to tell her about my visit to the squat. 'Debbie's talking about going away with that bloke she's staying with. Brian something.'

'It's her choice, Anna,' Brenda says on the other end of the line. 'I'll log it, but unless Debbie contacts me herself, there's little more I can do.'

'There must be something.'

'Well, I could contact the council, but it would take months to evict them. I dare say she'll be long gone by then.'

'So, there's nothing?'

'I think you should leave it. If Debbie wants to get in touch, she will.'

I disconnect and start to ring Zoe, but I hang up before she answers. I was going to tell her about Matt being unreasonable, but is he? This is his flat. When he asked me to move in a year ago and I'd left Zoe in the lurch, she hadn't complained. What if it's me who's selfish? Perhaps I am my mother's daughter?

I put a slice of granary bread in the toaster and flick on the kettle. Were Mum and Dad right all along? Should I be the one apologising? Once the toast pops up, I spread it with peanut butter, make myself a coffee and carry my breakfast over to the sofa to work on an email to my parents. After spending half an hour drafting it, I delete it before pressing 'send'. I type *foundling hospital* into the search engine to try to find out more, but I can't concentrate. My head aches, so I curl up on the sofa with a blanket over me and close my eyes.

I'm running down dark, narrow streets. Filthy water gushes along the gulley, such a foul stench. A rat keeps pace at my feet and I almost trip over it, but I can't stop. I must get to the child. I turn into a passageway. At the end is a door. Lifting the latch, I find myself in a long and dimly lit corridor. As I make my way along I hear crying, but the further I walk, the longer the corridor becomes. The child's sobs grow fainter. I run again.

I wake sweating, the blanket tangled around my legs. I check the time on my mobile – just gone twelve. Matt has football training after work, and then he and Iri will go for a drink. It'll be hours before he gets home. He won't be in any rush to see me.

Dressing down in jeans, tee shirt and an old hoodie, I tuck a credit card and my mobile in my pockets and set off for the station. On the way, I stop off at the cashpoint to draw out three hundred pounds. It means I'll have to sub from Matt or Zoe, but if Debbie's going away, she needs money. I can't let her be dependent on Bouncer Brian.

I take the train to Deptford and head for the squat. On the driveway I hesitate. There's no music coming from inside. Have they left already? I creep round the side of the house, squeezing past the old mattress to reach the side door. Finding it ajar, I push it open and step into the kitchen. The air is thick with marijuana, even worse than yesterday. I hear voices in the living room. I walk through, expecting to see Debbie and Brian, but two men are sprawled across the mattress. One leans against the wall, his head lolling about, eyes rolling like an arcade machine. He has a strap around his upper arm with

211

a needle sticking out. The second guy with a skeleton face and long greasy hair, is fastening a strap to his arm too. As he pulls it tight with his teeth, he looks up at me. His eyes go wide.

I'm grabbed from behind. I scream.

A third man has me in a vice-like grip. He pushes me towards the mattress and throws me down. Skeleton guy grabs me and holds me there. I kick my legs and flay my arms, but he doesn't let go. I stare up at the third man.

His bald head is shiny, his eyes wild. 'What have we here?'

I can't kick anymore as skeleton guy has pinned me firmly between his legs. 'I'm looking for Debbie,' I say in a shaky voice.

Baldy makes a show of looking around. 'No Debbie here. You seen a Debbie, Vince?'

Vince, aka skeleton guy, grabs my wrists and puts his mouth close to my ear. 'I don't see no Debbie. Just this little doll who's gone and dropped into my lap.'

His breath stinks of stale alcohol and his spittle lands on my cheek but I can't wipe it off. 'Please, let me go.'

'Please, let me go,' mimics Vince.

I thrash around again, trying to free my limbs.

Baldy drops to his knees and reaches out towards me.

I scream. Vince lets go of one wrist and claps his grubby hand over my mouth. I freeze.

Baldy's going through the pockets of my hoodie. I wave my free arm uselessly as he pulls out the wad of cash and my credit card. 'My, my.' His grin is lopsided. Stuffing the cash in his own pocket, he pats the pockets of my jeans where he finds my new mobile phone. He takes that too.

'Well, if little doll ain't bearing gifts,' Vince smirks.

The guy with the rolling eyes makes a weird noise, a cross between a gurgle and a whoop.

I yelp as he falls onto me with his face in my lap.

'Hey, wait your turn.' Vince loosens his grip to push the guy off.

I take my chance and roll sideways across the mattress, but Baldy reaches out and grabs me by the back of my thighs. His hand is on the back of my head squashing my face into the filthy mattress. I smell dampness, mold and decay. I'm experiencing déjà vu or was it a dream? *A dark place, ropes around my wrists and ankles, a leather strap around my waist, men laughing...*

'What's going on?' Bouncer Brian comes into the room.

Thank God.

The men stop pawing me.

'Let her go,' Brian orders.

They release me. I roll off the mattress onto my hands and knees and retch.

'Was only having a bit of fun,' says Vince.

'Don't look like she's having fun.' Brian pulls me to my feet. My legs shake so much I can barely stand. 'Thought we told you to fuck off?'

'I j-just wanted to see Debbie,' I stammer.

'She's gone,' says Brian. 'I suggest you do the same.'

'Gone where?' I ask.

Brian shrugs.

I stand straighter. 'If you've done something to her...'

'Oh yeah? What you gonna do? Perhaps I should leave them to it?' He nods towards the men.

I shake my head, swallowing bile. 'No, don't. Please don't.'

'Me and Debs was doing fine till you showed up. Fucking

213

kid, causing trouble…'

I stagger out to the kitchen. I've nearly reached the door when Brian calls out. 'Wait.'

I turn towards him and he chucks my mobile at me. I miss it and it crashes to the floor, cracking the screen. I bend to pick it up.

'Go on now, scarper,' Brian shouts. 'And don't come back.'

I stumble out of the house and run all the way to the station. Thankfully my Oyster card's still inside the phone case. I sob all the way back to the city. The other passengers on the train avert their gaze.

* * *

Janus hurries to the parlour with Khan at his heels. Janus kneels beside the couch, while Khan seats himself at a discreet distance.

As Janus takes her hand, Anna opens her eyes. 'Janus.'

'William has filled me in. Are you all right?'

'Yes, I… no…' Anna bursts into tears.

Janus puts his arms around her as Anna sobs into his shoulder. 'If it wasn't for Whistler…' She shudders. 'God knows what would have happened.'

Janus releases her and hands her his kerchief.

Anna glances over towards Khan. She looks back at Janus and gives him a weak smile. 'I'm so pleased you're back.'

He moves onto the couch and pats her hand. 'Tell me exactly what happened.'

As Anna recounts her story, Janus becoming increasingly agitated. 'What were they thinking? Wait until I get my hands on them. Shall I call a doctor?'

'I'll be fine. William and Ned have been taking care of me.'

'Where is Elizabeth?'

'She offered to stay with me until you returned from Colchester, but I persuaded her not to cancel her plans.'

Janus shakes his head. 'Why in God's name would Tweedie and Pestlemore do this?'

Khan clears his throat. 'Perhaps, Janus, they were unhappy that you have been somewhat distracted of late.'

'Distracted?' Janus stands up and faces him. 'Whatever do you mean?'

Khan shrugs. 'You have spent a lot of time with Mistress Stratton. Your colleagues may fear you are not giving the Prism group project sufficient attention.'

'And their solution is to kidnap her? Are they mad?' Janus paces the room. 'Tweedie and Pestlemore would never come up with such a harebrained scheme themselves. There is more to it than this. Khan, send word that I would meet with Pym and Quintar. I shall have this out with them.'

'As you wish.' Khan leaves the room.

Janus turns his attention back to Anna. 'I fail to understand it. Admittedly they are intent on achieving success with the experiment. That and finding this blessed phantom they keep talking about... unless...' He stares at Anna, seeing her clearly for the first time. 'Unless...' He grabs her arms and gazes into her eyes. 'Of course. How could I not have seen it? This explains everything. You are the phantom.'

He knows. 'I don't know how it happened. One minute I was on Westminster Bridge and then...' Anna sighs. 'I remember nothing but my name. Mercy rescued me and that's why I'm helping her. To be honest I didn't know what else to do.' Anna scrabbles for Janus's kerchief once more as her tears flow.

Janus crosses to the sideboard and pours himself a brandy. 'I can fill in some of the gaps. I fear my colleagues are entirely responsible. Those idiots Tweedie and Pestlemore were trialling our great discovery on Westminster Bridge. Without my permission, I hasten to add. I believe your predicament is a direct consequence of their actions.'

Anna wipes her eyes. 'If it was your invention that got me here, are you able to get me home?'

Janus shakes his head. 'I cannot believe I have been so slow to see.' He pours brandy into a second glass. 'Come, you need a drink as much as I.'

'Thank you.' Anna takes the proffered glass and sips the brandy. She coughs.

Janus crouches down in front of her once more. 'This is incredible. May I?' He reaches out, cupping her face in his hands. 'You feel real.'

'I am real.'

He caresses her cheeks. 'But this is fantastic. I did not anticipate the metamorphosis might create such material results.' Suddenly, as if realising what he's doing might be deemed inappropriate, Janus stands up.

Anna feels the loss of his touch. 'Unless this is some weird and elaborate dream.' She takes another sip of brandy. 'But, Janus, you didn't answer my question. Can you get me home?'

'I shall do my utmost to find a resolution. Meanwhile, it is imperative no-one else should hear of this. What have you told Mercy Benson?'

'She knows I had an accident, hit my head and lost my memory. Nothing more.'

'Good, good. Nearer the time I may have to confide in a few members of the Prism group.'

'Can we trust them?'

'Hmm, therein lies the question. I have known Tweedie and Pestlemore for years but their ambition to become fellows of the Royal Society clearly overrides your safety and well-being. You must stay here while I work out a way to get you home.' He picks up the brandy decanter. 'Top up?'

'No thank you. What about the others?'

'Quintar is a charmer and doubtless completely enamoured by you, but I am afraid he is a terrible gossip. For the moment we should keep this from him. Pym is arrogant but he's discreet and may be a possible confidant.' Janus fills his glass again. 'You always were a mystery. Unlike anyone I have met. When I heard Tweedie and Pestlemore recounting what happened I should have figured this out.' He spins around to face her. 'Tell me everything. The metamorphosis, how did it feel? Where do you hail from? What year?'

'I don't know. From the future, but I don't know what year. London is familiar, but not this London. I know my name, but I don't remember my family or my friends…' Tears course down her cheeks once more.

'Anna, I am sorry.' Janus sits down beside her, pulling her to him. 'Ignore me. Of course, you would not remember.'

She sobs in his arms.

'Ahem.'

Janus loosens his grip.

Khan is standing at the doorway. 'I have dispatched a messenger to Quintar and Pym as you asked.'

'Thank you.' Janus gets up. 'Anna, will you be all right alone for a while? I need to speak with Khan.'

'Yes.' She closes her eyes.

* * *

In his study, Janus sits down heavily behind his desk.

Khan remains standing. 'I have told Pym and Quintar to come the morrow.'

'Not today?'

'I believe you need time to process things before speaking with them.'

Janus shakes his head. 'You will not believe what I have just discovered.'

Khan eases himself into the Chesterfield chair and looks expectantly at Janus.

Janus stares at him. 'You already knew?'

'That Mistress Stratton is the phantom? I have had my suspicions.'

'Do the others know?'

'I cannot say. I would be surprised to find Tweedie and Pestlemore capable of working it out.'

'But Pym? And Quintar?'

Khan steeples his fingers. 'That I do not know.'

Janus slams his fist down on his desk. 'Can I be the only one not to have figured this out?'

'Not necessarily, and yet it is difficult to explain Mistress Stratton's kidnap in any other way.'

'Khan, you are right. Someone has been pulling the strings. I shall interrogate them all.'

'It might be better to keep your cards close to your chest.'

'You mean see if the culprit reveals himself? That is not a bad idea. I would like to find out what the devil they thought they were up to.'

218

* * *

Back in the parlour, Janus finds Anna dozing. For a few moments he watches her sleep.

Anna stirs, opening her eyes.

Janus smiles. 'How are you feeling?'

Anna stretches her arms and yawns. 'It's a relief now that you know. But you haven't told me about the mill owner yet. Did you discover anything?'

'There was no sign of the child. Denton did give us new information, but I fear you are too tired for a trip this afternoon.'

'Nonsense.' Anna pushes herself up from the chair. 'I want to come.'

'In that case I will explain on the way.' Janus takes her arm and leads her into the hallway. 'William?'

'Yes, sir?'

'We will be using the landau. Ask Ned to bring cushions and blankets to ensure Mistress Stratton's comfort.'

The driver of the landau swishes his whip. 'Ger on.'

As the horse trots along the road, Anna asks. 'Where are we going?'

'A fostering home in Barnet. The residence of a Mister Alfie Smythe.'

'Wasn't that one of the names Fripp mentioned?'

'Yes. According to Denton, Smythe has regular dealings with the Grey Man.'

'I am surprised Mister Khan is not joining us.'

Janus avoids eye contact. 'I have asked him to locate Whistler in order I can thank him properly for rescuing you.'

219

'What's wrong?' asks Anna.

'Nothing. It is just… Khan already knew about you.'

Anna gasps. 'How?'

'All is well. He will not tell a soul. Khan and I are as brothers.'

'As long as you're confident we can trust him.'

'I am. Look, I have been thinking, you must be careful what you say to any of us. We know not what damage your being here might do to the future. Undoubtedly you could tell us of amazing advances from your own time, but I think it is best that we develop things at their rightful time.'

After thirty minutes travelling north, the driver pulls up outside a collection of ramshackle buildings.

Anna stares out of the landau window. 'Can this really be a foster home?'

Two large dogs run out, froth hanging from their jaws. They leap up at the carriage door barking ferociously.

Anna backs into the corner. 'Are they rabid?'

'Get down,' Janus yells.

The dogs bare their teeth and snarl.

'Shut up yer buggers. Get down, down I say,' a voice calls.

Continuing to growl, the dogs crouch low on the ground.

''Tis no place for a child,' murmurs Janus.

'What d' yer want?' A man emerges from the barn.

Janus jumps down from the landau, his feet landing in mud. 'Mister Smythe?'

'Depends on yer business.' Smythe staggers towards them, his bent spine causing an unsteady gait.

'I come for information. I understand you have children here?'

Smythe hawks up phlegm and spits. 'What's it to you?'

'We mean you no trouble. We are here on a mission of some

220

delicacy.'

Smythe lurches closer. 'Are yer looking to make a purchase, sir?' He squints at Anna. 'Come to find yourselves a young 'un? I got one might be right for yer lady.'

Anna shudders. Smythe is scarier than his dogs.

'Let me see the child,' says Janus.

Anna stares down at the mud. 'Janus,' she calls.

Janus helps Anna down. Arm in arm they cross the yard, squelching through muck and horse shit.

As they approach an outhouse, Smythe calls out. 'Make yerself respectable, woman. We got company.'

Anna follows Janus through the open doorway, glancing around at the mud floor and open fire. The room is draughty and damp from the hole in the roof, the makeshift table appearing to be the only furniture.

A young woman, scarcely more than a child, slides down from a bale of hay.

Smythe gestures towards her. 'This be the missus.'

Janus tips his hat. 'Madam.'

Smythe carries a lantern towards a pile of old rags in the corner of the room. 'Out yer come,' he roars.

The heap moves and two small boys emerge from what must be their bed. They straighten up to stand before the visitors, skeletal and filthy.

Janus clears his throat. 'We seek one lad in particular. He would be a little under six years of age.'

Smythe cusses. 'Ain't got none that old. They's collected by time they's five.'

'Who collects them?' asks Janus.

'Who's asking? If neither of these lads suit yer' – Smythe points at the two boys – 'I think yer business 'ere is done.'

221

Janus taps his belt purse.

'Well' – Smythe scratches his ear – 'now I comes to think of it, s'pose I might be able to help.'

Janus takes two coins from his pouch and holds them out. 'Who collects the children. Is it the Grey Man?'

'Aye. He's the one what drops off the bairns. They's with us three, maybe four years. We takes good care of 'em, don't we Betsy?' As Smythe extends a hand towards Betsy, she and the little ones flinch.

'How do you contact the Grey Man?' asks Janus.

'He knows where we is.'

'When did you see him last?'

'Been a few months now, but that ain't unusual. Grey Man knows what age these two is. He'll be back when time's right.'

Janus removes another coin from his pouch. 'Where does he take them?'

Smythe shrugs.

'Come on, man. We know he delivers some to Denton's Mill but he must have more local places.'

Smythe wipes his nose on the back of his hand. 'I hear tell the Grey Man supplies the master sweeps.'

'And suppose I want to get hold of the Grey Man myself?'

Smythe stares at Janus's pouch. Janus pulls out a fourth coin.

'If he's in town, you'll likely find him in *The Mitre*. He has lodgings close by.' Smythe grabs the coins from Janus's hand. 'That's all I know. Now we is done and you'll be on yer way.'

Janus steps towards the door. Anna doesn't move. She continues to stare at the boys who gaze back without expectation or hope. Somewhere deep inside Anna's memories she recalls a childhood visit to a home for abandoned dogs. Some strays were young and eager to be chosen while others lay quietly in their pens as if they'd given up. These boys have that same look. She swallows. 'Janus, can't we...'

Janus shakes his head. He takes her arm and escorts her back to the landau.

'What a God forsaken hovel.' Janus wipes his hands on his kerchief as they drive away.

Anna bites her lip. 'I wanted to take those boys away from there.'

'I know.' Janus leans forward and brushes a strand of hair from her face. 'We might make one more stop.'

'The Mitre?'

He rearranges her cushions. 'Only if you feel up to it.'

Anna yawns. 'Yes, I'll be fine.' But the rocking motion of the carriage causes her eyelids to droop.

* * *

I get home and tear off my clothes. Stepping into the shower I let hot water cascade down my body as I relive what happened. How did I even get back from the tube station? It's a complete blank. I lather my hair three times and scrub my skin with the loofah, feeling like I'll never be clean again. Stepping out of the shower, I clip up my hair and wrap myself in one of our softest towels. I stand at the sink and brush my teeth until my gums bleed and I can no longer taste the mens' body odour.

I pad through to the living room. My hands shake as I pour myself a large gin. Matt hasn't called. I bet he'll stay out late to punish me. How will I explain the cracked screen on my new phone? I can't tell him I went back to Deptford. Brian had said Debbie's gone so where the hell is she? Had they argued?

223

Was it because of me? Should I report Debbie as a missing person?

I carry my drink through to the bedroom and check my mobile. Still nothing from Matt, but three texts from Zoe. I read the last message. *CALL ME*. I sigh. She'll be so mad at me for putting myself in danger. And the money, all that bloody money. It's pointless me ringing Brenda, she told me to leave it. This is all my own stupid fault.

I open the wardrobe and lift the shoebox from the top shelf. Inside, under the old photographs, I find the envelope. Sitting on the bed, I pull out the letter on blue notepaper.

Dear Anna,

First of all, know we love you and will always love you. You are the light of our lives and the most precious gift.

I may not be your birth mother, but I sang songs to you at two in the morning, lingering long after you'd gone back to sleep just to inhale your beautiful baby smell.

We have an album full of photos, your first tooth, your first steps, your first Christmas (when Dad gave you that giant teddy), your first day at school.

We may not be your birth parents, but we taught you to love books, nature, long walks in the countryside and the sea.

I was there with a hug when you fell from your scooter and it was Dad who taught you to ride a bike and caught you when you jumped into the swimming pool that first time.

We fought over when you could have a hamster, a TV in your room, your first mobile phone, your ears pierced (eventually giving in and letting you have them all).

I may not be your birth mother, but I comforted you when other kids were mean to you. I took you shopping for your first shoes and your first bra. It was me you called in the middle of the night and when you woke up after having that operation to reset your wrist.

We understand you want to find yourself and to know who you really are, but I can tell you... you are our daughter, and we are your parents. Although we respect your right to find your birth mother (and we will be forever grateful to her for giving us you), that is not the sum total of the wonderful girl you have become. You're more than your history, you are your present and your future.

We're so proud of you. You can be and do anything you want in this world. We want to celebrate with you when you get your first big promotion. I want to be there when you choose your wedding dress. Dad wants to walk you down the aisle and we want to meet our grandchildren.

To love you means letting you go out into the world and this we have done, but we will always be here for you, your Dad and me.

We will love you forever. xx

Dark spots appear on the paper from my tears. I curl up on the bed. I want my mum. Not Debbie. My real mum.

* * *

As they step inside *The Mitre*, Anna gags at the smell of stale tobacco, sweat and beer. Windowless stone walls and a dirt floor create the impression of being in a cave, while low beams intensify the darkness. Maybe it's early, but the tavern does not share the lively atmosphere of *The Three Cups*.

Janus moves across to the untended bar. He knocks at the counter. 'Landlord?'

A trap door behind the bar is open. It sounds like someone below is shifting barrels. Whoever it is pauses in their labour and muffled words float up from the hatch before they resume their toil.

'I suspect they are watering down the ale,' Janus mutters. 'Let us not bother to order sustenance.'

Three patrons sit at separate tables. They all look like they are drowning their sorrows. Janus nods towards a skinny man, dressed in grey from head to toe, drinking alone in the gloomiest corner. 'That is likely him.'

As they approach, the man looks up.

'Good afternoon, sir.' Janus tips his hat. 'Might I be addressing the Grey Man?'

The Grey Man inclines his head.

Janus drags over two stools, one for himself and one for Anna. After sitting down, he throws some coins onto the table.

The Grey Man puffs on his pipe, his eyes locked on Janus.

'We are trying to trace a child,' says Janus, 'taken as a bairn by a man named Fripp. The boy spent his first few years in a foster home in Harrow-on-the-Hill.'

'I visit many foster homes, some better than others.' The Grey Man turns to Anna. His smile is thin lipped. 'Terrible thing to lose a child.'

Anna opens her mouth to speak but Janus lifts his hand warning her not to respond.

'We have tried everywhere,' Janus continues. 'The child was moved around the age of five but then the trail goes cold. You might have picked him up? Delivered him somewhere? Perhaps a few months back?'

The Grey Man scratches his scrawny beard. ''Tis possible.'

Janus leans forward, lowering his voice. 'I would be grateful to learn where the lad might have ended up.'

The Grey Man sips his ale, resting his arm casually along the back of the settle. 'Hard to say. Were he a strong lad? Strong 'uns usually end up at Denton's Mill, Colchester way.'

'We have tried there,' says Janus.

'Five years old, you say? Too young for the ships, 'specially if he was a scrawny nipper. I'd say yer best chance is the master sweeps.'

Janus sighs. 'Alfie Smythe told us as much, but London is teaming with sweeps.'

'Perhaps you might try One-eyed Pete?' The Grey Man reaches forward to take the coins.

'Who on earth is One-eyed Pete?' asks Anna, as Janus helps her back into the landau.

Janus climbs up and sits beside her. 'I assume he is a master sweep. There are hundreds across the city, all employing small boys.'

Anna sighs. 'We're running out of time.'

'I will get Whistler on the case. If anyone can locate One-eyed Pete, I would put money on him.' Janus gazes at Anna.

'What?' she asks.

'Have you remembered anything more about your other life?'

'Not really. Just little flashes, usually triggered by something.'

He's still staring. Anna feels her cheeks burning.

* * *

When I wake, the bedroom's in darkness. I turn on the bedside light to check my mobile. Nothing from Matt. He'll be heading for the pub by now, probably confiding in Iri and complaining about what a selfish bitch I am. I can't tell Matt what happened, even if he was right. He'll blame me for going back to Deptford and putting myself at risk. I'll never hear the last of it. What shall I do about the stolen money though? I slide off the bed. I've been laying on Mum's letter; it's crumpled up on the duvet. I flatten it out, refold it and return it to the shoebox.

I walk through to the kitchen. I should eat. When I open the fridge door, a lock of my hair escapes from the clip. It still reeks of marijuana. Gross. I go through to the bathroom, turn on the taps and tip in a generous slug of bubble bath. While the bath is filling, I light candles and line them up around the rim. When did they become part of my routine? I ease myself down in the tub, closing my eyes to calm my racing heart. Images of 'what if' play across the back of my eyes like a scary movie. Several times I startle, opening my eyes to shoot glances at the bathroom door. I should have locked it. I could climb back out but instead I sink under the water and close my eyes again.

I hear the ringtone from my mobile. Damn, I've left it in the bedroom. I let it ring, but it's persistent. Perhaps it's Matt? I can't miss his call. We need to make up. Wrapping the towel around me, I pad through to the bedroom, soaking the carpet with my wet feet.

'Oh, so you *are* still alive?' Zoe sounds well narked. 'What's going on? We haven't spoken properly since Monday. You said you'd call me back.'

'I was just having a soak.'

'Oh well, pardon me for coming between you and your ablutions.'

'Sorry.'

'So? You went to Deptford? What happened?'

'I found Debbie.'

'That's great news.'

'But now she's gone again.'

'Oh.' Zoe's tone softens. 'I'm sorry, hun.'

'I wanted her to come back here and stay for a while.'

Zoe snorts. 'And Matt was okay with that?'

'Not exactly.'

She laughs. 'Well you can hardly blame him. I know she's your birth mother, Anna, but you barely know her.'

'Matt called her a drug addict. We had a big fight and he stormed out and now he's been avoiding me.' I glance through the open bathroom door to the flickering candles.

'He'll calm down,' says Zoe.

I stare at the candles.

Zoe's wittering on. She's taking Matt's side. 'I don't think he's being unreasonable…'

I'm finding the flames hypnotising.

'… do you?' Zoe asks.

I feel like I'm somewhere else.

'Anna?'

Where am I?

'Anna?'

My phone hits the floor.

* * *

'We will await dinner in the parlour,' says Janus. 'Send Ned in

229

with coffee.'

'Yes, sir.' William takes their cloaks.

Janus leads Anna to the couch. He places the footstool in front of her and elevates her foot. 'How are you feeling?'

She looks at her ankle. 'Oh, it's not so bad.'

'I was not referring to your injury. I was enquiring more generally. How do you feel in yourself?'

'I'm okay.'

'Would you say you feel stronger than when you first arrived? Or weaker?'

'Why are you asking me this?'

'Sorry, I...'

Ned comes in carrying a tray of refreshments.

'Thank you, Ned.' Janus sits down in his armchair while Ned serves coffee. After Ned has left, Janus continues. 'You were saying you only remember small flashes from your other life?'

'Yes,' says Anna.

'Triggered by events here.' Janus puts his coffee down and moves across to sit beside Anna. 'So, would you remember if there was anyone...'

'Ahem,' says William from the doorway.

Janus stands up quickly. 'Yes, William?'

'The boy is here, sir.'

'Good, good. Show him in.' Janus tops up his coffee cup and sits back in the armchair as Whistler shuffles into the room.

'I understand we have much to thank you for, boy,' says Janus.

Whistler's blush radiates despite his grubby face. 'It be no trouble. Hope you's recovered, Miss Anna?'

'I'm fine, Whistler. Thank you again for all you did.'

'There is something else,' says Janus. 'I assume you still cross paths with some of the climbing boys? I need to track down a master sweep. He goes by the name of One-eyed Pete. Have you heard of him?'

'Can't say that I has, Mister Greg.'

Janus downs the rest of his coffee and stands up. He pulls two coins from his pouch and drops them into Whistler's palm. 'Once again, I fear it is a matter of some urgency.'

William is hovering in the doorway.

'William, show the boy out,' says Janus. 'I take it dinner is served?'

'Yes, sir,' says William.

Janus holds out his hand to Anna. 'Well now, Mistress Stratton.' He winks. 'I believe it is time we joined the others.'

Elizabeth and Khan are already seated in the dining room.

'Ah, here they are,' says Elizabeth. 'How are you feeling, my dear? Come, sit beside me. Are you recovered?'

'I'm much better, thank you,' Anna replies.

Janus pulls out Anna's chair before seating himself at the head of the table. Ned serves the soup.

'And how was your trip to Colchester, brother?' Elizabeth lifts her spoon. 'Mister Khan has just been showing me his journal. I understand that you visited a mill? How intriguing. Please enlighten us.'

Janus helps himself to a slice of bread. 'Well, after bribing the mill owner, he became most obliging. He showed Khan and I around the apprentice house and allowed us to oversee the end of a shift.' Janus catches Anna's eye. 'All the lads were older than John Benson.'

Anna sighs. 'So, we don't have any real news for Mercy.'

'We will once we find One-eyed Pete.' Janus dunks bread into his bowl.

Elizabeth frowns. 'One-eyed Pete? Goodness me, the man sounds perfectly frightful. I hope, Janus, you are not planning on taking Anna anywhere unsavoury.'

Janus laughs, his eyes twinkling. Anna smiles back. There can't be many places less savoury than Smythe's.

They finish their soup. Ned moves around the table collecting the bowls and laying out the plates for the main course.

Elizabeth rearranges her napkin. 'I am not sure I understand why a foster home would send children to an apprentice house rather than back to the Foundling Hospital.'

'The Foundling Hospital pay by the week.' Janus passes the cold meat platter to the ladies. 'At the end of the fostering period most children return, but they accept some will not survive. In contrast, the apprentice houses pay for each healthy child on point of supply. If a few children should "pass away" before being returned to the Foundling Hospital, the foster parents can make a little extra money.'

Anna takes a small slice of meat from the platter. 'It's outrageous.'

'They must get the balance right.' Khan helps himself to vegetables from the serving dish. 'They have to convince the Foundling Hospital that the child died of natural causes rather than neglect. If they lose too many children, they will not be used again.'

'The cost of raising a foundling is high.' Janus takes the tureen dish from Khan. 'The Foundling Hospital will not worry too much if they lose a few, as long as the children were well cared for whilst they were alive.'

Elizabeth slices into her pork. 'I hope the factory owners provide these children with meals and a roof over their head.'

'I am afraid their life is grim,' says Janus. 'Breakfast and supper consist of onion porridge and an oat cake. They sleep three to a bed with one room for boys and one for girls. The stench of oily clothes and grease was enough to make me heave.'

Anna lays down her knife and fork. She wipes her mouth with the corner of her napkin.

Khan consults his journal beside his plate. ''Tis undoubtedly a hard life. *Sixteen-hour days, seven days a week.* And the work is dangerous. *The child starts as a scavenger, crawling under machinery to pick up loose cotton. Some lose fingers and many are unable to stand upright.'*

'Do they get paid?' asks Anna.

'Yes, but not until they have worked off the cost of the outlay to buy them in the first place. They are signed over to the factory owner and must work off the cost.' Janus looks at Anna's plate. 'You are not hungry, Mistress Stratton?'

Anna shakes her head. 'Not really.' She pushes her plate away. 'What you are describing, Janus, is slavery.'

'I agree.' Elizabeth dabs her mouth with her napkin. 'Life for the poor little mites must be most unpleasant.'

'If they survive the first few years,' Khan reads, *'they become piecers earning a few pence a week. Their lungs become filled with dust and fluff, many suffocate. If they survive that, they work until twenty-one to clear the debt.* It is too late then to do anything else.'

'Denton has built an apprentice house to take up to ninety youngsters. It is more economical for factory owners to employ children aged between five and ten years, cheaper than building homes for grown men and their families.' Janus lifts the last forkful from his plate. 'There will always be a plentiful supply of children from the likes of Fripp or the Grey Man.'

Khan moves his journal to one side. 'I shall meet with Gilbert next week and I intend to inform him of these appalling conditions. He may take it to the Commons Chamber for debate.'

'If John is somewhere like this, we have to find him,' says Anna. 'He won't survive. What shall I tell Mercy?'

Janus sips his wine. 'You can tell her it is still possible her child is alive.'

The front doorbell rings and moments later William stands at the dining room doorway. 'Mister Pym is here, sir.'

Elizabeth yawns theatrically. 'I am suddenly rather weary. I scarcely think any of us have the appetite for cheese. If you will excuse me, Janus, I might retire to the parlour. Anna, will you join me?'

Janus smiles. 'That is not a bad idea. William, show Pym into my study.' Janus holds out his arm and escorts Anna across the hallway. They pass Pym as William is relieving him of cloak and hat.

'Pym,' says Janus, 'I am getting the ladies settled. You will join Khan and I for coffee? Or a brandy perhaps?'

Pym focuses on Anna as she limps across the hallway. 'Mistress Stratton, you have had an accident since last I saw you?'

'I slipped on the front steps. I'll be right as rain in a couple of days.'

'I am glad to hear it.'

In the parlour, Janus leads Anna to the couch. 'Now, I would speak with Pym, but is there anything else you ladies need? Ned will bring you tea.'

Elizabeth sits in the armchair beside the fire. 'Do stop fussing, Janus, we are looking forward to a little peace.' She waves Janus away as he attempts to move the footstool close to Anna. 'Ned will do that. Away to your business, brother.'

* * *

Khan is pouring himself a cup of tea when Janus strides into the study to take his place behind the desk.

Pym, seated in the Chesterfield, lifts a glass from the tray proffered by William. 'I know you asked to see me the morrow, Gregory, but I was concerned that it might be urgent.'

Janus stares at him. 'Ha, so you know what happened. You had better explain yourself, sir.'

'What?' asks Pym.

'You know perfectly well that Mistress Stratton's injury did not occur on the steps.'

'Janus.' Khan shoots him a warning glance as he seats himself in the other chair.

Janus shakes his head. 'Pym, did you or did you not treat Mistress Stratton to your hospitality last night?'

'I am sorry?' Pym frowns. 'What is it you speak of?'

Janus stands up and leans across his desk. 'Are you the brains behind the kidnap? What the devil are you up to, man?'

Pym places his brandy glass carefully on the side table. 'I am afraid, Gregory, I have not the foggiest idea...'

'Oh, come off it. You expect me to believe Tweedie and Pestlemore came up with this madcap scheme? What were you thinking? Lock Mistress Stratton up and use her as an exhibit for the Royal Society to prove validity of our trials?'

Pym stands up. 'I assure you I know nothing of any plot to lock the young lady away.' He shakes his head. 'I am beginning to think, Gregory, that you may have lost your mind.'

'Janus.' Khan entreats his friend. 'There is no evidence that Pym was behind the plot.'

Janus exhales. 'You are right, of course. Pym, please accept my apologies.' Janus walks around the desk. He hands Pym his brandy glass and takes one from the tray for himself. 'William, we can manage now. Please see the ladies have some tea.' Janus collapses into his chair. 'Sorry, Pym. So much for keeping calm.'

Pym eases himself back down in his chair. 'But what is it you are telling me?'

'I suppose I have let the cat out of the bag now.' Janus sighs. 'Pym, Mistress Stratton is the phantom.'

Pym stares open-mouthed. 'I... I know not what to say.'

'Drink up. You may be needing another.'

Pym downs his brandy and twirls the glass thoughtfully in his hand. 'If this is true, at the risk of stating the obvious, you realise Mistress Stratton's presence endangers all our futures?'

'I am aware we must be mindful of the situation.' Janus sips his brandy. 'But her existence here is of our making.'

'We always maintained the principle that, should we be successful in our time travel experimentation, nothing would be disturbed.' Pym looks at Khan. 'Mistress Stratton may already have caused certain events to change.'

Khan pours another cup of tea. 'Pym makes a valid point.'

'How so?' Janus takes a drink, draining his glass.

'Such things are greater than our comprehension.' Khan sips his tea. 'We are bound to our respective properties and life spans.'

Janus pours himself another brandy. 'You are saying our actions go against God's will?'

'It is by Allah's will that the rules of the universe operate. He has responsibility for the day and the time, the chronology of all,' says Khan.

'But we will put things back as they should be.' Janus refills Pym's glass. 'We will restore things.'

'Only Allah has the authority to change things. This is *taqdeer*. It is not our place to meddle with destiny.'

'What might result if Mistress Stratton returns to her own time and speaks of these events?' says Pym. 'Is it not bad enough we caused her to come here?'

'Mayhap it was destiny she came and it is her destiny to return.' Janus laughs. 'I am sorry, gentlemen, but you cannot have it both ways. What would you have Mistress Stratton do? Stay here? How would that keep things to their allotted time and place?'

Pym shakes his head. 'So, Gregory, what is your plan?'

Janus sits forward. 'We must ensure Mistress Stratton returns to her own time as soon as possible. Are arrangements in hand for the second trial?'

'We have carried out preliminary calculations,' answers Pym. 'Tweedie believes the thirteenth is our best chance of creating the same conditions. It is the only night in the foreseeable future when the moon is once more in alignment.'

'So, Mistress Stratton has a few more days of our company,' says Janus. 'But can we do this on our own? Without the involvement of Tweedie and Pestlemore?'

''Twould be easier with their expertise,' says Pym.

'I would much prefer those fools were kept in the dark,

certainly for the time being.' Janus rubs his chin. 'They have caused enough trouble.'

* * *

Matt runs down the corridor, skidding to a halt in front of the lift. On the way up to the third floor, he is forced to stand still. His heart pounds. 'At least I'm in the best place to have a heart attack,' he mutters to himself. 'This bloody place is becoming too familiar over the last few days.'

He makes his way to Accident and Emergency, where he's greeted by a nurse in the reception area.

'Can I help you?' she asks.

'Anna Stratton. She's my girlfriend. I had a call to say she's been admitted?'

The nurse gestures towards the MediGel dispenser on the wall. Matt squirts a couple of drops onto his hands, rubbing them together impatiently as the nurse consults her computer screen.

'Bay Two. You can go in, but the doctors will be doing their rounds shortly and you may be asked to leave.'

Just try it. Matt pulls back the curtain and discovers Zoe sitting by the bed. Anna is motionless.

Zoe jumps up. 'Matt.'

'Zoe. How is she?'

'I don't know. She's sleeping. Oh, Matt, I didn't know what to do when I couldn't get hold of you.'

'The signal must have been bad. Iri and me had a drink after footie.'

'We were talking on the phone. Anna suddenly went quiet. I had a bad feeling and when you didn't answer your mobile, I hopped in an Uber. I used the key in the key safe to let myself in. Anna was on the floor.' Zoe puts her hand to her mouth. 'I couldn't get her to wake up.'

Matt moves closer to Zoe and puts his arms around her as she sobs. 'It's okay. She'll be okay.' He lets go and leans across to kiss Anna on the cheek. 'I'm here now, babe.'

'I called an ambulance, but they were ages.' Zoe blows her nose. 'I didn't know whether to call her mum and dad.'

'But you didn't?'

'No.'

'We'll wait a while.' Matt takes Zoe's seat and holds Anna's hand. 'Let's see what the doctor has to say.'

12th September

Matt's asleep in the chair beside Anna's bed. Zoe shakes his arm. 'Matt. Coffee.'

Matt opens his eyes. *Anna.* He scans her face. No change. He sighs. 'I hate hospitals.'

'I know.' Zoe passes him a Costa cup. 'Perhaps I should have stayed?'

'No.' Matt takes a sip, wincing as the coffee burns his tongue. 'It would have been pointless both of us staying.'

Zoe sets her own coffee on the bedside locker. 'Took me ages to find you. I didn't realise they'd moved Anna to a ward.'

'Oh shit.' Matt puts the cup down. 'Sorry, I should have texted.' He rubs his eyes. 'They've been in and out all night checking her obs. The doctor's supposed to be coming soon.'

As Matt speaks, a doctor arrives with his underling. 'Ah, yes.' The doctor applies MediGel to his hands. 'This one's a bit of a mystery.'

Matt stands up to give the doctor room.

'I'll give you some space.' Zoe picks up her coffee and moves away.

'This young lady was mugged,' the doctor says as he examines Anna. 'We've found nothing on her cranial scan and yet she's experienced a seizure of sorts.'

Matt clears his throat. 'What might it be?'

'Too soon to determine. I was thinking along the lines of diabetes or epilepsy, but blood tests rule that out.'

Matt frowns. 'Could it be something worse?'

'Nothing's shown up on the CT scan. Now, this fall...' The doctor leans forward to re-examine Anna's head. He straightens back up and turns to the junior doctor. 'Take a look at this abrasion, give me your thoughts.'

The junior doctor puts his notes on the bed and applies a liberal squirt of hand gel. He places his fingers carefully either side of the sutures on Anna's scalp. 'Intracranial hematoma?'

'Hmm.' The doctor shrugs his shoulders. 'If there was a bleed, the scan would pick it up. Perhaps the seizure is completely unrelated?' He turns to Matt. 'Any trips abroad to exotic places?'

Matt shakes his head. 'I wish. Why?'

'No mosquito bites? Tropical diseases? History of kidney or bladder problems?'

'No.'

'What's her emotional state? Has she been worried about anything? We need to rule out psychosomatic reasons for what's happening.'

Matt takes a deep breath, releasing it slowly. 'You think Anna's making this up?'

'No, that's not what I said at all. Psychosomatic illness can have very real physical symptoms. Any major trauma in her life? Bereavement? A falling out?' The doctor's stare intensifies.

'No. Well, she recently contacted her birth mother but....'

The doctor places a hand on his junior's shoulder. 'Puzzling, don't you agree?' He turns to Matt. 'Don't worry, we'll

241

continue to monitor her. I'm sure we'll get to the bottom of this.'

The junior doctor picks up Anna's file. They continue to discuss the case as they move on to their next patient.

Matt sits back down on the chair and sighs.

Zoe walks back over. 'So? What did they say?'

Matt leans forward and takes Anna's hand. 'They don't have a bloody clue.'

Eight a.m. and still no improvement. Anna hasn't woken up. Matt stretches his arms. *God, I ache.*

A nurse approaches Anna's bed. 'Morning. I thought you could do with a cuppa.' She passes him the beverage.

'Thanks.' Matt rubs his back.

'You're no good to your girlfriend if you make yourself ill. Why don't you pop home and get yourself something to eat? Freshen up a little?'

Matt gazes at Anna. 'I don't want to leave her.'

'We'll ring if there's any change. But before you go, I need to get some details.' Moments later the nurse returns with a clipboard and pen in her hands. She pulls the curtain around Anna's bed. 'I need to go through this checklist. Tell me about the bump on Anna's head. Does she suffer from epilepsy? How has she been sleeping? What about her diet?'

Matt's lost count of the times he's been asked these same questions, but he answers as best he can. 'Anna's not been dieting but she gets wobbly if she skips breakfast. Low blood sugar she tells me.' He runs a hand through his hair. 'She's going to be okay?'

The nurse smiles. 'You'll have to speak to the doctor.' She pulls back the curtain and leaves.

Matt sniffs his armpits. His slim-fit shirt proved unpractical worn overnight. Perhaps the nurse is right. It wouldn't hurt to go home, shower and grab some fresh clothes. His stomach rumbles. *I could kill for a bacon sarnie.*

* * *

Elizabeth leaves the half-eaten fruit bread on her plate and rises from the table. 'I must away. Are you sure, Anna, that I cannot tempt you to join me? My friends at *The Salon* would love to meet you.'

'Perhaps another time? Have a nice morning.'

Once Elizabeth has left, Anna finishes her hot chocolate and crosses the hallway to the parlour.

Janus looks up as she enters. He folds his newspaper. 'You are no longer limping?'

'My ankle is much improved. Elizabeth has left to meet her *Blue Stocking* friends.'

'Then come and join me.' Janus gets up and leads her over to the couch.

Anna lowers herself down. 'You were asking yesterday if I felt different?'

Janus sits beside her. 'Indeed, I was. Have you remembered any more?'

Anna shakes her head. 'Not really, only bits and pieces. But I do feel different.'

'In what way?'

'It's hard to explain. More awake, I suppose. More alive.'

Janus reaches for her hand. A shiver of excitement runs through her.

'Tell me, Janus, have you used the time travel apparatus yourself?'

'Yes, I trialled it once.'

'Where did you go?'

'To see someone who was special to me for a time.'

Anna squeezes his hand. 'What happened?'

'The trial was unsuccessful.' Janus stares into space. 'I was there but merely a shadow. I could see and hear everything going on, but had no capacity for interaction.' He sighs. 'No ability to change what was happening.'

Anna tries to catch his eye. 'So, you really were a phantom?'

Janus gives a half smile.

'Perhaps that's what it's like when you die,' muses Anna.

'I was not at all like you.' Janus gazes into her eyes. 'I can see you, hear you,' – he runs his fingers lightly up her arm – 'touch you.'

The tiny hairs on Anna's skin tingle. 'Why was your experience different?'

'I am not sure but,' – he pats her hand – 'I do have a theory.'

'Go on.'

'You have journeyed far back in time, whereas my visit was merely a few years hence. It is my hypothesis there may be some law of nature preventing the existence of two beings during one lifespan.'

'Do other members of the Prism group concur?'

'I have not yet discussed this with them.'

'And you haven't attempted time travel since?'

'There were adjustments to be made.' He smiles. 'And then you beat me to it.'

After a knock at the door, William comes in. 'The boy has returned, sir.'

As Whistler enters the room, Janus beckons him forward. 'Come in, come in. You have news?'

'Yes, Mister Greg. My mate Sid's brother works for a sweep. This is the fella.' Whistler reaches into his breeches, pulls out a crumpled piece of paper and hands it to Janus. 'Employs small boys, sir.' Whistler beams. 'Sid's brother Jack says they calls 'im Pete the Pirate, on account of 'im only having one eye.'

Janus flattens the paper out and reads aloud:

'Pete the Sweep. Extinwishes Chimenys on Fire with great care and Safty. Smoaky Jacks. Clean cloths. Little boys for small flues. Avalable day and night.'

'This is splendid, Whistler.' Janus claps the boy heartily on the shoulder, almost bowling him off his feet. 'It sounds as if this might be the chap.'

'Pete used to have a boy t' go up the small flues. Tom were his name.' Whistler rocks back on his heels. 'Awhile back he 'ad an accident.'

'What happened?' asks Anna.

'According to Jack, Pete's an evil bugger and oft sends his boys up hot flues.' Whistler shakes his head. 'If they don't go, he sticks pins in their feet.'

Anna winces.

'You ain't heard the best bit yet, miss.' Whistler licks his lips. 'One day, Tom were sent up a chimney that were aflame. Poor lad. He were a rat in a trap, hollering and shouting, afeared for his life. Well, he tries to climb up, but that flue's red hot and Tom's feet is blistering. He falls awkward-like and injures his leg so bad they says they might have t' cut it off at the ankle.'

Anna gasps. 'Oh no.'

'Sorry, miss. Anyways, Jack's too big to go up the small

flues, so Pete had to take on a new lad.' Whistler chuckles. 'Apparently this lad has curly dark hair and once he's got a layer of soot on 'im, he looks like one of 'em little black boys you ladies like to play with.'

Janus shakes his head.

Whistler turns back to Anna. 'Didn't mean to offend you none, miss.' He swallows. 'Anyways, I wondered if this lad might be the one you's lookin' for?'

'Well done, Whistler. This is good work.' Janus stands up, slips the boy a coin and ruffles his hair.

'Thank you, Mister Greg.'

'Can you see Whistler out, please William?'

'Certainly, sir. This way, boy.' William and Whistler leave the room.

Janus sits back down beside Anna. 'That boy,' – Janus shakes his head – 'he never lets me down.'

Anna takes his hand. 'So, what are the chances the lad is Mercy's son?'

'Whistler's information is usually sound.'

The front door slams. Elizabeth's voice floats in from the hallway. 'One in, one out. Who on earth is that child? I hope he has not dirtied the carpets. Oh, yes please, William, tea would be wonderful. Where is Janus?'

The door of the parlour is thrown open and Elizabeth enters. 'Ah, good, you are here.'

Janus stands to greet her. 'Back so soon, sister? You have scarcely been gone an hour. Come, catch your breath.'

Elizabeth sits down beside the hearth. 'I simply had to return immediately. You will never guess my news. It is Isabella Pym. She has quite disappeared.'

'Disappeared?' says Anna.

'Yes.' Elizabeth peels off her gloves. 'It was my dear friend, Audrey, who told me. She called on Isabella yesterday, only to find the servants closing up the house and the furniture already covered.'

'But where has she gone?' asks Anna.

'Well, according to Audrey, Isabella has been out of sorts for some time. I knew there was something wrong at the soirée. Did I not say, brother? Isabella was so pale and quiet. No-one seems to know where she is.'

'And what of Pym?' asks Janus.

'He was not there either and the housekeeper refused to say where he was.'

Anna frowns. 'But Pym was here yesterday.'

'It is a little odd,' says Janus.

'It is very odd.' Elizabeth glances at the door. 'Where is Ned with my tea?' She looks back at Janus. 'You recall where Isabella was when last described as being out of sorts?'

Janus rubs his chin. 'I do.'

Anna looks from one to the other. 'Where?'

'It was a few years ago.' Elizabeth stretches her hands towards the fire and rubs them together. 'Isabella lost a baby. It sent her a little mad.'

'I'm not surprised,' says Anna.

'Pym told us at the time Isabella had gone away to recuperate.' Elizabeth settles back in her chair. 'I always suspected he tried to have her put away.'

'Put away?' says Anna. 'You mean an asylum?'

'Most likely Bethlem. I will take a ride there today.' Janus looks at Anna. 'And before you ask, I will not take a lady to a place like that.'

* * *

I'm in the entrance hall of a grand house. The floor is tiled in a checkerboard of black and white. Two men stand, engaged in dialogue. Their lips move but I can't make out what they say. Ghost-like, I slip past them and ascend red-carpeted stairs. My footsteps make no sound. I reach the landing and a second flight of stairs giving way to a third. The floorboards are bare but I tiptoe on, a phantom casting no shadow. At the top is a door. I stand for a moment, my hand on the latch, and listen.

A trolley wakes me as it rumbles past my bed. It's the other side of the curtain so I can't tell whether it's food or medicine.

'Have we got the test results back?' asks a voice I don't recognise.

'No, still waiting on the psych report,' someone answers. Their footsteps move away.

What tests? There's a file in the rack at the foot of my bed. I wriggle towards it but I can't reach it because of the IV attached to my arm. As I lay back, a piece of card on the headboard behind me catches my eye. I snatch it down. *'Nil by mouth'*. What am I doing here?

Last night I heard screaming. Or was that a dream? No, it was too real. What are they doing to the people here? Is this some sort of asylum? I'm not mad. Why are they locking me away?

'Help,' I shout. 'Let me go.'

A nurse steps through the curtain. 'Hello Anna. I'm just going to check your obs.'

Shhh, act normal. 'Where's Matt?'

'He'll be back soon.' The nurse holds a thermometer to my

ear.

Did Matt bring me here? Is he in on this? I push the nurse away. 'No, no.'

'Now, now. Calm down, Anna.'

What are they plotting? The nurse is trying to keep me quiet. I've got to get out of here. I push her away, struggling to climb out of bed.

'Can I get some help in here?' The nurse presses a button on the wall and a male orderly appears.

'No,' I say as I float into darkness.

* * *

As the landau makes its way up the drive, Anna stares out at the domed clocktower and the imposing stone portico supported by six Georgian pillars. 'Wow. Not what I was expecting. It looks like a palace.'

'This is it, Bethlem,' Janus answers. 'The symmetrical façade gives it that palatial impression.' He steps from the carriage and helps Anna down. 'Come on.' Taking Anna arm, he escorts her through the main doorway.

A podgy young man tugs at the fastenings of his tailcoat as he approaches. 'You're here for the viewing, sir?'

'No.' Janus glances around the high-ceilinged entrance hall. 'We would like to speak with the superintendent.'

'I will see if he is available, sir.' The young man trots off.

'Viewing?' whispers Anna.

'I fear 'tis a popular pastime.' Janus frowns. 'For a few pennies, one might gawk at the inmates all day long.'

Anna gasps. 'No!'

The young man returns. 'Follow me, sir.' He leads them to

a small office.

As they enter, the superintendent rises from his desk. 'How may I assist you, sir?'

'I believe a lady, Isabella Pym, may have been admitted here in the last day or so?'

The superintendent opens his ledger and runs his finger down the page. 'No one by that name. There was a Bella Browning, brought in two nights ago by her husband.'

Janus glances at Anna and raises an eyebrow. 'Might we see the lady?' he asks the superintendent, dropping a small pouch of coins onto the desk.

The superintendent addresses the young man. 'Fetch Doctor Hasler.' He turns back to Janus. 'If you'd like to take a seat outside, sir, Doctor Hasler will be happy to escort you to see Mrs Browning.'

Anna perches on the bench outside the superintendent's office, while Janus paces up and down. 'Let us hope Doctor Hasler does not keep us waiting too long.'

They both turn at the sound of footsteps approaching from along the corridor. A bearded man hurries towards them. As he reaches Janus, he extends his hand. 'How do you do. I am Doctor Hasler.' He shakes their hands. 'I understand you wish to see Mrs Browning?'

'Indeed, we do,' replies Janus.

'This way, sir.'

Anna and Janus follow the doctor down a long passageway. They pass a wooden staircase, stopping to give way to a well-dressed couple descending.

'Thank you,' says the man tipping his hat.

As the couple make their way out, the man whispers

something in his companion's ear. She chortles with laughter.

Janus turns to Anna and points up the staircase. 'That is the viewing platform.'

Anna shudders as she peers up at the walkway above.

They continue to follow the doctor through a warren of corridors until finally he stops. He lifts a key from the chain around his waist and unlocks the door to a small square room. A narrow, glazed panel high up in the brickwork lets in the only light. A woman in a soiled nightgown is sitting cross-legged on the single cot. Her matted black hair hangs in rat tails down her back as she rocks backwards and forwards. Scratch marks on her upper arms look as if they've been caused from her fingernails digging into her flesh.

Anna gasps. 'Did you say she's only been here two days?'

'That is correct,' replies Doctor Hasler.

Anna approaches the bed and whispers, 'Isabella?'

The woman stops rocking and looks up, revealing her swollen face and blotchy eyes.

Anna turns to Janus with a quizzical expression.

'Doctor Hasler,' says Janus. 'There appears to have been a mistake. This is not Isabella Pym.'

'You asked to see the woman brought here by her husband. This is that woman, Bella Browning.'

Janus shakes his head and turns to Anna. 'We should leave.'

As they head for the door the woman points at Janus. 'I knows you.'

Janus clears his throat. 'Doctor Hasler, might we have a few minutes alone with Mrs Browning?'

'This is highly irregular.'

Janus slips a few coins into the doctor's hand.

'Well, perhaps a few minutes. Knock on the door when you

are ready to leave. I will be outside.' The doctor leaves the room.

Janus lowers himself down to the woman. 'You know me?'

She shrinks away.

'Let me try.' Anna takes a step towards the cot. 'Hello, Bella. We'd like to speak with you for a few moments if that's all right?'

The woman glares at Anna. 'I ain't Bella.'

Anna steps closer and perches on the edge of the straw mattress. 'Then, what is your name?'

'Edith.'

'Don't be afraid, Edith.' Anna takes Edith's hand. 'We just want to ask you a few questions. Do you know a Nathanial Pym?'

'No, miss.' Tears stream down Edith's face.

'Mister Pym didn't bring you here?'

Edith shakes her head. 'No, 'twere my gentleman. He's abandoned me, that's what he's done.' Pulling away from Anna, she covers her face with her hands. 'I been a fool, tricked and duped. I ain't saying no more, I ain't saying nothing. He says I'll be in trouble for what I done but he's the one what should be in trouble.'

'Edith.' Anna speaks with a gentle tone. 'We want to understand. To see if we can help.'

'I ain't saying no more.' Edith removes her hands from her face and her eyes narrow. 'I don't know you. Who are yer?' Her eyes shift to Janus again, her voice rising to a high-pitched shrill. 'But I seen you afore.'

The key turns in the lock and the doctor re-enters the room. 'I think it is clear the patient is becoming distressed. I am afraid I must ask you to leave.'

Anna steps towards Janus. 'Perhaps it's your presence,' she whispers. 'I feel sure she'd say more if we were on our own.'

Janus protests. 'I cannot let you do that.'

'I'll be fine. You go.' Anna pushes him towards the door.

Once the men have left, Anna sits again on the bed next to Edith and hands her a linen kerchief.

Edith takes it. She examines the lace border before blowing her nose and offering it back.

'You keep it. Edith, you say you know Mister Gregory?'

'I seen him. At the Foundling Hospital with that Mister Wilkes.'

'But it wasn't Mister Pym who brought you here?'

'I already told yer, I don't know no Mister Pym.' Edith sniffs. 'It were Henry Quinn. He's the one what took advantage of me.'

'Henry Quinn? Do you mean Henri Quintar?'

'Henri? Stuff and nonsense. He's always been plain Henry to me. Known 'im since he were a nipper. His ma too, God rest her soul.'

'His mother's dead?'

'Died of consumption when he were nowt but a lad. My Henry was always gonna make something of himself.' Edith smiles. 'Talked his way up and got hisself a good job. Went abroad, he did. To France. That's where he picked up them fancy airs and graces. But not with me, never with his Edith. He's always been my Henry.'

'You and Henry are a couple?' Anna tries to keep incredulity from her voice. 'Edith, you said you'd seen Mister Gregory at the Foundling Hospital?'

Edith nods. ''Twere my Henry that got me the job. Course, he were after something. I had t' pass on information, see?

253

Perhaps I knowed too much?' Her sob shudders through her. 'Henry tricked me. He brought me here and got me locked away. The more I protest, the more it confirms what he's told that doctor.' Edith digs her fingernails into her arm.

Anna reaches out, taking Edith's hand to stop her.

'They says best chance I got of getting out is to admit I'm his wife. Wife?' Edith's laugh is manic. 'Chance 'ud be a fine thing. As if Henry would marry me. Got hisself a fancy woman over in Paris, so I hear. Runs the same racket out there.'

'I'm sorry.' Anna squeezes Edith's fingers.

'Henry's my gentleman. I know'd it wouldn't go nowhere, but I never dreamed he'd betray me like this. Not after all I done.'

'What did you do, Edith?'

'Alerted him which ones were ready to be moved. He picked the best ones and sold 'em. Got a good price for 'em on the ships once I'd fattened 'em up. Poor little sods, I gived 'em extra rations, see? Once they'd got some strength in 'em, they were good to go up the mills or down the mines. Now my Henry's gone and abandoned me.' Edith breaks down, blowing her nose noisily into the kerchief once more.

'Leave it to me, Edith.' Anna stands up. 'I'll do all I can to get you out of here.' She knocks on the door signalling she's ready to leave.

Doctor Hasler escorts Anna to his office where they find Janus sitting at the desk, poring over a ledger.

Janus looks up as they enter, addressing the doctor. 'Five more minutes?'

Doctor Hasler leaves them alone.

'You're not going to believe this.' Anna perches on the desk.

'It was Quintar who had Edith locked up.'

'Quintar?' Janus stands up. 'Surely not.'

'Edith worked at the Foundling Hospital. That's why she recognised you. She used to tip Quintar off when there were children suitable to sell.'

'So Quintar has been creaming off the strongest foundlings?' Janus paces the small room. 'But this makes no sense.'

'Apparently, Henry, as Edith calls him, runs a similar scam in Paris. Edith thinks he's got a woman there doing the same thing as her.'

'*l'Hôpital des Enfants-Trouvés.* It is near Notre Dame. Quintar's experience in Paris was the reason the London Foundling Hospital engaged him as a financial consultant.' Janus returns to the ledger, running his finger across an entry. 'This says Isabella Pym was here a few years ago, checked in under the fake name of Bella Browning. Hasler did not work here back then; Isabella was in the care of a Doctor Jamieson. Hasler says Jamieson retired to Scotland last year. Could Quintar have somehow acquired her medical records so he could make out that Edith was Isabella? If so, Pym must be in on this.' Janus shakes his head. 'I cannot believe they are working together. Why?'

'Money?'

'Money certainly equates to power. You saw how easily I persuaded the superintendent and the doctor to let us in.' Janus paces again. 'No wonder Quintar was reluctant for me to help you with the search for John Benson. He suspected I might discover what he was up to. I would not be surprised if it was him who persuaded Tweedie and Pestlemore to kidnap you.'

'Why would they want me out of the way?'

255

'You are a valuable commodity. Think how much you could tell the world about the future? The Royal Society would be most interested.'

'But what was Quintar's scheme? Can he really make that much money from foundlings?'

'Selling on the stronger foundlings from the hospital as well as using alternative foster homes to rear children and sell them to mill owners and master sweeps. Quite lucrative I would think, especially if operating in both London and Paris.'

'It's immoral.'

Janus shrugs. 'I suppose 'tis not all bad. Nine out of ten children without a stable home die in their first year.'

'You're not saying Quintar has helped these children?'

'No, of course not, but some children suffer a worse fate. What I cannot work out is what hold Quintar has over Pym. Yes, Isabella spent time here a few years ago, but that would not be enough for Quintar to blackmail Pym into handing over her medical records.'

'What about Edith?'

'Once we get to the bottom of this, I am sure I will be able to get her released.' Janus pulls a watch from his waistcoat. 'I need to locate Pym, but first we must visit One-eyed Pete.'

'Can we take Mercy with us? She's the only one who can identify John.'

'Certainly. We will pick up Khan on the way too.'

'Where do we find One-eyed Pete?'

'The Rookery, St Giles. Be prepared, for 'tis not a desirable place for a lady.'

* * *

Matt closes his eyes, letting steaming water cascade over his stiff shoulders. If only they hadn't argued... but Debbie was bad news and he couldn't let Anna get sucked into that again. He shouldn't have got angry, but how did Anna expect him to react when she compared Debbie with his own mother? That was crossing a line.

He steps out of the shower, towels himself dry and walks through to the bedroom to check his mobile. Nothing from the hospital. After getting dressed, he heads for the kitchen, flicks the switch on the kettle and drops two slices of bread in the toaster. He reaches to take the milk from the fridge and grabs a packet of bacon.

Matt enters Ward 14 to find Anna's bed stripped bare. He checks his watch. Ten-thirty – he's only been gone a couple of hours. His heart pounds. 'Where is she?' he yells.

A nurse he hasn't met hurries across from the other side of the ward. 'Excuse me, sir, you're disturbing the patients. Take a seat and I'll be with you shortly.'

Matt huffs as he sits down on the plastic chair beside the empty bed.

After a few moments, the nurse returns. 'Who was it you were looking for?'

'Anna Stratton.' Matt puts his hand to his head. 'I don't understand, I've not been gone long. She was right here.'

'All right, sir, we'll sort it out.'

Matt follows the nurse over to the nurses' station where she taps the computer keyboard and scans the screen. 'Ah, there we are, Anna Stratton. She's been transferred to Ward 22.'

'Thanks.' Matt races to the lift, stopping before stepping in to consult the map on the wall. *You are here,* it helpfully informs him. Ward 22, shown in orange, is on the sixth floor. Matt refers to the key. Orange is a Psych ward.

He steps into the lift, pushes the button and leans against the wall. What the hell happened while he was gone? And why didn't they call him?

The reception area is positioned beside big double doors. 'Can I help you?' asks a formidable looking receptionist.

'I'm here to see Anna Stratton. She's been transferred up from Ward 14.'

'Visiting hours are three until five.' The receptionist returns her attention to the computer.

Matt raises himself to his full six feet two inches. 'I want to see her now. I also want to know why the fuck no-one rang to say they were transferring her.'

The receptionist stands up. 'You need to calm down, sir,' – she takes a deep breath – 'or I shall be forced to call security.'

Matt deflates like a punctured balloon. 'Sorry, sorry.'

'That's better. Now, why don't you get yourself some water from the drinking fountain over there while I see if I can find someone to speak with you.'

Matt walks across to the fountain and fills a cone with water. After gulping it down, he wipes his brow, refills the cone and moves back to sit on a seat adjacent to the desk.

A few minutes later the doors open and a female doctor emerges. 'I understand you're here to see Anna Stratton. Why don't we have a chat?'

Avoiding further eye contact with the receptionist, Matt follows the doctor through the doors and along the corridor to a small meeting room.

'Please, take a seat.' The doctor sits down in one of two comfy chairs and gestures for Matt to join her. 'My name's Doctor Lawrence. I'm one of the hospital's resident psychiatrists and I'm in charge of this unit. And you are?'

Matt sits in the other chair. 'I'm Anna's boyfriend, Matthew Vine. I'm her next of kin. Her parents live abroad.'

'Right, good. Can I get you anything? Cup of tea? Coffee?'

'No thanks.' Matt eyes the box of tissues on the coffee table.

Doctor Lawrence opens a buff folder. 'It must have come as quite a shock to find Anna had been moved up here.'

'No-one rang me.'

'I'm sorry about that. It's always a bit hectic in the mornings. Someone would have been in touch later today.'

Matt sits forward. 'Why's she been moved?'

'I'm afraid she became increasingly agitated.'

'She woke up?'

'Anna awoke very confused.' Doctor Lawrence peers at Matt over her glasses. 'She said something about having been bound and gagged.'

'What the hell are you suggesting?'

'I'm not suggesting anything, Mr Vines. Hallucinations can happen when someone's been unconscious for a while.' The doctor thumbs through the notes. 'I see she was confused when admitted? I understand they had to sedate her.'

'Sedated? I thought she was asleep.'

'No. Look, sometimes the hospital has to make decisions in the best interests of the patient and other patients around them. Earlier this morning it was in Anna's best interests to be moved here for observation.'

'But she will be okay?'

'Well, that's what we're trying to establish. There doesn't seem to be any clinical reason for her seizures. At the moment we're examining all possibilities. The staff up here are better

259

equipped to deal with patients who present as confused.'

'Can I see her?'

'Yes, yes of course. But I have to warn you, Anna is heavily sedated. She'll be out of it for a few hours. Why don't you go and get yourself something to eat? Take a walk, come back later.'

'No, I'm not leaving her again.'

'I understand.' Doctor Lawrence picks up Anna's file and stands up. 'Let's go and find her then, shall we?'

* * *

The landau pulls up outside the Astleys' house and Anna gets out. She runs down the basement stairs and knocks on the door.

Mercy answers. 'Miss Anna?'

Anna takes Mercy's hands. 'Fetch your shawl, Mercy. There's a chance we've tracked down your John.'

Janus is holding open the carriage door. 'Mistress Benson.'

Mercy blushes as she clambers aboard. She sits beside Anna while Janus takes the seat next to Khan.

Anna reaches for Mercy's hand. 'We don't know for certain that it's John. That's why we're bringing you along. To see if you recognise him.'

'It be me boy.' Mercy pats her chest. 'I feels it in me heart.' She closes her eyes and moves her lips in silent prayer.

They head into the Rookery, a maze of passageways and dead ends with wooden houses crammed together like a shanty town. As their route becomes increasingly impossible to navigate, they are forced to abandon the landau and walk.

Khan takes the lead along narrow alleys while the others follow. Gutters are overflowing with slops and the stench is overpowering. Janus hands Anna his kerchief to cover her mouth and nose.

As they round a corner, Anna gasps at the sight in front of them. A couple, the woman's skirts lifted high as the man thrusts her against a wall. Further on they pass another woman, hair matted and clothed in rags, she swigs from an earthenware jar while two small children play barefoot in the filth at her feet.

'Gin.' Mercy shakes her head.

They reach a row of wretched houses, broken windows patched with rags and paper.

Khan halts. 'This is One-eyed Pete's abode.'

Janus raps sharply on a wooden door.

A young woman, wearing a dirty woollen skirt and shawl, opens the door. She curtseys. 'Evening to you, sir. You be wanting my Pete? He's settling the boys, but I can call him for yer?'

Janus tips his hat. 'Might we come in?'

The woman shrinks back against the wall. 'Pete,' she yells, 'there be gentlefolk 'ere.'

They step past her and enter a room so small they immediately fill it. The straw-filled mattress suggests this is the only living space, with a chair in front of the grate and a pot of what smells like vegetable stew suspended above the fire.

A man wearing a patch over his left eye appears from a doorway at the back. Ignoring Anna, Mercy and Khan, he addresses Janus. 'Yes, sir. What can I be doing for yer? If you's in need of yer chimneys swept, most gentlefolk send their servants to make arrangements.'

261

'We are here on a delicate matter.' Janus removes his hat. 'We would like to see your boys.'

'Me boys, sir?' One-eyed Pete puffs his chest. 'I don't want no trouble now. If one of me boys has taken something from yer, sir, weren't nowt to do wi' me.'

'We're not here to accuse anyone of anything.' Anna links arms with Mercy. 'It's possible that one of your boys is the son of this woman.'

Pete's cheeks turn crimson. His right eye bulges as he raises his fists.

Janus steps forward. 'As Mistress Stratton has said, we are not here to cause trouble. If it should turn out that this woman's son is in your employ, you will, of course, be reimbursed.'

Pete drops his arms to his sides. 'Well, sir. Me boys are valuable.' He scratches his ear. ''Twould have to be a fair sum.'

Janus inclines his head.

Pete leads them outside to a squalid backyard where a lean-to precariously clings to the back wall of the house.

'He surely doesn't keep children here,' murmurs Anna.

Pete cusses as he struggles to slide the rusty bolt. 'Come on, yer bugger.'

''Tis not unusual,' whispers Janus.

Having succeeded, Pete yanks open the door.

Anna steps forward, squinting into the gloom. The shed is full of chimney sweeping paraphernalia, long rods and brushes and… two pairs of eyes stare back at her. Anna gasps. 'They live in there?'

Pete folds his arms. 'They's fed ain't they? Sleeping black they is. Helps t' toughen the skin.'

Anna shakes her head. 'Their lungs must be full of soot.'

Pete gestures towards a tin bath hanging from the wall. 'Me missus gives 'em a bath once a week.' Pete raises his voice. 'Come on out, boys. These gentlefolk want t' take a look at yer.'

The boys crawl from their makeshift bed of sacking, the first emerging on hands and knees. As the scrawny lad unfolds, he is surprisingly tall and covered in soot from the top of his head to his bare feet.

'This 'ere be Jack.' Pete stands with hands on his hips. 'He's a good lad. Been with me four years or more.'

'You must be Sid's brother,' says Anna.

Jack blinks. 'Yes, miss.'

'Let us be sure.' Janus nods at Khan. 'Please, do the honours.'

Khan reaches for Jack by the scruff of his collar. 'Head f'ward.' Pulling a kerchief from his sleeve, Khan rubs at a patch of skin at the back of the boy's neck. Under the soot his flesh is pale. Khan spits on the kerchief and rubs even harder at the boy's hairline revealing a ginger hue to his hair. Khan turns to Janus. 'This appears to be Jack.'

Pete scoffs. 'Didn't I tell yer as much?'

The second child still cowers in the doorway.

'Come out, boy,' bellows Pete.

The child shuffles forward on his knees, his hands over his ears.

'What is this child's name?' asks Janus.

Pete scratches his head. 'Ain't got no name. I jest calls 'im boy.'

Mercy takes a step forward, her hands clasped to her chest.

Khan pulls the boy up and repeats the process. Unlike Jack's neck, the boy's skin tone is olive. Khan scrubs at the soot on the boy's head, but his hair remains black as night.

'It be me boy,' Mercy cries. 'This be my John.' She grabs the boy to her and hugs him tight.

The boy holds himself rigid in her embrace.

'Well now, sir, I can't be doing me job without this 'un.' Pete scratches his stubbly chin. 'He's small, see? Just the ticket for 'em small flues.'

Janus puts an arm across Pete's shoulder and leads him the few steps to the back of the yard.

After a short exchange of words, Pete spits on his palm and holds it out to shake Janus's hand. 'Pleasure doing business wi' yer, sir.' Pete takes the small bag of coins from Janus and tucks it into his shirt. 'Now, if you should be wantin' any more lads, you knows where I is.'

Janus puts his hat on his head, signalling they should leave. Khan lifts the boy up and throws him over his shoulder like a sack of potatoes. Hastened by the sounds of squabbling and swearing from the dwellings on either side, they weave their way back through the honeycomb of blind alleys.

Mercy trots along at Khan's heels. 'Don't be going so fast, you'll make 'im dizzy. Mind 'is head on that wall…'

On reaching the landau, the ladies scramble aboard and Khan deposits the child on the seat between them. The boy's eyes are wide and he's shivering from head to toe.

Like rescuing a mistreated animal, thinks Anna, passing Mercy a blanket.

Mercy wraps the boy up and strokes his head. 'Soon have yer home,' she whispers. 'Told yer I'd come.'

The boy buries his face in Mercy's cloak. He doesn't look up.

It is dusk by the time they arrive back at Duke Street. Khan lifts out the boy and places him at the top of the basement steps. Mercy climbs down to join him. The front of her travelling cloak is covered in soot.

Anna leans out of the carriage window. 'I'll come and see you in the morning, Mercy.'

As they drive away, Anna leans back in her seat. 'Is the boy really her John?'

Janus smiles. 'You witnessed the expression on Mercy Benson's face? She believes that he is.'

Khan tuts. 'Does it matter? You saw the conditions the boy was living in. If the Benson woman is willing to give him a home, that has to be better for the child.'

13th September

Janus and Elizabeth are chatting in the hallway when Anna comes downstairs.

Janus turns to Anna. 'I told William not to disturb you.'

'Well, my dear.' Elizabeth kisses Anna on both cheeks. 'I am mighty glad to have the chance to bid you farewell.'

Anna glances at the grandfather clock. 'You're away early. Have you eaten?'

'I prefer an early start when I am travelling.' Elizabeth buttons up her cloak.

'Mrs Lawson has provided Elizabeth with a basketful of goodies. She will not go hungry on the journey.' Janus takes Elizabeth's hands. 'Well, sister. Your bags are loaded and your carriage awaits.'

Elizabeth embraces him. 'You do look after me, brother. Now, promise to come down to Tunbridge Wells at the beginning of next month for Ernest's birthday?' She turns to Anna. 'We shall be having a small gathering. I hope you will make the journey too? I have become quite fond of you.'

'And I you, but I'm afraid I won't be here next month.'

'Mistress Anna travels herself very soon.' Janus wears a mournful smile. 'I fear she will be away for some time.'

'Oh Janus. Why do you relay such bad news, just as I am

about to depart? Now I feel quite out of sorts.'

Janus leads his sister out to the waiting carriage, holding her hand to help her to board.

Anna waves as the post chaise disappears into Brook Street.

'How are you?' Janus asks as he pours two cups of tea in the breakfast room.

'I feel,' – Anna sits down at the table – 'like a burden has been lifted.'

'Because we found the boy?'

'If it's really him.'

Janus places a cup in front of Anna before taking a seat to join her.

'Thank you.' Anna sips her tea. 'Any news of Pym?'

'Not yet. Elizabeth was right. Pym and Isabella do indeed appear to have vanished.'

'And where is Mister Khan this morning?'

'I sent him along to the Foundling Hospital to see what he might discover.' Janus drums his fingertips on the arm of the carver.

Anna grins. 'Hopefully he'll be some time.'

Janus frowns.

'Sorry.' She glances at him. 'Is something the matter?'

'Khan and I had words. I hate it when we are out of step.' Janus sighs. 'The trouble is he does have a point.'

Anna places her cup down on the table. 'What was your disagreement about?'

'Khan suspects I have become too involved with you.'

Anna blushes. 'And have you?'

Janus gazes at her. 'What do you think?'

Anna swallows. 'Do you think Mister Khan will uncover

267

the evidence you need?'

'I hope so. A person of Quintar's standing engaging in such skullduggery cannot go unnoticed.'

'Do you mean his relationship with Edith?'

'Well, yes.' Janus picks up his cup, holding it ready to drink. 'But also if he had the audacity to meet with Fripp at the Foundling Hospital, then someone must know something.' Janus sips his tea. 'I fear I have been played for a fool and I do not appreciate disloyalty.' He grimaces. 'I am in need of something stronger.' Getting up, he strides across to the sideboard.

'Did you manage to secure Edith's release from the Bethlem?'

'I shall be drafting a stern letter to the superintendent this very morning.' Janus pours a brandy and waves the decanter. 'Would you like one?'

Anna frowns. 'No, thank you. It's too early for me. And anyway, I need to go and see Mercy.'

Janus sits back down. 'You intend to raise doubt in her mind?'

'Not necessarily.' Anna sighs. 'She looked so happy, so convinced.'

'And yet?' He swirls his brandy around the glass.

'It's just… I think she should be able to know for sure that the boy is hers.'

'How do you propose we prove that?'

Anna gets up from her chair. 'I don't know. Perhaps you and Khan are right. Whether the boy is hers or not, she will give him a loving home.'

'Khan has the landau.'

'That's fine, I'll walk.'

* * *

Matt spends a second night in a chair beside Anna's bed. She stirs occasionally, at one point opening her eyes. Matt's sure she tries to smile at him before closing them once more.

Matt watches as nurses come and go, taking Anna's obs. His mobile rings. Moving out into the corridor, Matt presses the answer button. 'Hi Zoe.'

'Thought I'd give you a quick call before I head off for work. How is she?'

'Still out of it. Can you believe that they've moved her to a psych ward?'

'What the fuck? Why?'

'I don't know. They said she was confused.' He lowers his voice. 'I'm not sure they know what they're doing.'

'I should have come back last night.'

'It wouldn't have made any difference.'

'How are you doing?'

'I'm okay.' Matt rubs his eyes.

'Did you speak to her mum and dad?'

'Not yet.'

'Don't you think they need to know?'

'No, not yet.'

A doctor is striding down the corridor towards him.

'Look, I've got to go. I'll call you later.' Matt ends the call as the doctor reaches Anna's door.

'Mr Vines?'

'Yes.' Matt slides the phone into his jeans pocket as he follows the doctor into Anna's room.

The doctor turns to face him. 'I'm Doctor Ashmael. I'm a neurologist. I'm sorry about the mix up yesterday. It must have been a shock to find Anna had been moved up here.'

'You can say that again.'

'Anna was very disturbed, which forced the duty doctor to take the decision to move her. However, I tend to agree with you that the psych unit is not necessarily the best place for her.'

Matt exhales. 'Great.'

'No, Mr Vines, I'm afraid you misunderstand me. Data from Anna's obs shows signs of deterioration. If things don't improve, I shall be moving her to ITU, that's medical ITU. The paranoia might be an indicator of a neurological problem. There could be something pressing against her brain.'

Matt grabs the back of the chair to steady his legs. 'A tumour?'

'We can't rule that out. Alternatively, it could be a bleed to the brain caused by the fall. Or possibly an infection. We need to decide what to try next. Perhaps a spinal tap.'

'When will you move her?'

'As soon as we have a bed. We'll keep a close eye on her over the next couple of hours.' Doctor Ashmael pats Matt's shoulder before walking towards the door. He turns back. 'Mr Vines? Does Anna have other family you should call?'

Matt slumps into the chair and stares at the floor. After a few moments, he pulls out his mobile and presses a button. 'Zoe?'

* * *

Anna turns into Duke Street and spots a post chaise down the road. Is it outside the Astleys' house? She jogs the last few steps.

'Wilt thou be long, lad?' the driver calls to a young man loading the luggage.

The young man heaves another trunk onto the rack. 'Mercy?' he yells over his shoulder. 'You and the lad ready?'

'Stop mithering, Simkins. We's coming fast as we can.' Mercy runs up the basement steps. Her face lights up when she sees Anna. 'Oh, miss. I'm that pleased to see yer. I feared we might not meet again.'

'I couldn't let you go without saying goodbye.' Anna takes Mercy's hands. 'You look happy.'

Mercy beams. 'I be grand now I got me boy.' She turns back to the house. 'Come on, John.'

The boy emerges, squinting in the morning sun.

Anna grins. 'He's cleaned up well.'

'I near enough scrubbed the skin from his back.' Mercy pats his head. 'Look how his hair glows?'

'You've transformed him.'

Mercy adjusts the boy's jacket. 'I been saving these clothes… see how well they do fit?'

Mrs Marsh emerges with one last bag. She hands it to Simkins and stands waiting with her arms folded.

Simkins tuts as he surveys the loaded luggage rack.

'Never mind, I'll take it in wi' us.' Mercy grabs the bag and turns to Anna. 'I best get John aboard.' She ushers the boy into the carriage and places the bag on the floor.

The boy squashes his nose against the glass to peer out at Mercy through the window.

'That's right, I's coming.' Mercy hesitates a moment longer before stepping forward and flinging her arms around Anna. 'Oh, Miss Anna. I can never thank yer enough for what you done. I be forever in yer debt.'

'Nonsense.' Anna hugs Mercy back.

'You'll pass on my thanks to Mister Gregory? He's such a gent.'

'Of course.' Anna pulls away gently. 'John's doing okay, then?'

'It'll take time before he settles. 'Tis all an adventure. Don't think he's quite grasped we be leaving London for good.'

The horses are skittish. The driver cusses as he tugs at the reins.

'We needs to be off,' says Simkins.

'Mercy,' – Anna lowers her voice – 'have you told John that he's your son?'

Mercy shakes her head. 'Not yet. We's taking it slow. He don't even know his name. That sweep just called him "boy". We got a lot of catching up to do. But I'd know my John anywhere. Look at his dark curls, just like my beau's.'

Mrs Marsh catches Anna's eye.

Anna swallows. 'Mercy, I wonder…'

Simkins clambers up to sit beside the driver. 'Ready, Mercy?'

'Just about. Well, can't stand around here all day.' Mercy turns to hug Mrs Marsh.

Mrs Marsh drops her head and closes her eyes.

Mercy steps away and climbs into the carriage. Mrs Marsh slams the door, and the driver swishes his whip.

Anna waves as the post chaise pulls away and disappears around the corner. 'She's so sure.'

'Yes, and that be the main thing. It be a new start for the both of 'em.' Mrs Marsh rubs her hands together. 'Well, I must get on. Lord and Lady Astley return in a few days and this house won't ready itself.'

272

* * *

Zoe walks onto Ward 22 waving a brown paper bag. 'Lunch. BLT and a latte?'

'You're a star, I'm starving.' Matt takes the bag.

Zoe drags a chair over to the other side of Anna's bed and sits down. 'No change then?'

'No, and apart from going to the loo, I haven't left her.' Matt bites into his sandwich. 'Did you get hold of her mum and dad?'

'Yeah, I managed to Facetime them on the yacht.' Zoe frowns. 'They've booked a flight, but it'll take hours for them to get back to harbour and drive to the airport.'

Matt groans. 'Why didn't I ring them before?'

'Because you didn't know how serious this would get. No-one did. Christ, Anna was out with me the other day. No-one could have predicted this.'

'I should have known.' Matt pulls the lid from his latte and stirs it. 'I should have seen it coming, insisted they do more tests.'

'You can't know everything, Matt.'

He smiles. 'You sound just like Anna.'

'Sorry.'

'It's okay, I know she talks to you. She's always telling me I try to fix everything.'

Matt lifts the second sandwich to his mouth.

Zoe removes the empty sandwich wrapper from the bed.

'It's only because I love her,' Matt continues, 'because I care.'

Zoe concentrates on folding the cardboard wrapper into triangles.

'What?' asks Matt.

Zoe sighs. 'This is not the time…'

'No, go on.'

'Well, it's just… Anna's not a kid. She makes mistakes, we all do. Perhaps you need to give her the space to make them?'

'Oh shit.' Matt rubs his face. 'Am I going to lose her?'

'She's going to be fine.' Zoe gets up and chucks the wrapper into the bin. 'Anyway, what about letting Debbie know?'

'I've spoken to that Brenda woman.' Matt blows his nose on the paper serviette. 'Did you know Anna's been emailing her again? Apparently, Debbie's done a runner and they've no way of contacting her. Maybe it's just as well with Anna's mum and dad on the way.'

'Anna's in the best possible hands. From what you've told me, this Doctor Ashmael seems to know what he's talking about.'

'Yeah.'

A nurse sticks her head around the door. 'The team are on their way now to move Anna to ITU.' She smiles apologetically at Zoe. 'I'm afraid visiting is very restricted up there.'

'It's okay. I'm going anyway.' Zoe leans over Anna and kisses her cheek. 'See you soon, hun. Stop all this buggering about.' She puts a hand to her mouth as her voice breaks. Her eyes glaze as she turns to hug Matt. 'You know where I am.'

* * *

William greets Anna at the door. 'Ah, Mistress Anna. Mister Gregory has been awaiting your return.' William takes her cloak and ushers her in.

Janus and Pym are seated in the drawing room. Janus gets up as she enters. 'Mistress Stratton. Please, come and sit

274

down.' He turns to Pym. 'Perhaps you might repeat what you have just told me.'

Pym takes a deep breath before looking Anna in the eye. 'I am afraid I did play a small part in your abduction and for that I am truly sorry.'

Anna stares at him. 'But why would you do that?'

Pym shrugs. 'I had no choice. To refuse would have put my family at risk. I assure you no harm would have come to you. It was simply a means of getting the Prism project back on track.'

Janus slams his fist against the arm of his chair. 'You seriously believed I might focus more on our project with Mistress Stratton out of the way? Ye gods, what were you thinking?'

Pym looks down at his hands.

Janus exhales. 'I find it hard to understand why you were helping Quintar with his exploitation of the foundlings. It is not as if you needed the money.'

Pym raises his head. 'It was never about money.'

Anna exchanges a glance with Janus.

'For years I have watched those desperate women going to any lengths to get rid of their babies. Before moving to London, I lived in Surrey.' Pym looks at Janus. 'You will recall I sat on the Magistrate's Panel?'

Janus sits forward. 'I remember.'

'A dreadful case came before the prosecution. A young girl living with a well-to-do farmer. When he found out she was pregnant he wanted nothing more to do with her, so she travelled to a nearby county to ask relatives for help. On the way she went into labour. She was writhing in pain when a magistrate rode by. Not wanting the cost of another child on his doorstep, he told her if she didn't move along, she'd be thrown in gaol.'

Anna puts her hand to her mouth. 'That's terrible. Could he really do that?'

Pym mops his brow with a kerchief. 'The girl did not get far before she gave birth. As she sat by the river, her baby in her arms, she pondered her fate. If she were free of the baby she could work.' Pym swallows. 'She hit the baby's head against a fallen tree, tied it in her apron and threw it in the river.'

Anna gasps. 'Oh my God.'

'Her own child,' continues Pym. 'She told us there was nothing else she could do.'

'What happened to the mother?' asks Janus.

'Hung for the crime of infanticide.' Pym shakes his head. 'Dozens of women each year are hung for this crime. How many more leave babies on rubbish tips, never to be discovered? So, Janus, do not ask why I get involved. I do them a favour. Yes, children who go to foster homes have a hard life, but at least they have a chance.' Pym stands up. 'Which is better? To tell them we have no room or find another way to relieve women of their burden?'

Janus shakes his head. 'You cannot tell me Quintar is not in this for the money.'

Pym's cheeks flush. 'I took no money for my part.'

Anna sighs. 'I still don't understand. Why give Isabella's medical records to Monsieur Quintar?'

Pym shrugs. 'Quintar had an acquaintance in similar circumstances. He wanted to engage the services of the Scottish doctor who helped Isabella. My discretion was paramount.'

'I remain unconvinced.' Janus gets up and takes Pym's arm.

'Come with me. Khan is presently at the Foundling Hospital going through the ledgers. I am determined to get to the bottom of this.'

Anna rises from her seat. 'What about me?'

Janus turns to her. 'I think you should stay here. Ned will serve you luncheon. I will be back in good time for your departure.'

* * *

Janus strides into the records office at the Foundling Hospital. Pym follows with a little more reluctance.

'*Mes amis.*' Quintar greets them as they enter the small room. 'Come, join us.' Quintar gestures to the table where Khan is poring over the ledgers. 'Monsieur Khan has been through the books. He is more than satisfied there is nothing untoward to be discovered.'

Khan looks up. 'Certainly, these ledgers are perfectly in order. However, I am not convinced that I have yet viewed all relevant records.'

Quintar glances at Janus. 'What is Monsieur Khan's meaning?'

'He means that it is over, Quintar.' Janus lifts his chin. 'Pym has told us everything.'

Quintar twiddles his moustache. 'Everything? Then I'm sure Monsieur Pym will have reassured you that what we do here is for the good of *les enfants, n'est-ce pas?*'

'Pym may have acted in good faith, but I suspect, Quintar, your motives are less pure.' Janus steps forward. 'Or should I call you Henry Quinn? You can drop the French accent, for we have spoken with Edith and know all about your business

277

interests, both here and in Paris.'

'That is not all.' Khan pulls a bulky envelope from his jacket. 'These letters and receipts reveal a significant diversion of donations received under the auspices of the Magdalen Project.'

Quintar lurches forward. 'How did you acquire those?'

Khan whisks the envelope from his grasp. 'Mr Thorpe was kind enough to furnish me with them.'

'You blackamoor,' snarls Quintar. 'What business is this of yours?'

'It is my business when I believe my friend is being deceived.' Khan tucks the letters back in his jacket.

Janus tuts. 'No wonder you tried to stop me meeting with Thorpe. You were siphoning off funds from Magdalen.'

Quintar puffs out his chest. 'So, Gregory, what do you intend? Will you call for one of Fielding's "thief takers"? Put me in front of the Bow Street magistrates?'

'Why in God's name would you get involved in all of this?' Janus shakes his head. 'I believed you to be one of my closest friends.'

'Perhaps you do not know me as well as you think?' Quintar laughs. 'But, alas, if I go down, I shall take Mister Pym with me.'

'You blaggard…' Pym lunges forward.

Janus steps between him and Quintar.

Quintar smirks. 'Are you sure, Pym, that you have told Gregory everything? If you have revealed your little secret, I wonder your conscience is not lighter?'

Pym swings his fist, landing a blow on Quintar's chin.

Quintar staggers back. 'You will regret that.'

'Enough,' shouts Janus. 'I will inform the authorities.

Quintar will suffer the consequences of his actions.'

Quintar rubs his chin. 'Perhaps you will not act so hastily, Gregory. There is much I could tell the authorities about the Prism group and your experiments.'

Janus sneers. 'Do your worst.'

'It is a strange coincidence, is it not?' Quintar continues. 'Mistress Stratton arriving at the same time as your underlings summon up a phantom?'

Janus stares at him. 'What do you infer?'

'Come, I am no fool.' Quintar smiles. 'You intend sending the girl back from whence she came. However, that might be a pity. Her presence would be of considerable interest to the Royal Society. Indeed, to the authorities in general.'

Janus pales. 'What is it you want?'

'Ha.' Quintar laughs. 'I believe we may yet strike a deal. Is it not this very night you intend to re-enact the experiment? 'Twould be a pity if that were disrupted.' Quintar straightens his jacket. 'Let me go. The morrow you may do whatever your moral standards dictate. By then I shall be long gone.'

Khan steps forward. 'You cannot allow him to blackmail you, Janus.'

Janus slumps down into a chair. 'What choice do I have?'

Quintar picks up his cloak and cane. At the door he looks back at Janus, tipping his hat. *'Bonne chance, mon ami.'*

* * *

A junior doctor walks into the Intensive Care Unit. He's accompanied by a nurse wheeling a trolley.

'What's all that?' Matt asks as they rig up electrodes to Anna's skull. 'You've already been monitoring her heart rate and she has an IV.'

'EEG,' says the doctor. 'We'll be measuring brain activity for the next couple of hours.'

The nurse smiles at Matt as she feels for Anna's pulse.

After they've gone, Matt takes Anna's hand. 'Come on, babe. Can you hear me?'

The monitors bleep every few seconds. Anna's breathing is deep but not laboured. They can't be too worried, Matt reasons to himself, or they'd be doing more.

The nurse comes back. She tears a strip of paper from one of the machines. The doctor wanders in. The nurse hands him the readings and he checks them before fiddling with a dial on the equipment. He says something to the nurse, but Matt doesn't quite catch it. The nurse nods, and she and the doctor walk off down the ward.

Another nurse comes in and straightens Anna's sheets for the umpteenth time.

Matt sighs, running his hands through his hair.

It's like Mum all over again. Anna's right, he'd tried to fix that too. But you can't fix breast cancer. Dad did his best. During Mum's first rounds of chemo, Dad wore himself out emotionally and physically. When the cancer came back ten years later – stage 4 and terminal – Dad couldn't face a second battle. Instead he found himself a new partner, leaving his son to pick up the pieces. No-one could have tried harder than Matt, but nothing had worked. Perhaps it was Karma, but Dad was dead himself within the year, leaving Matt an orphan.

Matt's mobile pings with a text. He calls back.

'How is she?' asks Zoe

'She's been doing that rapid eye movement thing again. The bleeping from the monitor keeps fluctuating but even when it bleeps fast, no-one comes. I just wish I knew what it meant.'

'They've done more tests?'

'She's had an MRI and they've taken fluid from her spine.'

'What's all that for?'

'They still don't know what's causing it.' Matt sighs. 'I Googled her symptoms again and all the tests they're doing. I think the lumbar puncture is to rule out meningitis.'

Zoe exhales. 'Oh shit.'

'They won't know for a couple of hours.'

'Want me to come back?'

'They won't let you in. I'll call you if there's any change.' Matt hangs up and puts his phone down on the bedside cabinet. He holds Anna's hand. 'Come on, Anna. Wake up.'

* * *

The parlour door is thrown open. William coughs. 'Excuse me, Mistress Stratton. Mister Pym has returned alone.'

Anna hurries out to the hallway. 'Mister Pym. Did you find Monsieur Quintar? Where is Janus?'

'No, I said that I will keep it on…' Pym disengages from the butler's attempts to relieve him of cloak and hat. 'Ah, Mistress Stratton. Yes, we found Monsieur Quintar but were unable to detain him.'

'Please, come through.' Anna leads the way into the parlour. 'Take a seat, Mister Pym, catch your breath.'

'Thank you, but no. There has been a change of plan. I need you to accompany me.'

281

Anna clasps her hands together. 'Janus told me to wait here.'

Pym nods. 'I anticipated this. I warned Gregory you would be unwilling to come. He gave me this.'

Anna takes the note from Pym and breaks the seal.

Anna. Go with Pym. I will meet you there shortly. Janus

'I have a hackney outside,' Pym gestures with his hand. 'We need to leave at once.'

'I'll be coming back here?'

'In all likelihood, but time is of the essence. We must depart right away.'

When Anna rings the bell, William responds immediately.

'William, I'm leaving now with Mister Pym. Mister Gregory is aware. I hope to be back later and then…'

Pym is already by the front door. 'Mistress Stratton, we must go.'

'Yes, sorry.' She gives William a small smile.

Pym guides Anna out to the hackney. The horses stamp their hooves. Pym and Anna climb in and the carriage speeds away.

'Where are we going and what's the rush?' Anna grabs the side of the coach as she's thrown from side to side.

'I apologise for the secrecy. All will be explained.' Pym stares out of the window.

In less than twenty minutes, they pull up outside a large house. Pym steps onto the drive holding out his hand to help Anna down.

'Where are we? Is Janus here?'

'This is the home of my sister-in-law, but she is presently abroad.' Pym rings the bell. 'Gregory will meet us soon.'

The door is opened by a servant. 'Good afternoon, sir.'

'Thank you, Edward.' Pym leads the way to a small drawing

room. 'Please, Mistress Stratton, wait here. I must check everything is in order.'

Left alone, Anna admires a beautiful portrait above the fireplace. Two women, one is Isabella and the other must be her sister as their features are so similar. The artist has skillfully captured sadness in Isabella's eyes. Is that why Pym is always so protective? He never left her alone at the soirée.

'Please, Mistress Stratton, come this way,' Pym says as he returns. 'There is something I want you to see.' He escorts Anna back through the entrance hall and up a fine staircase. They make their way along a corridor. Pym stops and pushes open a door. Putting a finger to his lips, he nods towards the tableau by the window.

Isabella is on the floor with a most enchanting child with curly fair hair sitting beside her. A spinning top entertains them. Isabella spins it across the bare wooden boards. The child claps his chubby hands in glee. His laughter tinkles across to Anna and Pym.

Anna makes to step forward, but Pym bars her way. As they watch the joyful scene, the child suddenly becomes aware of their presence. He smiles in delight, gets up and with arms outstretched, takes wobbly steps towards Pym.

Isabella looks up. She rushes over and scoops the child into her arms as if Anna were a threat.

Whispering into Isabella's ear, Pym wraps his arms around his wife and the child. Isabella's shoulders visibly relax as Pym playfully tweaks the child's nose. He gestures to Anna to leave and quietly they withdraw, making their way back downstairs.

Anna follows Pym into the drawing room. He heads straight for the sideboard. 'Please sit down. I have ordered you some tea.' He pours himself a brandy from the decanter.

Anna makes herself comfortable on the couch. 'Your family are delightful, Mister Pym.'

'Yes, they are both very dear to me.' Pym has his back to Anna. He replenishes his drink, then steps away from the sideboard and slumps down in the armchair facing her.

After a tap on the drawing room door, a maid comes in with refreshments. She sets the tray on the occasional table and pours Anna a cup of tea.

Anna takes the cup proffered. 'Thank you.'

The maid gives a little curtsey and leaves the room.

Anna glances at the clock. 'Where's Janus? You said he'd meet us here?'

'What?' Pym glances up at her. 'Yes, soon.'

'Mister Pym. It is, of course, a great pleasure to see your family but why could we not speak to Isabella? And why did she look so scared?'

Pym sighs. 'I am afraid, Mistress Stratton, Isabella is terrified the child will be taken from her.'

'But why would she think that?'

'Because the child is not theirs.' Recognising the voice, Anna spins around to see Janus enter the room. Pym glances up before turning his attention back to his drink.

'I don't understand,' Anna says as she places her cup back on the tray.

'Tell her, Pym.' Janus pours himself a brandy before sitting down. 'It might do you good to offload your burden.'

Pym exhales deeply. 'Isabella and I wanted a child more than anything. We were so happy when she conceived and delighted when she later gave birth to our beautiful daughter. However, there were complications. Isabella was confined for several days. She lost a lot of blood and the physician told me to prepare myself.' Pym drains the last of his brandy. 'Thank the Lord, Isabella pulled through, but we knew the child would be our first and last. Sadly, within a month, our daughter had grown increasingly sick. I came home one night to find my wife clutching the baby to her breast, the child quite motionless.'

Anna stifles a gasp.

Janus tops up Pym's glass.

Pym continues. 'Isabella was distraught.'

Anna wipes away a tear. 'I'm so sorry.'

Pym takes another sip of brandy. 'She lost her mind. I took her to a doctor to get help.'

'Bella Browning?' Anna looks at Janus for confirmation.

Janus nods. 'Pym did not want Isabella's malady to be common knowledge.'

'She was incarcerated for months and when I brought her home,' – Pym shakes his head – 'I feared for her. She tried several times to take her own life.'

'So,' says Janus. 'You found her another child.'

'Yes, but not from the Foundling Hospital.' Pym answers in an earnest tone. 'Our records are meticulous. In any case, I would not abuse my position in such a way.' He hesitates before continuing. 'Are you acquainted with the foundling wheel at the Convent of St Mary's?'

'I have heard of it,' replies Janus.

'I merely had to await my opportunity.' Pym knocks back the rest of his drink. 'Isabella was overjoyed when I brought the child home.'

Anna puts her hand to her mouth. 'You stole a child?'

Pym ignores her as he reaches out to clutch Janus's arm.

'You must understand, Gregory, I genuinely believed it was the only thing I could do to save my wife. For a while Isabella was confused. She kept referring to the child by our daughter's name.' Pym releases Janus and falls back into his chair. 'The situation has improved. Isabella is a perfect mother. It is only when away from the child that she becomes agitated. In the company of strangers her paranoia returns. She fears everyone is trying to take the child away from her.'

Janus finishes his brandy. 'Quintar figured out your secret.'

'Yes, the swine was blackmailing me.'

'What if the mother should return to claim her son?' asks Anna.

Pym sits forward. 'Neither St Mary's nor the Foundling Hospital have a record. The mother would conclude her child is lost.'

Anna sighs. 'As you expected Mercy to do.'

'Yes, as with the Benson woman.' Pym gets up and points out of the window. 'Look at the life we offer in comparison. How can this be wrong?'

Anna raises her voice. 'But he's not your child.'

Pym smiles. 'Is he not?'

Anna looks out over the extensive gardens. The child is toddling around the flower beds, Isabella chasing after him.

'Look how happy she is. The gardens here relax her. This was once Isabella's childhood home.' Pym turns back to Janus. 'So, tell me, which action is the more noble? Return the child to the hardship of the Foundling Hospital, or leave him where he is happy and loved?'

'But you have risked your reputation and integrity,' says Janus.

'If I have, it was worth it.' Pym sighs. 'What will you do?'

'I will consider the matter.' Janus gazes out at the family scene. 'My priority now is to get Anna home.' He guides Anna to the door, then turns back to Pym. 'Will you join us later?'

Pym continues to look outside and shakes his head.

'Where were you?' Anna asks as she and Janus ride back in the landau.

Janus pats her hand. 'I stayed on at the Foundling Hospital to talk to Wilkes. I am reassured he knew nothing of Quintar's deception or his ill-gotten gains. Wilkes will ensure charges are brought against Quintar and that will prevent him from operating in London in the future.'

'Pym said you were unable to detain Monsieur Quintar?'

'Unfortunately, that is correct.' Janus glances out of the carriage window. 'Wilkes is sending word to his counterpart in Paris in case Quintar should turn up there.'

'How did you find out about Pym and Isabella's child?' asks Anna.

'I asked Doctor Hasler to make further inquiries. Doctor Jamieson's notes from three years ago revealed that Isabella could have no more children.'

'And yet they had a young son.'

'Pym kept the details of Isabella's confinement a secret. Even Elizabeth, one of Isabella's dearest friends, was surprised. With hindsight it was obvious something underhand had taken place. Quintar must have learnt of it and, realising Pym could not risk anyone finding out, exploited the situation.'

'What will you do about Pym?'

'His involvement with the Foundling Hospital goes way back. He has always supported Coram's mission of a hospital for the maintenance and education of deserted children.

287

Quintar deserves to suffer the consequences but Pym's mis-doings are another matter. The child will certainly have everything he needs if he stays with Pym, at least all the time Isabella stays sane. And yet...' Janus sighs.

They travel the rest of the way deep in thought. It is dark as they arrive back in Grevil Street.

Janus shrugs off his cloak as they enter the house. 'William, we will take supper in the parlour.'

'Very good, sir. Mister Khan awaits you in the study.'

Janus puts his hand on Anna's arm. 'Go on into the parlour. I will join you shortly.'

* * *

Khan jumps up as Janus enters the study. 'Did the boy find you with Pym?'

'Whistler? No, I have not seen him. Why?'

'We have a problem. The prism is missing.'

'How can that be? I left it in your care.'

'There has been a substitution.' Khan opens the wooden box and lifts out a glass sphere. 'As you see, the real prism has been substituted.'

'Ye gods.' Janus rubs his chin. 'Can those scoundrels Tweedie and Pestlemore be responsible?'

'I imagine so. That is why I sent Whistler to intercept you. Pym may yet track them down.'

Janus glances at the clock. 'Time is slipping.'

'Pym is the best chance.'

'Have the watchmen been taken care of?'

'All pedestrians and carriages will be diverted to London

Bridge for one hour.' Khan picks up his hat and cloak. 'I will go ahead to ensure everything is made ready. Have faith and patience.' Khan gives a wry smile. 'Although I fear they have never been your strong suits.'

Janus pats Khan's shoulder. 'And yet, my friend, optimism is.'

* * *

Janus joins Anna in the parlour as Ned arrives with a loaded supper tray. Janus sits beside Anna. 'Come, let us enjoy one last meal together.'

Ned pours the tea. Janus offers Anna a slice of fruit cake.

Anna rubs her stomach. 'I'm not very hungry – butterflies – but I'll take some tea. You need to distract me. Tell me about how the time travel apparatus works.'

Janus passes her a cup. 'I am afraid it is a little complicated.'

'Try me.'

'Very well. Our invention stands on the shoulders of the greatest men, Harrison's work on navigation and Bose's discovery of electrostatics. Newton held that the speed of light was finite but we discovered, by tilting light using a prism, we could achieve deflection and thus open a doorway to a different time.'

'So, this doorway? Is it like a black hole?'

Janus frowns. 'Black hole?'

'Never mind, I've probably said too much.' Anna puts down her cup. 'This is probably inappropriate, but I'm feeling nervous. Would you mind giving me a hug?'

Janus sets down his own cup and puts his arm around her.

Anna rests her head on his shoulder, listening to his heart

beating. Closing her eyes, she stays like that, enjoying the moment. 'Sometimes,' she murmurs, 'I wonder if I even want to go back.'

Janus lifts her chin and looks into her eyes. 'Why?'

'I don't know what I'm going back to. Has time passed while I've been away?'

'You have not been away, Anna.'

'But I've been here eleven days. Time must have passed in my world.'

'Yes.'

'Perhaps someone's been worried about me. Won't they wonder why I just disappeared?'

'You did not disappear.'

'What do you mean?'

'That is not how it works.'

'I don't understand.'

'You believe you left your own world to travel here?'

'How else do you explain it?'

'Your essence divided. You became two beings travelling parallel paths. You are not missing from your own life, Anna, you are still there.'

'But how can that be?'

Janus chuckles. 'You accept travel through time and yet you will not believe your soul or spirit can divide?'

'So, what's happening in my world? And who's the person living my life?'

'She is still you, Anna,' he answers in a husky voice.

'Does she know I'm here?'

'That I do not know.'

Her heart beats faster. 'Then couldn't one version of me stay here with you?'

'That cannot happen.'

Anna clutches his arms. 'But why not?'

'As far as I am aware, no-one has sustained duality for so long.' Janus shakes his head. 'I fear you will be in grave danger if you stay. Something catastrophic might happen.'

'Like what?'

'It is not possible to exist indefinitely in two realms. You might start to fragment.'

'That doesn't sound good.'

He gazes into her eyes. 'I will not let that happen.'

Anna swallows. 'What about me being here? Does it change things? History, I mean?'

'In terms of history, I shall take care of it.' Janus wraps both arms around her waist. 'In terms of your effect on me, Anna,' he whispers in her ear, 'I am forever changed.'

Anna feels his warm breath on her skin. She doesn't want to go anywhere.

'Ahem.'

'William.' Janus moves quickly away.

'The boy is here, sir.'

'Whistler? Show him in.'

Whistler shuffles into the room. 'I just come to say, Mister Greg, that I delivered the message. Mister Pym says he'll sort it and he'll meet you on the bridge.'

'Good lad. William, make sure Whistler is fed before he goes back out in the cold.' Janus checks the clock. He stands up. 'Anna, it is time.'

'Already?'

Janus holds out his hands and pulls her up from the couch. She follows him into the hallway as William emerges from the lower stairs.

291

'William.' Anna shakes his hand. 'I wanted to say thank you for all you've done, and please pass on my thanks to Ned and Mrs Lawson.'

William inclines his head. 'You will be needing your cloak, Mistress Stratton.' He places the travelling cloak gently over her shoulders.

* * *

It is dark as the landau approaches the gate on the west side of Westminster Bridge. Janus raises his hand. The watchmen wave them through. They pull up halfway across the bridge where Khan is guarding a stack of wooden boxes.

Janus looks around. 'No sign of Pym?'

Khan pats his shoulder. '*Inshallah*, he will be here soon.'

'Come, Anna.' Janus takes her hand. 'You might enjoy a final look at my great city.'

As if we have all the time in the world, thinks Anna. Perhaps we have?

They amble along the deserted bridge. Below them, watermen steer loaded barges through the last of the river traffic. Others call out from their wherries, competing for late night passengers seeking passage across the water.

Anna points to three boys scrabbling about in the mud at the water's edge. 'What are those children doing out so late?'

'Mudlarks,' says Janus, 'scavenging for whatever they can find.'

Minutes slip by. The bridge is eerily quiet with no pedestrians or carriages. Janus and Anna stand side by side, gazing at the stars.

Anna smiles. 'Perhaps I'll have to stay after all?'

Janus strokes the back of her hand with his thumb as a hackney pulls up. Pym alights with Tweedie and Pestlemore in tow. 'I think you will be needing this.' Pym holds up a crystal. Each of its multiple faces emits a ray of light, reflecting across the dark waters below.

'Just in time.' Janus slaps Pym on the shoulder. 'How did you know where to find these rogues?'

'Soon after the boy left, Tweedie and Pestlemore turned up at the house. They had figured out Mistress Stratton was the phantom and came to persuade me we should detain her as evidence of our experiment.'

'Well, Tweedie, Pestlemore.' Janus's voice is stern. 'What have you to say for yourselves?'

'I am s-sorry Gregory,' stammers Pestlemore. 'I believe we may have got a little c-carried away.'

Tweedie clears his throat. 'You must admit, Gregory, Mistress Stratton makes convincing proof. Her presence would ensure we all became Fellows of the Royal Society.'

Janus clenches his fists. 'If you wheeled Mistress Stratton in, do you seriously believe they would let her leave? She would be regarded as nothing more than a laboratory rat.'

Pestlemore's face drains of colour. 'P-perhaps we had not f-fully thought things through.'

Anna lays a hand on Janus's arm. He relaxes. 'No, clearly you had not.'

Tweedie stares at Anna. 'The result of the trial was remarkable though, Gregory, was it not?'

Janus turns to gaze at Anna. 'Remarkable indeed.'

Pestlemore takes a tentative step forward. 'It is as Mitchell said. 'Twas the appearance of the blue moon made all the difference.'

Tweedie nods. 'Mayhap.'

'Well.' Janus places a hand on each of their shoulders. 'Now you are here, you can make yourselves useful and assemble the equipment.'

Tweedie and Pestlemore step forward and begin to unpack items from the boxes. Pym lays the prism down carefully in its wooden box.

'Thank you, Mister Pym,' says Anna.

Pym smiles. 'Perhaps, Mistress Stratton, we might be of mutual assistance to one another?' He gestures towards Janus.

They set up the apparatus. Anna recognises the hollow sphere from the replica model in Janus's study. High above them, stars are bright and the moon clearly visible. Janus supervises while Tweedie aligns the telescope with a particularly dark patch of sky.

'Janus.' Anna moves closer. 'Do you have to inform the authorities about Pym and Isabella's child?'

Janus turns around. 'Was it not you who was concerned about the real mother showing up?'

'It's not likely though, is it? And even if she did, I'm sure you'd work out what to do. Perhaps it's better for the child to enjoy the life he has rather than being raised in the Foundling Hospital?'

'For the sake of the child' – Janus smiles – 'but more so for you, I will think on it.'

* * *

Matt checks the time on his mobile – seven p.m. Surely the doctors should have done their evening rounds? Easing himself up from the plastic chair he stretches. He looks across to the nurses' station where Doctor Ashmael and a colleague are going through a file. Occasionally they look up and glance towards Anna's bed. Matt struggles to hear what they're saying.

'... results ...inconclusive.'

'... brain biopsy ...fifty-fifty.'

Dr Ashmael is heading towards Matt. 'Mr Vines?'

'Yes?'

'I'm afraid there's been further deterioration. Anna's heart rhythms are abnormal.'

'But she opened her eyes earlier. She didn't speak but, opening her eyes, that's a good sign, right?'

Doctor Ashmael shakes his head. 'Not necessarily. You need to understand that Anna's in a coma. To begin with it was drug induced, but as we've reduced her medication, she should have been showing signs of waking up.'

Matt frowns. 'I don't get what you mean?'

'She's at what we refer to as level seven on the Glasgow scale. Basically, Anna's able to respond to pain, and her eyes occasionally open as you've observed, but she's not making any verbal responses. It's as if she has no awareness of where she is or what's happening to her.'

'So.' Matt swallows. 'What happens next?'

Doctor Ashmael sighs. 'I'm going to treat her for encephalitis. I'm not convinced that's the cause, but we're running out of options and we have to try something. Nurse?'

The ward nurse steps forward.

'I'm prescribing Aciclovir – 400mg every four hours.' The doctor puts his hand on Matt's shoulder. 'If this doesn't work, we may have to put Anna on a respirator.'

Matt sits back down to stop his legs shaking.

Dr Ashmael rubs his beard. 'It's odd. It's almost as though she's given up. Keep talking to her. Perhaps she has some favourite music you could play? Did you manage to contact her parents?'

'They're on the way,' mumbles Matt.

* * *

I'm without form or body, travelling along a path of white light. The pulsing sound grows louder and louder, more a vibration. Up ahead a hairpin bend draws closer and closer. As I arrive at the point of no return, I'm tugged from all directions, pulled apart. I hear a cry, a howl of agony. Is it me? No. There is no me.

* * *

Anna stands on the spot Janus marked. Gusts of wind blow up from the Thames. She shivers as her travelling cloak billows around her ankles. Janus and Tweedie conduct a final inspection of the equipment while Pym and Pestlemore crane their necks to observe. Khan stands a few yards away, eyes closed, hands open in prayer. The prism is in place. Everything is ready.

Anna stares up at the moon, silvery blue against a dark sky. She turns back to watch Janus checking and rechecking. 'Janus,' she calls.

'Yes?'

'Will it hurt?'

His smile reassures her. 'No.'

'That time when you tried the apparatus yourself. Where

did you go?'

Janus rubs his brow. 'Anna, I…'

'You went to see her, didn't you? Ramia?'

'Yes.'

'Perhaps you'll visit me one day? Janus, I will see you.'

Their eyes lock.

At the periphery of her vision, Anna notices tiny flecks of light dancing across the bridge towards her. They ripple and shimmer, licking at her toes like tiny waves until she is surrounded by rays. Tickling and tingling, they merge with her flesh. Anna lifts her hands and examines them. They are translucent. She's overwhelmed by a sense of calmness.

Anna and the light become one. She reflects, *perhaps she is an angel after all?*

14th September 2019

'Anna?'

Is that Matt? I blink. The room is so bright.

'Nurse. I think she's waking up.'

'Matt? Where am I?'

'Anna, it's okay. You're going to be fine.'

Epilogue

Matt joins me at the table. 'Flat white with almond milk, right?'

'Thanks.' I check the departures board for the umpteenth time.

'It's okay,' he says. 'You've plenty of time.'

The Sunday papers lay unread on the seat between us. I imagine Matt will read them once I've boarded.

He studies me. 'You sure you're okay?'

I smile. 'I'm fine.'

Matt adds sugar to his latte and stirs it. 'You don't remember anything?'

'Candles around the bath, talking to Zoe, then everything's a blank.' I watch him as he sips his coffee. There is something else, but I can't tell Matt about the handsome dark-haired man who visits me in my dreams...

Matt's saying something.

'Sorry, what?'

He grins. 'You were miles away. I said, at least Zoe managed to head your parents off before they stepped on the plane in Malaga.'

'Yeah, I don't think I was ready to deal with them then.'

'You sure you want to do this on your own?'

'Bit late now.'

'No.' Matt pulls his passport from his jacket pocket. 'I've got my credit card. Say the word and I'll grab a ticket. Come with you.'

'The flight's full. Anyway, your CEO will go mad if you don't show up tomorrow. You've missed enough days already.'

Matt stares out across the concourse. 'Sure that's all it is?'

'What do you mean?'

He turns and takes my hands. 'What's going on?'

'You know what's going on. I have to put things right with Mum and Dad. You're the one who's been going on about it.'

'I mean with us. Where are we?'

I pull my hands away. 'Honestly? Right now, I don't know.'

'What did I do?'

'I'm not sure that you did anything. It just feels like everything's changed.'

'How can I fix this?'

'You can't Matt. That's kind of the point. You can't fix everything and you can't fix me.'

'I'm not trying to fix you.'

'Then why does it feel like you are?' I sip my drink. 'Sorry, I didn't intend for us to argue.'

I check through my bag again. Passport, boarding pass, money. It reassures me when my fingers brush against my copy of *Coram's Children*. I've not given up on writing my story, but I need to figure out another way to get it out there.

'What are you thinking?' Matt asks.

'Nothing really.' I sigh. 'I was just wondering if I'll see her again.'

'For sure.' Matt squinches his eyes. 'You couldn't have done any more. Debbie will surface when she's ready.'

I check the board. 'That's my flight.' I get up. 'I need to go.'

Matt stands up. He puts his arms around me and kisses my forehead. 'See you soon babe.'

Afterword

In 325 A.D. the Julian Calendar was adopted by the Nicene Council. Unfortunately, due to a flaw in calculations, the Julian Calendar exceeded the Solar year by eleven minutes per year. In 1582, in an attempt to put things right, Pope Gregory XIII decreed that a new calendar should be adopted. This was named the Gregorian Calendar. However, by 1752 the calendar in England was eleven days out of sync with the rest of Europe and so the government of the day decided, in order to sort this out once and for all, eleven days should be removed from September 1752.

Consequently, Wednesday 2 September 1752 was followed by Thursday 14 September 1752. The eleven days, 3rd September to 13th September 1752, do not exist.

About the Author

Suzi Bamblett lives with her partner Colin in Crowborough, East Sussex. She has three grown up children, two stepchildren, fifteen grandchildren and three great grandchildren. In 2019, Suzi graduated with a distinction for her MA in Creative Writing (University of Brighton).

Suzi writes psychological thrillers and suspense stories for adults and young adults. She's a huge fan of Daphne du Maurier and her *Imagined Dialogue with Daphne* can be found on the Daphne du Maurier website. Suzi's writing has been published in literary magazines and anthologies. *The Travelling Philanthropist* is her debut novel.

Suzi's second novel will be released later in 2021. For more information, please visit her website where you can also sign up to receive news.

You can connect with me on:
- https://broodleroo.com
- https://twitter.com/Suzibambi
- https://www.facebook.com/broodleroo

Printed in Great Britain
by Amazon

55489146R00187